PENGUIN BOOKS

WHOSE CITIES?

Mark Fisher, Labour MP for Stoke-on-Trent Central since 1983, was born in 1944, and has been the Shadow Minister for Arts and Media since 1987. He read English at Trinity College, Cambridge, and was a documentary film producer and scriptwriter from 1966–74, and Principal of Tattenhall Centre for Education in Cheshire from 1974–83. He became a Staffordshire County Councillor in 1981, where he was Chairman of the Libraries Committee. He was a member of the Treasury and Civil Service Select Committee from 1985–7. Mark Fisher is co-author of *City Centres, City Cultures* (1988) and author of two plays, *Brave New Town* (1974) and *The Cutting Room* (1990). He is married with two sons and two daughters and lives in Stoke-on-Trent and London.

Ursula Owen was born in Oxford and spent the first eighteen months of her life in Berlin. After reading physiology at St Hugh's College, Oxford, she spent five years in social work and research into psychiatric problems in the community. For two years she lived in the Middle East, teaching at the American University in Cairo. In the early seventies she worked as an editor in various publishing companies and in 1974 became a founder member of Virago Press, where she was Editorial Director and later Joint Managing Director. In 1991 she left to become Cultural Policy Adviser to the Labour Party and Director of the Paul Hamlyn Fund. She is the editor of *Fathers: Reflections by Daughters* (1983) and a contributor to *Publishing: the Future* (1988). She has one daughter and lives in London.

WHOSE CITIES?

EDITED BY
MARK FISHER AND URSULA OWEN

PENGUIN BOOKS

PENGUIN BOOKS

Published by the Penguin Group
Penguin Books Ltd, 27 Wrights Lane, London W8 5TZ, England
Penguin Books USA Inc., 375 Hudson Street, New York, New York 10014, USA
Penguin Books Australia Ltd, Ringwood, Victoria, Australia
Penguin Books Canada Ltd, 10 Alcorn Avenue, Toronto, Ontario, Canada M4V 3B2
Penguin Books (NZ) Ltd, 182–190 Wairau Road, Auckland 10, New Zealand

Penguin Books Ltd, Registered Offices: Harmondsworth, Middlesex, England

First published 1991
1 3 5 7 9 10 8 6 4 2

Set in 10/12 pt Monophoto Baskerville

Printed in England by Clays Ltd, St Ives plc

CONTENTS

MARK FISHER

Introduction

A hare astride a horse stares out at Dundee. It's a stone sculpture by Lisanne Wood, part of a public art project that has transformed the Blackness district of the city over the past eight years. The arts are helping to change cities all over Britain. As the intercity train draws into Wakefield Station, you are carried the length of the platform past a sculpture by Charles Quick. Down in the Isle of Wight the building of the new St Mary's hospital by architect Richard Burton incorporates work by more than two dozen artists in the form of murals, sculptures, prints, paintings, fabrics and landscaping. In Lewisham a mortuary has been converted into a Music Academy to which people from all over south London come to learn instruments, to sing and to master the techniques of recording.

Projects like these enrich cities. They add to enjoyment, they give cause for people to be proud of their neighbourhood. These are some of the things we look for in city life: variety, quality, surprise. Of course we want work and a house, and good schools, safe streets and reliable transport, but we ask for considerably more from cities. They should offer public places, squares and parks and waterfronts, in which it is a pleasure to be. There should be choices, of theatres and cinemas, of book and record shops, of bars and restaurants. Most of all there should be other people to meet, with whom to share these amenities. These are the elements that make up a city's life and its culture, which determine whether a community enjoys itself or simply survives.

It is the work of artists, designers and architects which can often give expression to, and meets, these needs. In Leicester the city council is supporting an International Festival of Dance; in Carlisle they have just opened a new art gallery, Tully House; in Brighton the support for Carousel provides dance and drama for people with disabilities. Glasgow and Birmingham may capture the headlines with new symphony halls and multi-million-pound investment in the arts, but at the same time a new text for the arts is being written as small-scale projects are developed in almost every city in the country.

This expansion has taken place when nationally the arts are having to mark time, under pressure from a government that demands they should cut their budgets and be more market-oriented, and when local authority finances are under constant attack. So why and how has this cultural explosion happened?

These essays explore people's experiences of cities and the diversity of city cultures. They start from a wider definition of culture, which extends beyond individual artefacts or perform-ances in dance, drama, fine arts or writing, and encompasses such factors as the new technologies of broadcasting, cable and video, and the design of a city's public spaces and architecture. What happens outside theatres and libraries is as important as what happens inside them.

This wider view presupposes a different and more active relationship between people and culture. While the arts are seen to take place solely in theatres, art galleries and concert halls, they can be provided as the gift of an enlightened patron or local authority. Once they are recognized as being part of everyday life, in which all can participate, they begin to grow out of communities rather than being imposed on them. Exciting though the new Symphony Hall in Birmingham is, the beautiful pave-ment outside it in Centenary Square, designed by the artist Tess Jaray, may well become as much part of the lives of Birmingham people as the concerts conducted by Simon Rattle inside the Hall.

The driving forces behind such initiatives and behind this significant change of attitude toward the arts and culture are complicated and prosaic, sometimes pragmatic, but always con-cerned with local identity.

During the last decade almost every major city saw its manufacturing base decline or disappear. It was these industries, shipbuilding in Glasgow, fishing in Hull, steel in Sheffield, which had given communities their identity, which had made them distinct. In the 80s, as the Government removed credit controls, the one area of economic growth was in consumer spending. Glitzy new shopping malls sprang up in city centres but these offered consumer distraction rather than an alternative identity. Since only national retail chains could afford the high rents, every centre had the same mix of food shops, bookshops, shoe shops, novelty shops.

The need for a new individuality became intense. For many the established emblems of local identity, the civic theatre and the city's football club, retained a potency. But for others they were no longer sufficient. The diversity of city life experienced by women, the young, the elderly, those with disabilities, those with different ethnic cultures, demanded more various ways of expressing local culture and identity.

There are as many ways to address such needs as there are cities but it is not surprising that councils have turned to the arts for part of the answer. Each theatre company, artists' studio, dance group is different. Arts projects can express the character of a community, indeed they literally give voice to it. In doing so, they are not merely decorative, they often capture the distinction between a community's identity and its image. It is true that some cities, such as Glasgow, have used their investment in the arts to promote or market a new image, but the renewal of confidence, the pride and the involvement of people in a city's cultural life goes deeper than mere image-making. At a time when inner-city areas are faced by problems on every side, people have a sharp appetite for the sense of achievement and enjoyment that a successful arts project can create.

This expansion has not been part of some national masterplan. These initiatives have arisen haphazard. Few of them existed a decade ago. In that year, 1981, a new Labour administration was elected to run the Greater London Council (GLC). The annual arts budget it inherited was £9 million, for a city of seven million people.

3

The new Chair of the Arts Committee, Tony Banks, soon altered that. Specialist officers were employed, grants advertised and processed, the budget boomed. By the end of the first year the GLC was spending £18.5 million and Londoners were beginning to enjoy themselves. Not surprisingly the policy proved popular. At the same time as its editorials were demonizing the GLC leader as Red Ken, the *Evening Standard* was moved to grudging praise for the council's arts programme. More crucially people and communities all over the city were discovering a voice. For the first time London's ethnic communities began to be, and to feel, a part of the capital's cultural life.

In the space of two years, London changed from a city whose artistic life was dominated almost entirely by the great national institutions such as the Royal Academy and the British Museum to one in which over 150 new community arts projects were competing for audiences. The speed with which this happened meant that expansion tended to take precedence over a considered strategy, but the air crackled with new ideas.

Not that London was alone, or even first, in discovering the joys of investing in the arts. Swindon had been spending 6 per cent of its total municipal budget on the arts for years. The 1983 opening of the new Burrell Museum in Glasgow, to which Glasgow's 1980s renaissance can be traced, goes back properly to 1971 when the two-stage architectural competition for the building was won by Barry Gasson. But London was not only investing, it was beginning to ask new questions: what were the cultural needs of the elderly or the young or the housebound; how could these developments be linked to the capital's broadcasting media; what were the implications for the city's employment and economy of this expansion of the arts and cultural industries?

In the decade since, whether through an arts centre like the Leadmill in Sheffield offering a live music venue for the city's bands, or the South Humberside Dance Project introducing everyone from children to grannies to the joys of dance, or the Belgrave Centre's arts activities in the middle of Leicester's Asian community, cities have been trying to answer these questions in practical ways by introducing new opportunities to people who've been untouched by the municipal rep or the touring orchestra.

Such initiatives send out a message that things can change quickly, even in the most difficult of times, that people can express themselves and in doing so reclaim their city.

How can you justify such expenditure when housing and social services and education are being starved of resources? Cities like Glasgow and Birmingham give two answers. First, a city needs both housing *and* theatre, social services *and* public libraries; second, the arts are an essential part of a city's identity, neither more nor less important than other civic services. Then there remains the perennial question about spending money on the arts. How can you justify a concert hall to which a lot of people never go or an art exhibition that many will not see?

The studies by economist John Myerscough for the Policy Studies Institute (PSI) in 1988 showed that the arts were major employers and boosted local economies by attracting people back into city centres. The Museum of Photography, Film and Television opened in Bradford in 1984. By the end of the decade over 800,000 people were visiting it each year, spending money in local restaurants, bars, hotels, car parks and shops. What would become of the economy of Stratford-on-Avon without the Royal Shakespeare Company? Arts policies have a further, though less direct, effect in attracting industrial and commercial investment. If a German or Japanese company is seeking a location for a new factory, they will tend to choose a city offering to their employees an attractive and varied environment, which includes the arts.

It is a lesson which cities all over Europe are learning. Frankfurt is opening thirteen major new museums, Barcelona is building a National Theatre of Catalonia and a new symphony hall, and Montpellier hosts specialist arts festivals throughout the year. Cultural competition between cities is a serious business, not just for tourists and for prestige, but also for a share of the new technologies and cultural industries, particularly broadcasting. Sheffield has established a Cultural Industries quarter on the southern edge of the city centre which brings together music recording and independent film. Like Edinburgh, Liverpool and others, Sheffield ran a major national campaign in pursuit of the nomination for the location for Channel 5, the new terrestrial TV channel whose franchise remains unallocated.

Such attempts to re-establish local roots for broadcasting are not easy to achieve. The scale of investment, in television and satellite if not in cable or radio, may mean that the move in broadcasting towards the international is unstoppable. But the tendency towards the global in broadcasting is precisely what provokes the search for greater local expression. Viewers and listeners undoubtedly want stations that can give them news and sports coverage instantly from around the world, but they also want to hear local issues reported and debated. To achieve this will involve some rebalancing of the axis of broadcasting in Britain away from London, by developing local neighbourhood and community radio stations, as in Australia, and by creating a television channel, Channel 5, which carries a serious amount of local news and views.

This highlights one of the most significant aspects of the expansion of city cultures. It is beginning to redistribute opportunities for both artists and audiences away from London. For years our cultural life, like almost every other aspect of British life, has been hugely weighted towards the South-East. Despite cities like Manchester developing a strong cultural voice, the capital has kept most things to itself, theatres, galleries, television companies, publishing houses, agents, work, investment. Now other cities are fighting back.

With these new opportunities comes new confidence. At last we are learning the lessons that European regions, like Catalonia, Bavaria, Tuscany and Brittany, have been trying to teach us for years: that regions are not a sub-species of nations, they are simply different and they offer the most effective way of preventing us slipping into a monoculture whose most insidious characteristic is that, within it, only the national and international are valued and given authority. The view from the region is seen as parochial. There is no room for local voices. In such a world there is a real danger that local people and their needs will be forgotten, left standing on the pavement as the cultural juggernaut thunders by.

Raymond Williams said that culture is ordinary. That is a fine aspiration, but we have a long way to go before we achieve it. Only when as much care and attention is given to the design of the local health centre or primary school or bus station as is put into the local theatre will art truly and finally have become ordinary, and thus extraordinary. Only when it becomes commonplace in this way will these policies command the widespread support necessary to sustain them.

The most successful cities are trying to achieve this by building their arts policies from bottom up, in response to local needs and demands. To date, the investment has come entirely from local taxation. Unlike housing or education or social services, the arts receive no matching funding at present from central government by means of the Revenue Support Grant. If we want this cultural expansion at city level to continue, that will have to change. For the last twelve years the Government's implacable hostility to any local-authority expenditure has made such support impossible. In such hard times, who needs a hare astride a horse in Dundee, they ask?

Town Hall and arts organizations can give a lead, but ultimately the only response to that question must come from the electorate, from people saying, 'We want concerts in the parks, and writers in libraries. We want theatre in education companies, and local festivals. We want arts projects for those with disabilities, and we want funding for amateur drama groups. These are our cities and this is our culture.'

It is this new involvement of people, whether as audiences, participants or artists, which offers the most exciting possibilities for the 1990s and which begins to address the question this book poses – 'whose cities?'

I

VIEWS FROM THE BRIDGE

JEANETTE WINTERSON

Dreams and Buildings

Great cities are born not made. The buildings we delight in, the squares and parks that give us so much pleasure, are not the product of town planning, social conscience or even good business. The monuments and spaces that we return to in daylight and in dreams are the unlikely offspring of civilization's most ecstatic romance: the grand union of money and vanity. Money and vanity built Westminster Abbey and St Paul's Cathedral, laid out Hyde Park, swarmed up the Eiffel Tower, and raised the Helmsley and the Chrysler buildings. What have the terraces of Nash or the splendours of Bauhaus to do with necessity? It is certain that we need buildings and that in some great cities, like New York, those buildings must go upwards. Yet it is a fact that the romance of old New York is precisely that: romance. Not the practical drive to fit so much into so little but the intoxication of showing off. New York wears her heart on her sleeve. London, though by far the older sister, is well known for her excess, and it is the thrills and frills of her bricks and mortar beauty that make our capital the preferred holiday haunt of New Yorkers and friends world wide. To put it another way, with thanks to the lady in the floral print outside the Houses of Parliament, 'Snap it Harry, it's culture.'

It is, but to what extent can we rest on the achievements of history? If London is to be more than an architectural museum we will have to meet the challenge perplexing most other great cities: her new buildings must be a match for her old. This is not

simply a problem for architects and social historians. It is
dilemma with wide implications. The city we inhabit inhabits us.

In this essay I want to think about the links between ou
internal and external constructions and the role of the imaginatio
in shaping ourselves as individuals, as a people and as a natior
Politics and metaphysics, like dreams and buildings, go togethe:
If in doubt consult either Machiavelli or Peter Palumbo. Mear
while I shall continue my inquiries in a political context, focusin
on an essential difference in thinking between Labour and th
Tories, a difference which is quite new and which is informin
policies on either side. During the last few years the Labour Part
has overhauled its philosophical underpinning and it should b
praised for doing so. Mrs Thatcher did the same with her party
indeed she pushed it round rapid right-angles while claiming tha
she alone was the face of stability and continuity. That Labou
has had the courage to look closely at itself, its policies and th
people it can stand up for makes it stronger, not weaker. The blin
old Labour rhetoric, so predictable and insular, is now givin
way to an imaginative dialogue with the voters. Labour, unlike th
Tories, is not telling us what to think but requiring that we shoul
think. After twelve years of Tory nannying we are being asked 1
conceive of Britain in a profoundly different way. It's a policy c
reconstruction with new and creative foundations. Against Tor
totalitarianism, Labour has become the party of the imagination

This is shocking, especially so since Labour and not the Tori
seems most able to restore a sense of personal well-being an
national pride. I'm not talking about arrogance or jingoisn
We've had plenty of both in the me decade and the result ha
been a psychotic obsession with winning in the narrowest sen
and losing much of great value. The Tories, while advertisin
themselves as the party of individual fulfilment, have forgotte
about happiness. Perhaps because you can't buy it.

Other things too cannot be bought: generosity, communit
social responsibility, public spiritedness. They cannot be bougl
but strangely they can be sold and as the Tories have brick b
brick dismantled and disposed of so many of our national interes
and much of our system of public welfare it seems that the idea
and aspirations that were their real foundations have disappeare

along with the hospitals, schools, theatres and charitable housing. Our hearts are derelict.

London, we have been told again and again, will be recon- structed with private money. That's what Docklands was sup- posed to be about, what King's Cross is meant to be about. Private money will be found for the Opera House extension and to support all those London theatres that have had their grants cut and don't want to put on musicals. In practice it's not so simple. Gifts to the nation are hard to find, the problem being that Thatcher-style capitalism has so winched up the notion of the profit-motive that it seems like a far more glamorous and elevated persuasion than straightforward greed. Making money, which used to be thought of as a means, has become an end. Why bother building a hospital or a body of safe, cheap housing that trumpets the name of Peabody or Guinness when nowadays simply to be a Guinness or a Maxwell or a Murdoch, i.e. very very rich, is enough redress for the vainest soul? London, old London, the London we love is absolutely a product of money and vanity, the wish to leave some conspicuous mark of success. This impulse can be made to work for the public good but only in a climate where wealth has *defacto* obligations. The Tories have traded social responsibility for a pair of tickets to the charity ball.

Great cities are born not made. To get beyond a nostalgic past and a stagnating present we will need more this time than patrons and architects. We will need ourselves. The inner city is just as much the city we carry inside us as the city whose bricks and mortar we obey. That buildings affect the way we work and very often the way we feel is well known. We are powerfully tied to our surroundings, and yet it is true too that our surroundings are umbilically tied to us. For instance, most of us complain bitterly about traffic congestion in London and most of us know too that we are still going no faster in real terms than our vanished ancestors in their horse-drawn carts. And yet how many of us will admit that our imaginations are at fault? That we cannot see beyond four doors and a windscreen? We sit day after day in a long, long line of stuffy discontent, we creep through the choked air past buildings covered in exhaust grime, we arrive often late and usually frayed having paid the price of a take-away lunch to park, and when challenged we call this hell freedom, independence, necessity and economy. The Government has pledged twelve billion pounds to make hell more hellish, which will include widening that bower of bliss, the M 25, and carving through the ancient silences of Oxleas Wood. There's no point blaming industry; there are about half a million goods vehicles regularly on our roads and over twenty million private cars. You and I are going to have to imagine a London that is not being designed around the car. A London where shops and schools and hospitals can be reached easily by the kind of cheap efficient public transport that, say, Amsterdam enjoys. For decades now we have worshipped rubber on the road. Since the fifties, popular imagination has fuelled the car quite as much as refined crude. In the nineties, we'll have to find a creative way out of what has become a very prosaic nightmare.

Creativity is the key. Whatever we can imagine we can bring to pass. Our future isn't in the hands of boffins, architects, Bovis Homes, or even Government. All of these interested parties rely on us either to give them the lead or to go along with what they decide. It has suited the Tory Government very well to render the British people more and more inert. Inertia is a danger and clearly there is some part of our individual and national consciousness which longs for inertia, which sighs with relief when big, strong people muscle in and paint up signs saying Right and Wrong and proceed to tell us exactly what we need. Labour has chosen not to do this. In this decision lies their greatest strength and also the possible seeds of their defeat. It is hard to know quite how inert and unimaginative the British have become. Three times we have voted in the Tories and the chance now to vote them out seems based on the same kind of limited selfishness that has kept them there so far. I worry about this. It's the little Englander, little Londoner, me-and-mine philosophy that is anathema to anything progressive or new. If the city we carry about inside us is small and mean, made up of doors that are always closing, then the city we live in will certainly become so. We generate our environment. We make it what it is. I do not accept that we are powerless, that life is done unto us. It does look that way right now because we have a government that does not listen and that rides roughshod over any protest against its policies. But we all have to take responsibility for this mess. It is not an accident of fate that the Tories have been in power for so long. They are not a volcano that erupted over our peaceful lives. They are a democratic choice. To say 'I didn't vote for them' is a shoddy response. There are countless opportunities to challenge a Government whilst it is in power and if you oppose a Government then you cannot do so passively. It's not enough to rush to the polling station then shrug ones shoulders for five years. How can our voices be heard if we do not raise them?

To conceive of Britain in a profoundly different way will mean conceiving of ourselves in a profoundly different way. If we want to enjoy a capital city that is a thriving centre of culture and finance (there is no reason why the two should be at odds), a capital where people can afford to live and afford to visit without being slung into a doss house in King's Cross. A capital where young people seeking new prospects are not most likely to end up on the streets and a capital that considers human beings as its life blood not as an afterthought, then we are first and foremost going to have to find that city in ourselves. We must desire it, dream of it, talk about it, work together to bring it into being. This is the only way to get free from the pincers of apathy and nostalgia. Just as there is a real fear that London may become an architectural museum, a city of the past with new buildings as drab as any in Eastern Europe, so there is too, the worse terror that its people may not care. It's not only that our building programme needs to be revitalized but that we too need to reach out to the future.

At an individual and societal level we could start imagining ourselves. We could stop being told what our priorities are and start working them out for ourselves. We could decide what quality of life actually means and force our elected representatives to put our views into practice. How often, when grinding through London's filthy streets, dodging the detritus of yet another redundant office block craning upwards, do we hear older people remembering 'the good old days' when there was decent public housing, plenty of buses, less crime, fewer cars, more community? Then, go round a corner into a wine bar and the Thatcher generation are beginning to question the bootstraps and bicycle wisdom. They pulled themselves up, moved with the work, were aggressive, competitive and now they can't manage the mortgage and there are no decent schools for the kids. Well, I'm not a nostalgia-monger myself and I don't know about those 'good old days', but I do know that wherever you listen and look there is tremendous discontent. Labour's task, and the task for which I believe the party is equipped, is to turn this discontent into a dream-vision. While the Tory Party is promising to rescue the people of Britain from all kinds of monsters – inflation, unemployment, Europe, the world, it is the Labour Party that is urging people to rescue themselves. This isn't the bootstraps and bicycles mentality; rather, it is an intelligent and proper response to the feelings of powerlessness that so many of us experience. The Tories have noticed this powerlessness, they call it 'frustration', the sort of word you use for a five year old who can't get their own way. Indeed we are bound to feel powerless. For twelve years we have handed over our power to the nanny in the sky and it's now a bit difficult to ask for it back. The Tories understand, of course they do, and their message is 'trust us'. Labour's response is neither so facile nor so obvious, and this might make it difficult for a Britain used to being told what's what. The idea that we, the people, can change things, that we should change things, that it is desirable to do so and that there should be plenty of debate on doing so is frightening as well as exhilarating. The chattering classes have become the discredited classes. The Tories have succeeded in squashing argument and restricting the platforms of dispute. They don't want questions they want faith. Thatcherism was a religion and many still prefer that old time gospel to the burdens of personal choice. Quite how the Tories have persuaded people that choice is what they've got is one of the more sinister miracles of the modern age.

The grand union of money and vanity. Do we really want it back? Doesn't it smack of feudalism, patronage, an unequal society of just the kind the Tories, in spite of their utterances, have worked to encourage? I think not. Even if the large estates of inherited wealth are broken up, it is always going to be the case that some people will still have serious money. What Labour has to do is to make sure that a good deal of that money endows the nation. Taxation is the obvious answer but not the only answer. Yes, we need progressive taxation but we also need a system that encourages people to give; to give because they want to and because they believe it is right to do so. This is not a yucky handing over from the haves to the have-nots but, certainly as far as London is concerned, a sensible approach to the problems of a stagnating capital city. London needs building that the public purse cannot and should not buy.

Money and vanity are not only the preserve of the rich. There is no reason why a Government should not set out an agenda for the things London needs and raise the money by public subscription. Well-publicized boosts from wealthy individuals would set an optimistic beginning and then we could build up a mega fund, a grand version of those thermometers you see on church walls, the red line creeping steadily upwards. This kind of communal effort would engender tremendous pride, a feeling of achievement and control, not of powerlessness. Needless to say, these public endeavours should be lodged under trust so that they could never be sold off or privatized. If, for instance, the people of London, the rich and the not so rich, had bought the King's Cross site by public subscription, not only would British Rail have been forced to go to Stratford for the Channel Tunnel terminus, where they are needed, but we could also have drawn up a development scheme that would genuinely benefit local people and London as a whole. Who knows, we might have laid the first new grand park for over a hundred years. In a smaller way, the Coin Street development on the South Bank has proved how much can be achieved when people get together and insist on what they want and are prepared to refuse all compromises to get it.

Will responsibility come back into fashion? Will it prove more enduring than fashion? It didn't take the Tories long to completely undermine it, to replace it with a nauseating smash and grab individualism which for some years wore responsibility's clothes but which now stalks naked. I don't know why our better natures have been so easily overruled but I am confident that a new impetus from a new government could remind us of ourselves.

I cannot accept that human nature is as small and mean as a trip through the streets of London would suggest.

We shall shortly be going to the Polls (At least some of us will; why not make voting compulsory?) That will be the first step in deciding what sort of a people we want to be. Are we going to imagine ourselves as responsible, powerful, in control, with ideas that will find a voice, or are we going to hand ourselves over yet again? There are some who think that imagination is only fantasy or game playing. There are others who don't understand its relationship to reason. Yet it remains the case that whatever exists existed first in the imagination. Every invention, every discovery, every work of art, every great building found its crucial life in somebody's thoughts. We have a choice: either we participate in this imaginative structure and bring ourselves and our surroundings into being over and over again (the imaginative life is a continuous life). Or we opt out and let someone else do it for us. But we should choose carefully because there isn't much time. In dreams begin responsibilities.

DAVID EDGAR

From Metroland to the Medicis:
The Cultural Politics of the City State

As we speak, there is a general consensus in the West that we are
moving towards an increasingly federalized Europe, and a feeling
that 'Europe' means more than a bureaucracy in Brussels, but
necessarily embraces certain universal principles of liberty, democracy, justice, civilization and the like. And it is felt (again in the
West) that, by limiting the role of the nation-states, this move
may well assist in the development of civilized, democratic and
legal forms of autonomy for those oppressed nationalities (the
Scots, the Basques) within their borders.

Meanwhile, in the East, something rather different is happening. Here supranational institutions are being demolished and
states fragmented. The slogan of 'Europe' itself is coined as a
code for the dividing line between civilization and the barbarian
hordes (giving the continent a strangely mutable frontier: beyond
the Elbe, it appears that 'Europe' ends twenty kilometres to the
east of wherever one happens to be). It's no surprise that both
anti-gypsy and anti-Jewish feeling are more active and virulent now
than at any time since 1945 (in the latter case, all the way from
Moscow to Marseilles). And having redesigned the currency and
recomposed the national anthem, the first thing a good Slovakian
or Ukrainian or Azerbaijani nationalist plans to do with independence is to withdraw from their minorities (Hungarians, Poles,
Armenians) the rights that they themselves have been denied.

While behind the enlightened Beethovian rhetoric of the new
Europe, the far right grows in strength, liberated Germans attack

liberated Poles, and shadowy ministerial working-groups meet to plan ways to stem the flow of immigration from the third world (and perhaps the second). As the borders go down within the new Europe, they are built ever higher around it.[1]

The consequences of these developments are at their most acute in the cities. It is here that communities of Iranians, Colombians, Filipinos and Sudanese have migrated, to clean houses and offices, to serve petrol and Big Macs. It is here too (of course) that earlier waves of Turkish and Algerian 'guest-workers' have settled, and (in Britain's case) Pakistanis, Indians, Bangladeshis and Afro-Caribbeans have made their home. It is also in the cities that internal migration has formed communities of interest around employment, gender, 'lifestyle' and sexuality – communities that may well feel they have more in common with their equivalents in other countries than they do with their national compatriots.

In other words, there is a crisis of alignment and identity, which goes way beyond Saatchi and Saatchi's well-known maxim that 'there are more social differences between mid-town Manhattan and the Bronx than between Manhattan and the seventh *arrondissement* of Paris'.[2] How, for example, does a Turkish Cypriot in Manchester relate to a Greek Cypriot in Marseilles – or in Nicosia? Particularly if that Cypriot is gay, or a woman (or both)? How do alignments based on locality, origin, religion, sexuality work with each other? What are the cultural consequences of a continent increasingly defined by migration and the breaking-down of traditional patterns of affinity?

Well, the answer is: they are contradictory. On the one hand, 'universal' or national cultures have fractured outwards and inwards (outwards to world music, satellite television, fax art and the internationalization of food; inwards to specific gay cultures, community arts, black performance and music, and religious fundamentalism – the two movements meeting, one might say, to the tune of a Satanic Verse). Further, the unwoven strands have reknitted themselves into strange new patterns. Of course, there is something unpleasantly smug about the old saw that 'you can always tell a Brummie by the shamrock in his turban' (particularly from the city that gave us the Birmingham Six *and* the 'rivers of blood' speech). But most of us write our lives on a palimpsest of national, regional and local cultures, there is a Welsh-speaking black reggae band in Cardiff, and the Scottish writer John Byrne has made a career out of exploring the strangely obsessive relationship between Glaswegian instrumentalists and American popular musical forms.

On the other hand, there has in the face of this fragmentation been a reassertion of traditional (and exclusive) national cultures. In Britain, this has been seen in both the onslaught against modernism by 'high art' critics like Roger Scruton and the late Peter Fuller, and in the more down-market phenomena of heritage theme parks, the pastiche 'traditional' in architecture and interior decoration, and the simulation of the exclusive pleasures of the country-house weekend and the London Club.

What the diverse culture of the cities and the kitsch traditional have in common is their distance from those cultural forms that have been smiled upon and encouraged by subsidy and commission over the last twenty years. From the mid-1960s to the early 1980s, the aim of arts and cultural policy has been to make the contemporary expressions of high-art forms universally available through subsidy: both hiphop and heritage, on the other hand, were market led. When migrant and minority voices *were* heard in the high arts, it was as likely to be in the 'commercial' form of the novel (Rushdie, Ishiguro, Mo) or the movie (Kureishi, Jarman) as in the traditional (and subsidized) performing arts. Overall, when the emergent forms of the 1980s were contemporary they weren't seen as 'universal'(black and gay art), and where they were 'universal' they tended increasingly to be old-fashioned in form and conservative in content (figurative arts, classical architecture and opera, wall-to-wall renderings of *The Seagull* and *Twelfth Night*).

This tension between the new cultural expressions and the pull of tradition has been reflected in arts policy. In Thatcherism's laboratory period, the market was seen as the sole motor of arts development, for ostensibly libertarian reasons. In 1978, the economic-liberal Selsdon Group produced a pamphlet whose simple message was contained in its title: 'A Policy for the Arts: Just Cut Taxes'. Its argument was that if more money was left in the pockets of the people, then consumers could pay the market price for arts products, and private patrons enabled to make up any shortfall in production; its implication was that by releasing the Arts from the dead stranglehold of state control it would usher in a new age of radicalism and innovation.

This view was confirmed by Mrs Thatcher's first Arts Minister, Norman St John Stevas, speaking less than a fortnight after the election victory. For Stevas, private funding not only provided 'an alternative source of finance' but also had the merit of 'avoiding or neutralizing some of the dangers of state patronage, such as censorship and conformity and the promotion of what I might venture to call "establishment art"'.[3]

This 'let a hundred flowers bloom' view of arts privatization was countered by a much more conservative perspective, in which the market was not so much a liberator as a policeman. A year after the Selsdon pamphlet, Kingsley Amis wrote a pamphlet (entitled 'An Arts Policy?') that blamed subsidy not for stifling innovation but for encouraging the aesthetic self-indulgence of an avant-garde that doesn't need to satisfy the public. After a somewhat desultory rehearsal of the anti-statist argument, Amis moved quickly on to his real targets: 'plays without plots, a canvas entirely covered with black paint offered as a picture, poems that are meaningless patterns of letters – I needn't go on'.

Increasingly, it was the Amis rather than the Selsdon view that won through. Shortly after the 1987 General Election, Stevas's successor Richard Luce made his famous attack on those in the arts world 'who have yet to be weaned away from the welfare-state mentality – the attitude that the taxpayer owes them a living'; going on to say that 'the only real test of our ability to succeed is whether or not we attract enough customers'.[4] Similarly, Douglas Mason (of the impeccably libertarian Adam Smith Institute) criticizes subsidy not for stifling initiative and invention but rather for encouraging 'élitism' and 'self-indulgence'.[5]

The success of the market-as-policeman model can be seen in starkest form in the theatre. Long resistant to the Great Bourgeois Cultural Revolution, when the theatre finally succumbed it did so with a vengeance. Under pressure from the funding bodies, theatres up and down the land set to, preparing business plans, drawing up mission statements and opening corporate sponsorship suites (a mechanism for providing the least committed section of the audience with superior front-of-house facilities). The renamed 'Royal' National Theatre offered sponsoring firms 'increased corporate awareness' and 'prestigious entertainment facilities'; the equally Royal Shakespeare Company assured businessmen that it 'can tailor a project to suit a company's individuality and offer a high return on a sponsorship investment'.

Not surprisingly, marketization has had an effect on what is being marketed. The RSC has always believed that the classics need to be recaptured and made new for every generation. In the late 1970s, it put that belief into spectacular effect with Trevor Nunn's triumphant musical version of *The Comedy of Errors*, which led the same director (in collaboration with John Caird and me) to seek to revitalize another minor work of a great writer and adapt Dickens's early comic novel *Nicholas Nickleby* for stage performance. Fired by that success, the same two directors set about to reclaim another dusty and ill-used classic by stripping the pantomime varnish off J. M. Barrie's *Peter Pan*, and exposing the original, with all its complexity and ambivalence, to the light of day.

What all of these projects had in common was that they devoted the same degree of rigour, commitment, innovatory zeal and, crucially, sense of purpose to the production of consciously popular theatre as the RSC dedicates to Shakespeare. But ten years on, things had changed. In the late 1980s, the company presented three perhaps unintentionally equivalent productions: another Shakespearian offshoot (*Kiss Me Kate*), a second children's classic (*The Wizard of Oz*) and a further adaptation (of the Stephen King horror-yarn *Carrie*). The difference between the second trio and the first was not merely that the latter had all been major films. It was that between the first trio and the second the RSC had presented its hit-musical version of Hugo's *Les Miserables* and as a consequence of that success had come to rely – financially and in a real way psychologically – on similar achievement in the commercial sector. The very genuine zeal to reclaim and to reinvent, the sense of campaigning purpose that informed *The Comedy of Errors*, *Nicholas Nickleby* and *Peter Pan* had within two or three years of *Les Miserables*' undoubted triumph mutated into the equally compulsive but creatively damaging urge to prove work in the 'real world' of the market place. One of the most striking differences between the first trio and the second was that the projects became progressively less inventive, less innovatory, more and more bound by given notions of what in particular musical theatre is, meaning of course what it has been thus far. In order to succeed in the subsidized sector, the RSC rightly felt itself obliged to innovate; to win in the market place, it seems constrained to be conservative.

Finally, the theatre began to change its attitude to its audience. Instead of addressing 'playgoers', who might expect the experience of playgoing to be challenging as well as confirming, actors were serving 'customers' (*pace* Richard Luce), who as we know are always right. The English repertory movement began as a crusade for the renewal of particular cultural identities (the very first, A. E. Horniman's Gaiety Theatre in Manchester, was inspired by the revival of the Irish dramatic movement at the Abbey in Dublin; over half the plays were new). By the end of the 1980s, however, it was often hard to tell rep programmes apart. The amount of main-house new work nearly halved, much of the slack was taken up by adaptations of novels, and if you went to an English rep in 1988 and *didn't* see *The Tempest* or *Gaslight* they gave you a small cash prize. In short, as students of American experience had found, privately sponsored and market-led arts lead not to a profusion of blooms, but to a limitation of programming and a narrowing of choice.[6]

So what developed in the 1980s was a kind of cultural Easter Egg: the top half of the shell consisted of an increasingly conventional and unchallenging reading of the 'establishment' high arts, and the bottom half an echoingly homogeneous articulation of the national heritage across the range of Viking villages, medieval banquets, Blitz experiences and indeed Metroland shopping malls; with the shell as a whole concealing a much richer assortment of confectionery within (its ingredients international, its flavours intriguing, its centres hard as well as soft).

How then should a progressive political party respond to these developments? First, it seems clear that you can't make a socialist arts policy without cracking the egg at least enough to expose the wonders within. Second, such a policy should encourage, promote and enable arts that challenge, oppose and call to account the dominant culture of the times.

I appreciate that this is not a currently fashionable view of the role of the arts or the nature of socialism. But I am sustained in it by a brilliant analysis of the latter by Zygmunt Bauman,[7] in which he argues that throughout the modern period the real purpose of socialism has been to act as a critical opposition to capitalism, exposing its failure to live up to modernity's ideals (notably the French revolutionary trio of liberty, equality and fraternity). In that sense, socialism was both an expression of and a challenge to the prevailing characteristics of the epoch. (In the same way, though Bauman doesn't use this analogy, feminism was both an outgrowth of and a challenge to the counterculture of the late 1960s.)

Now, Bauman contends, we are in a new era, whose guiding principles are no longer liberty, equality and fraternity, but rather (as he defines it) liberty, diversity and tolerance. And if socialism is to have a postmodern role, then it will be (again) the questioning of capitalism's ability to live up to those ideals. So, socialists should now be pointing out that liberty still appears to be restricted to economic liberty, diversity to that which can be serviced individually and commercially, and that tolerance can all too easily degenerate into indifference and neglect of others.

Comparably (though not of course identically) one can see Britain's contemporary market culture making a series of superficially attractive claims for itself (popularity, plurality, accessibility, a healthy concern with our national historical roots). Against those claims it might be asserted that without genuine participation popularity turns into populism, that surface plurality is often no more than sameness reclad, that where accessibility is based on ability to pay, it actually *implies* exclusion (the security guard at the entrance to the shopping mall; the bouncer outside the sponsor's bar), that the heritage industry turns history into a costume parade. And while it is important that such a challenge is posed in the columns of learned journals and from college lecterns, it could be (and of course it *always has been*) the role of the arts themselves to call the surrounding culture to account, to note its ideals and challenge its record in realizing them. In other words, in this model the arts could and should have the same role in and against the prevailing culture as socialism should have in and against the political economy.

It's my belief that by forcing the arts more and more into the commercial market-place, the Conservative Government has sought to discourage the arts from performing this role. It is important that an incoming Labour Government comes to the rescue of many arts institutions whose role in the culture has always been (or has in some cases recently become) essentially supportive. But it is also important that a progressive Government should encourage those elements and practices in the arts that are likely to challenge that culture most forcibly.

First, Labour arts policy should encourage arts that are effectively participatory, that break down the division between the professional and the amateur, and that challenge the traditional division between the pre-electric forms and contemporary disciplines like cinema, photography and popular music.

Second, and consequently, it should promote arts practices that are genuinely plural, in that they should express and articulate minority identities, and give voice to the powerless and the invisible.

Third, however, a radical arts policy should take heed of the frustrations with life in the ghetto of those minorities who want to universalize the minority experience and by doing so to confront the idea that there is a universal 'high art' up there, expressing a universally agreed set of cultural principles to which all particularities ultimately aspire. (This is the view which holds that a touring rap version of the *Macbeth* story, or a classical orchestra playing jazz in a school, or indeed the V & A's socks exhibition are but preliminary stages in a process of acclimatization by which the masses will be gradually weaned off the *Sun* and on to Schoenberg.) Indeed, there is a growing feeling across the spectrum that the time has now come for some mixing of the palette: that the experience of women's, gay and black theatre should begin to change as well as to challenge the way that the high arts are presented, not least in order to present a view of the past that reflects the experience of the marginalized and the excluded.

It should be no surprise that such policies are being most effectively implemented by local authority arts and leisure committees in provincial cities. First, because it is in the cities that the actuality of diversity is most obvious. Second, because most cities are run by Labour councils, most of which have now come round to the view that the arts needn't be the preserve of an affected and lordly élite. Third, because Labour councils have noted the skew of national funding towards the national institutions in central London and see their own spending as one way to counteract it. But fourth, and paradoxically, it is precisely because the cities do not have responsibility for the whole range of the high arts that they are able to pursue arts policies that are distinctive and diverse.

The Arts Council of Great Britain continues to have considerable problems with multiform work (particularly black performance art which embraces drama, dance, the visual arts and music) and with amateur performance (it has still found no effective way of financing the mushrooming number of professionally written and directed community plays). The electronic media are (largely) beyond the Arts Council's remit and it appears to be uncomfortable with crafts. In the performing arts it feels itself required to encourage provision across the board (the best examples from the widest field). The fact that one can see its point in all of these matters is not to underestimate the limitations it places on arts policy in our times.

The cities on the other hand are not required to cover the board, and they can specialize (as has Bradford with photography, Glasgow with Mackintosh and environmental theatre, Sheffield with film and video, and Birmingham with dance). This process could indeed go further, with cities fostering and promoting the cultural life of particular constituencies (as Manchester might with youth culture and music, or as Bradford already does with its Asian cuisines). In a region like Merseyside or the West Midlands, for instance, where provision of a balanced dramatic repertoire is guaranteed within a thirty-mile radius, it would be perfectly feasible for an imaginative local authority to give its repertory theatre over, say, to the Women's Playhouse Trust or to a Black or Asian company or to large-scale new writing.

Nor do the cities have to bother about the demarcation lines that cause such problems to the national funders. Following the GLC's pioneering support for non-traditional areas like community radio, record and video distribution, and ethnic newspapers,[8] places like Bradford, Sheffield and Newcastle have put money into the development of cultural-industry districts providing infrastructural support for the media (on the model of the ceramic and clothing industry milieux of northern Italy), without worrying overmuch about where art stops, craft takes over and small-scale manufacturing carries on.

And the cities might also pay less attention than the Arts Council to the distinction between amateur and professional activity, and show less concern about the accusation of 'social work' or 'therapy' directed against arts provision in which the process is more important than the product. (Such accusation can on occasions come a little adrift: in the *Sunday Telegraph*, the critic Derwent May gleefully reported, in the tone of voice that Peter Simple uses when listing the grant recipients of north-east London boroughs, the existence of a 'Dorchester Community Play Association' as a more than usually risible example of Arts Council financed 'social and educational "good works" that had hardly anything to do with art'.[9] In fact, the Dorchester Community Play is an outgrowth of Ann Jellicoe's Colway Theatre Trust, notorious for its obsession with artistic standards, and employing Charles Wood, Fay Weldon, Howard Barker, Arnold Wesker, John Godber, Jane Thornton and me as its writers.)

The 'therapy' point is important in one particular respect. There are four accusations generally levelled at culture-led revivals of old industrial cities, all of which have been prominent in the 'morning after' debate following Glasgow's year as European City of Culture. The first is that events are overpriced and exclude the ordinary citizens who ultimately pay for them; the second is that the events themselves are élitist in content (particularly if limited to the high arts). The third is that cultural regeneration 'yuppifies' city centres and changes their nature (the dire Glaswegian spectre of the Sauchiehall Street wine bar), while the fourth is that city-centre arts provision pays little attention to the needs of the most deprived areas of the city (in Glasgow terms: 'what about Easterhouse?').

All four problems are real and need to be addressed if cities are to take their citizens with them. On the first, there seems to be no problem with a two-tier pricing scheme for the out of town public and the local residents, which some cities are considering; on the second, the accusation of élitism is much easier to counter if councils are financing work which is genuinely artistically original, expresses divisions within as well as between cities, has local roots and is occasionally free.

The problems of the increasing divide between urban gentrification and blight are beyond arts and cultural policy as they have proved beyond much else. There is a view that any spending on the arts while water is running down the walls of council properties is a dalliance. But insofar as the funded arts have a role in the regeneration of the estates that role is surely dependent on not making too fine a distinction between process and product, animation and social work, arts and therapy, hobby and job. What is Simon Rattle's musical work with deaf children in Birmingham? Or the Birmingham Royal Ballet's work with Afro-Caribbean and Asian children in Handsworth? Or indeed the uncharacteristically long-lived partnership between community arts and job-creation in Greater Easterhouse itself?

From all of this it will be clear that I see the cities as being uniquely fitted to encourage and enable those artistic activities that express and challenge the Way We Live Now. There are already precedents for the successful pursuit of a contemporary arts policy by imaginative local authorities both here and abroad (the Roman Summer Festivals organized by the communist city administration in the late 1970s effectively combined mass-popular and 'high art' forms, often against the background of the Forum, the Colosseum and the Circus Maximus[10]). Those arts which cross conventional discipline boundaries, challenge conventional relationships between artist and audience, articulate identity, and express the experience of disjuncture and migration, are at the leading edge of the contemporary experience.

However, such forms should complement and not replace the traditional institutions (not least because the border between them is and should be an open one). National arts policy should enable the provision of the full breadth of arts activities. If I am less convinced than I should be by the efficacy of an expanded regional tier, it is because I suspect that Sheffield and Liverpool may have more in common than – say – Birmingham and Henley-in-Arden. But the point is that a plural arts policy implies a plural funding policy. The limits of private sponsorship are clear and admitted by its keenest advocates. The way to answer Norman St John Stevas's fears that public funding will lead to censorship and conformity is to provide alternative sources within the public sector.

I live in one of the provincial cities that has been transformed over the last decade by the imaginative policies of a Labour council, where the spirit of Metroland has been confronted if not yet defeated by the new municipal Medicis. Such policies have been promoted on the excellent grounds of economic development, urban regeneration and local morale; but it seems to me that there are even more fundamental reasons for encouraging their development.

As our traditional regional identities have declined, and our urban environment has become more and more homogeneous (with its ring-roads and tower blocks, atriums and Arndales), so culture has become more and more important as a means of locating ourselves. Indeed, you could say that culture in its broadest sense is as central to what people are about at the end of this century as the means of industrial production was to the people of its early and middle years. It is what both distinguishes and binds together the disparate, mobile, uncertain and inquisitive peoples of our continent, and those who have left other continents to join them. Culture *is* where they're coming from, where they're at and where they're going. And it is in the cities that those cultures meet, clash and, who knows, may eventually cohere.

In his book *Europe, Europe*, Hans Magnus Enzensberger makes the unlikely assertion that there are 100,000 magicians in Italy, and that those of them resident in Turin earn more than the Fiat factories. I am not sure I believe this, but I am sure I want to. And I think it would be best for us all in the long run if we behaved as if it were so.

NOTES

1   See 'Europe: variations on a theme of racism', *Race and Class*, Jan.–Mar. 1991.

2   Quoted by Kevin Robins in *Marxism Today*, December 1989.

3   Speech at the Royal Academy, 15 May 1979.

4   Speech at Newcastle on Tyne, 8 July 1987.

5   Open Mind, *BBC Radio 3*, 4 December 1988.

6   In a study by Simon Crine of the National Campaign for the Arts, reported in the *Guardian*, 21 July 1989.

7   'From Pillars to Post', *Marxism Today*, February 1990.

8   See Franco Bianchini: 'GLC R. I. P. Cultural Policies in London 1981–1986' *New Formations* No. 1, 1987, pp. 103–17.

9   *Sunday Telegraph*, 18 February 1990.

10 See Franco Bianchini: 'Cultural Policy and Urban Social Movements: The Response of the "New Left" in Rome (1976–85) and London (1981–86)', in Bramham *et al*, *Leisure and Urban Processes: Critical studies of leisure policy in Western European cities*, Routledge, London, 1989, pp. 24–9.

MARGARET DRABBLE

A Vision of the Real City

I was recently talking with friends about which of the arts has the most powerful and direct effect upon the emotions. The rival claims of music and poetry found the most powerful advocates, until one unexpectedly nominated architecture. A surprised and respectful silence fell. Architecture? Did she really mean architecture? Did *buildings* make her want to weep or sing with joy? We questioned her and, yes, she did mean buildings; she meant cathedrals and country houses and churches and skyscrapers.

I have thought back to this discussion many times, and now consider this friend's point is less eccentric than at first appeared. Some of the greatest and grandest emotional and aesthetic experiences of life come from architecture. Who can forget a first vision of Venice, of Rome, of Istanbul, of Marrakesh, of Carthage, of Tangiers, of Paris, of Rio de Janeiro, of Moscow, of Sydney, of Cape Town? Who can fail to be stirred by the grandeur of New York and Chicago? All these cities have burst upon me with an extraordinary impact, far outstripping any postcard or celluloid image of them, outstripping even representations by Guardi and Turner and Whistler. Cities are beautiful. Cities are powerful. They are our largest, our most diverse and complex and passionate works of art, assembled from many interlocking visions, and with many intricate moving parts.

Visitors to London, not yet dulled by delays on the Northern Line or IRA threats or rage with parking restrictions or knee-deep garbage, may still receive the impression of a grand and beautiful city. One can still cross Westminster Bridge and feel something of what even that profoundly rural northerner Wordsworth felt as he stood there. Dull would we be of soul not to respond to the river at night or early morning, the view of the City from Parliament Hill, the South Bank, the Lloyds building in Lime Street, the window displays of Liberty's, the Mall, the Henry Moores by the Serpentine and at Spring Gardens, the squares of Kensington, the dome of St Paul's, the curve of Regent's Street.

Yet we are very dull of soul, and often we do not respond to these beauties at all. It is not entirely our own fault. It is hard to feel an uplifting of the spirit when standing at a bus stop watching motionless traffic in the pouring rain, or while picking one's way through the black bags of Soho or along the treacherous pavements of Camden Town. It is hard not to notice that the fountains in Trafalgar Square rarely play, that the brand-new statue at Seven Dials seems permanently concealed in some kind of hoarding, that County Hall stands empty seemingly forever, that the building of the new British Library has been delayed and curtailed and may never reach its promised shape. These are our public places, our would-be show pieces. Many of our private places, our blocks of flats, our council estates, our suburban neighbourhood shopping streets, are in far worse condition.

Some of the mess in London is the direct result of the bitter feud of the past decade between government and local government. Some of it springs from a sort of stubborn English philistinism about architecture and city life, encouraged by the wilder utterances of the Prince of Wales. Not for us the pride of Paris in its pyramid, in its brave and soaring arch; not for us the multi-coloured panache of Stirling's Staatsgalerie in Stuttgart. We are timid and mean.

One of the reasons for our current architectural timidity lies in the failure of post-war high-rise and deck-access council building, symbolized by such episodes as the collapse of Ronan Point and the murder at Broadwater Farm. Justified complaints about housing have spilled over into attitudes towards public buildings. We all accept now that most people – and particularly families with small children – do not want to live in high-rise blocks on vast ghetto estates with dangerous open spaces. They want to live in mixed developments preferably in homes with pitched roofs designed on a human scale. But this does not mean that our public monuments should have pitched roofs and domestic proportions. We do not want St Paul's to look like a Swiss cottage or a village church. We do not want the Stock Exchange to look like a high-street bank. A twentieth-century concert hall need not resemble a seventeenth-century barn.

City dwellers and city visitors enjoy handsome and well-designed big buildings, both ancient and modern. They find them exciting. A city should offer a variety of scale, a range of styles. A city grows and changes, and can encompass many ages and stages of development. Why shouldn't a commercial glass palace soar above a preserved Shakespearean stone? Planners need not impose uniformity or cramp diversity and ambition. When offered architectural excitement, people forget their affectation of philistinism, and gaze about them with delight.

Some cities, like Venice and Istanbul and even my home town of Sheffield, have natural geographical advantages. They are well sited and offer fine vistas. Good architecture enhances their natural beauty. Venice without its buildings wouldn't be worth putting on a postcard, and Istanbul without Haghia Sophia and the cafés and stalls and thronging human traffic of the Galata Bridge wouldn't be one of the wonders of the world. I don't claim that Sheffield is either a Renaissance miracle or an industrial Utopia, but it can look good and it could look better. In the past it has employed some imaginative civic architects, and it continues to show an interest in bold and good design. And it has tried to stick to one of the most frequently abandoned virtues of a thriving city – it has kept a living centre. People still live on estates a few minutes' walk from the shops. You can walk to the market or to the Crucible Theatre. There is no vast acreage of dead down-town space. It does not empty at night. And public transport is still relatively cheap and frequent.

On a recent visit, on a crisp wintry day, I took in three of Sheffield's new architectural developments. The first was Blackwell Court at Bard Street, a small model block of sheltered housing, complete with warden, special bathrooms and buttons and telephones, laundry and hairdressing and chiropody facilities,

34

prettily decorated guest suite and all the conveniences of custom-built space for the elderly and the disabled. Over sandwiches and cake we praised its virtues, before some of the residents had to rush off to other Christmas parties in other blocks. They are a sociable lot on the Bard Street estate. We even spoke of the arts, and two women gave me leaflets of poetry they had written, encouraged by the weekly creative-writing class. A good time was had by all, and few complaints – except about water rates – surfaced. Here was a building that seemed good to live in.

Then I was whisked off, at my own request, to see the huge new shopping mall of the Meadowhall Centre, which has recently arisen in the derelict manufacturing area of the Lower Don valley. Where once the steelworks prospered and stained the night sky red, now the clean and glittering domes of consumerism arise. Here it seems that you can find a branch of every building society and every large store in the land (except, as some mutter, the sage John Lewis): here you can buy clothes and furniture and greetings cards and chocolates and fluffy toys and perambulators and refrigerators. Here golden plaster cherubs swoop over your head with swags of fruits and flowers, and fountains frolic, and escalators ceaselessly rise and descend, and cheery notices inform you where to find your car-park level or your lost offspring. Here you can eat American-style, Italian-style, Mexican-style. Here, in short, you might as well be in Edmonton or Dallas.

I must say I had sensed a certain disapproval when I admitted to my hosts in the Housing Department my desire to see this City of Temptation, this Vanity Fair of the 1990s. I would have been morally better regarded, I felt, had I asked to see a restored industrial hamlet. But there is no doubt that people, and here I include myself, are fascinated by this kind of venture. Shopping malls have become a new, day-out tourist destination. People go out of curiosity, not necessarily to shop but to gape and marvel at the sheer lavishness of the display. A friend of my aunt's had been to the Meadowhall Centre on a coach tour from Lincolnshire. We have progressed a long and affluent way from the somewhat dour Arndale centres of the 1960s, with their forbidding cement walls and slit windows. ('Shoppers don't need natural light; building windows is a waste of money,' property developer Sam

Chippindale once told me as he proudly showed me round his centres at Luton and Bradford.) I prefer the glitz of Meadowhall. It is cheery, it is big and bright and light, it is extravagant. And it is for us. It has no other function, no higher calling. No wonder people like it.

It is also, of course, a threat to the life of the old city centre. It is a threat to traditional retailers. It is a threat to the delicate web of interconnection between the domestic and the commercial, between homes and shopping space. The city centre, if it wishes to continue to attract custom, must make itself beautiful and glamorous too. Why should citizens be fobbed off with dowdiness, with litter, with traffic chaos, with ugly buildings and bad planning and hideous multi-storey car-parks on prime sites? (Sheffield, like all big cities, is guilty of car-park offences. Could we not learn from the ingenious burrowing Japanese, or even from our own excavations beneath Hyde Park and Bloomsbury Square? I love the car-park under Bloomsbury Square, in the form of a double helix: it is a good shape, it is easy to park in, it works, and from street level you cannot even see it is there.)

My third Sheffield tour on this December day was of the old Lyceum Theatre. Here my family would come for its one annual visit to a live cultural event. We never went to a concert or a gallery or a play at the Playhouse, but along with thousands of our fellow citizens we used to go to the Lyceum pantomime. This was an immensely glamorous occasion, and the theatre building itself was an essential ingredient of the glamour. Built to the grand designs of W. G. R. Sprague, it opened in 1897, and was a marvel of luxury. The ceiling decorations, the rosettes and nymphs and cherubs, the lamps and chandeliers, the red velvet curtains and gold braid were glorious and so were Davy's Real Ices, Morecambe and Wise, Frankie Howerd, Jewell and Warris, and all those undifferentiated principal boys in spangled tights, and those chorus girls with glowing faces painted bright pink and brown with magical Five and Nine. The excitement was tremendous. This was a real night out.

But the Lyceum, along with so many of the grand Victorian theatres of the regions, began to fall into disrepair. As live theatre in the fifties and sixties felt the threat of television, so audiences dwindled. Eventually money was raised for rebuilding and renovation. And now the Lyceum, helped by a major grant from the European Regional Development Fund, has been lovingly restored and is more beautiful than ever. It is to be a touring theatre, run in tandem with the neighbouring 1960s-built production theatre-in-the-round, the Crucible, famous for Clare Venables and for snooker.

Others can argue the merits of productions and performances and programmes in these buildings: others can write about theatre subsidy and the balance between snooker, Shakespeare and Stoppard. My case here is more concerned with the effect of these theatres as buildings and meeting points, with their contribution to the visual texture and vitality of the city. The space of Tudor Square outside the Lyceum, when I last saw it, was a paved pedestrian area, which in a milder climate or a good summer would encourage the spontaneous sprouting of little café tables and street events. Even on a winter's day it seemed full of possibilities. People like to walk in streets and courtyards that are safe, lively and aesthetically interesting. City walks can and should be as enjoyable as country walks. It is not a question of postmodernist versus modernist, of kitsch versus brutal, of mock-classical versus high-tech. It is a question of boring versus interesting, of meanness versus courage. The restored Lyceum raises the spirits. So do brave new buildings, surprising sculptures. They can coexist happily.

What we do not want are the meannesses and shabbinesses that so often we seem prepared dully to accept. Why should we put up with the dinginess of the peeling Bingo hall and the insanitary disco, with the abattoir conditions of the football terrace? There is big money in Bingo and discos and football. Why not plough more of it back for the pleasure of those who pay? Fun should be fun. It shouldn't be a grey battle against fire risks and our fellow citizens. Some of our entertainments look more like punishments. They are an insult to the ticket-purchasing fun-seeker and to the eye of the freely wandering pedestrian. At least Meadowhall and the restored Lyceum and London's South Bank look like fun. Those who believe more people could enjoy the arts should have more faith in the city as art form. The beautiful city could educate us all.

Perhaps we all have some kind of vision of the ideal city, the Utopian city. Renaissance painters and architects played with the concept of a city where the buildings would be of such harmonious proportions that they would burst into the music of the spheres. Occasionally we catch a glimpse of this ideal classical city; elements of it linger in my own vision. But for me they are superimposed by and infused with a vision that I think probably owes more to our own William Morris (and possibly therefore a little to Ruskin, who is also celebrated in Sheffield's Tudor Square). By this, I do not mean a rustic city papered with honeysuckle and lilies, lit by stained glass windows, and walled with medieval frescos. The Morris vision has more to do with the people of the future than with the artefacts of the past.

In this city of the future, the people will be healthy and well clothed and well fed. Merely from looking at them you will not be able to distinguish those who sweep the streets, those who walk the streets, and those who own the streets. There will be no more servant faces, no more master faces. There will be no more undernourished, underprivileged, miserable stunted citizens. There will be no more cardboard cities, no more huddled, blanketed bodies in cement underpasses. There will be no more dirty peeling halls with broken decorations and fused light bulbs; there will be no more shops with iron grids or hardboard nailed over their windows. There will be no more overflowing trash cans of junk-food wrappings. There will be no more urine-stinking lifts with violent graffiti. There will be no more fear on the street corner, no more terror on the tube.

T. S. Eliot, in *The Waste Land*, had a vision of the nightmare city, the Unreal City, where the undead crowd of what we now call commuters flowed over London Bridge:

> so many,
> I had not thought death had undone so many.
> Sighs, short and infrequent, were exhaled,
> And each man fixed his eyes before his feet.

We all know that city. It is the city of the overcrowded nightmare journey to work, of the snatched sandwich and polystyrene tea, of the tedious office routine, of the cancelled train and the traffic jam and the pinched bottom and the bomb scare and the Clapham rail disaster. Eliot's city is the city of the wage slave. He paints a city inhabited by carbuncular young men, by typists living in boarding houses with drying combinations spread on the windowsill, by the damp souls of housemaids. Some of these condemned figures have been swept away by history but others linger on, abused by the city itself as well as by their impoverished working lives. We must do away with all of that: with all that contempt, with all that snobbery, with all that pity. We have the means. Society has phased out the damp housemaids already; society should cease to exploit ranks of second-class workers and unemployed drifters.

William Morris believed that people were capable of better and deserved better. He believed that socialism could bring them a better city and a better life. He believed, as I believe, that the aesthetic and the moral and the physical are all intimately, inextricably connected. There is nothing particularly novel about this point of view. Most of us believe that poor living and poor working conditions contribute to poor health and physique. We cleared the slums to give peopled a fairer physical chance in life. But you only have to use your eyes to see that we did not go far enough. Our streets are still peopled by the conspicuously disadvantaged. Inadvertently, we created new slums. We put our trust in square feet of bedroom space and bathrooms and central heating. All these things are good, but we did not have enough faith in the principle of beauty. We did not give the arts enough of a role to play. Morris would have known better. Our building programmes perpetuated a divided society, and the past ten years have created deeper and more severe division. Ugliness breeds schism and despair.

I cling to the possibility of the redeemed city, the earthly Jerusalem, where our bold and beautiful public buildings and work places will be matched by comfortable and attractive domestic architecture, where transport will be clean and safe and easy, where streets will be pleasant. I have always liked the idea of large multi-purpose buildings that allow you to buy your supper or have a haircut in your lunch break; I like Bush House on the Aldwych, and well-stocked Leadenhall Market with its highly decorated glass roofed arcades built in 1881, I love the magnificent and romantic Palmer House that is a city in itself in Chicago, and I wish that the new British Library could incorporate a greengrocer and a deli. When offices are relocated, one of the first questions a working woman will ask of the new workplace is 'What's the shopping like?' And a well-stocked fishmonger's is a work of art.

Incidentally – or perhaps not incidentally? – I must say how much I disapprove of the fashionable notion that safe cities are dull. Safety depends on a good and interesting mix. We don't need a chorus of thieves and beggars and murderers to entertain us.

And let us also do away with the idea that good architecture, modern sculpture and imaginative design are somehow élitist and extravagant. It is always easy to find a philistine *vox pop.* to protest in the name of the Common Man and Commonsense against any form of new building or scheme. It is easy to save money by telling the people to tell themselves that they don't want Henry Moore or an opera house, they want a cheap cement multi-storey car-park. The truth is that many people are suspicious of the new, and are unwilling (or, as in my case, unable) to see from an architectural plan or drawing what a finished building will really look like. It is easier to sneer than to applaud. It is easier to approve the familiar than the surprising. It is easier still to do nothing at all. Yet when we do admit into our cities our Henry Moores and our Elizabeth Frinks and our Barbara Hepworths and our Picassos, we soon learn to love them. I firmly believe that the people of Leeds would have come to love that endearingly eccentric proposal for the Holbeck Man. Designed by sculptor Tony Gormley, Holbeck Man was a huge brick man who would have towered benevolently over a derelict area behind Leeds station. But to build him somebody had to take the risk. And somebody was afraid.

We need more incentives, financial incentives, to encourage local authorities and private enterprise to commission sculptures and fountains. Some countries have them. Why can't we? Because we are of little faith. Because we think it doesn't matter. But it does.

There is a lesson for us all in Sydney Opera House. How it got itself built at all is something of a miracle. What can its elliptic paraboloids have suggested on paper, to the uninformed eye? When Danish architect Joern Utzon's sketches won the competition for the building in 1957, there were mutterings from several directions – about expense, scale, style. Some even thought it would be pallid and boring, and the philistines predictably made jokes about a building that looked more like 'nuns-in-a-scrum' than the promised 'sails-in-a-harbour'. It was a risky building if ever there was one, but look how magnificently the risk paid off. It is a triumph. It looks wonderful, it is fun to visit, it enhances the landscape and it has put Sydney on the map of the world. Sydney would have been immeasurably the loser if timidity had triumphed at the planning stage. Instead we are all the richer, even those of us on the other side of the world, for that act of corporate courage. There are no losers.

It is a great pity that the notion of planning has got itself such a bad name. It is true that planners of different and indeed opposing ideologies have been guilty of environmental atrocities and delays and heritage nostalgia, but the free market and the uncontrolled profit motive have also destroyed some fine sites and buildings and erected some monstrosities. For any kind of coherent grand design, some kind of planning is obviously necessary. It is, I repeat, a pity that we no longer trust the vision of our planners or the concept of planning. It was not always so.

Today, for the first time for more than forty years, I visited the Monument in the City of London, and climbed up its 311 steps to the public balcony. The view has changed somewhat.

The Monument was built, as every tourist knows, to commemorate the Great Fire of London, which in 1666 destroyed 13,200 houses and eighty-nine churches. Its simple fluted Doric column is in itself an object of beauty, and one can see why Christopher Wren initially thought a phoenix would be an appropriate crowning symbol. (The phoenix was rejected because it would be 'not easily understood at that height, and worse understood at a distance'.) On the south panel of the base is a Latin inscription which tells us that Charles the Second 'commiserating the deplorable state of things, whilst the ruins were yet smoking provided for the comfort of his citizens, and the ornament of his city; remitted their taxes, and referred the petitions of the magistrates and inhabitants of London to the Parliament; ... immediately passed an Act, that public works should be restored to greater beauty, with public money, to be raised by an imposition on coals; that churches, and the cathedral of St Paul's should be rebuilt from their foundations, with all magnificence; that the bridges, gates and prisons should be new made, the sewers cleansed, the streets made straight and regular, such as were steep levelled and those too narrow made wider, market and shambles removed to separate places.'

And all this was done, and thus the Great Fire gave us town-planning and St Paul's Cathedral and also rid London of the plague. Beauty, magnificence and health were restored by the restored king.

Yes, you may say, but we do not have the likes of Sir Christopher Wren around today, and we do not have the money to build as he built.

Gazing from the public balcony of the Monument over the City, and up and down the river, it seemed to me that in the late twentieth century we have a great deal of money, some amazing and occasionally eye-delighting new building technology, at least a few fine architects, and that these things can sometimes come together. There is a splendid view, for those who have no tendency to vertigo, of Richard Rogers's extraordinary Lloyds building, with its glittering silver bravura. This is an exciting building from every angle. It is possible to build boldly and beautifully and practically.

Some six thousand people work in Lloyds. Does the glamour of the environment make them feel less like wage slaves, less like T. S. Eliot's wasteland commuters? I hope so.

It shouldn't be beyond the wit of man and woman to create cities which are at once prosperous, practical and beautiful, where we can enjoy both work and leisure. We all have an interest in this. The vision of the Real city concerns us all.

RUTH WISHART

Fashioning the Future: Glasgow

---

n the middle of the 1980s nine British cities put forward their
espective claims to the Office of Arts and Libraries to represent
Britain in 1990 as Cultural Capital of Europe. Most of the
contenders were predictable: among them the aesthetically pleas-
ng Cambridge and Bath and Edinburgh, already firmly estab-
ished as the home of the world's premier arts festival.

In the event the nomination went to Glasgow, a city not
mmediately synonymous with the popular concept of culture!
But if outsiders were shocked – and in Edinburgh outrage and
disbelief went off all known scales – the citizenry in the 'dear,
green place' itself pronounced the selection entirely appropriate.
The application, after all, had post-dated one of the most success-
ul civic self-marketing exercises since the I Love New York campaign.

The pun, 'Glasgow's Miles Better', accompanied by a smiling
cartoon logo had, as it happened, been principally devised to
make a sales pitch abroad and in the deep, dark south-east of
England where the natives still doubted that the razor gangs of
1930s mythology had bequeathed their fiefdoms to more civilly
inclined successors. As subsequent research was to prove, the
campaign was highly successful in persuading record numbers of
new tourists to include Glasgow as a destination in its own right
in addition to its function as a logical base for exploring much of
central and south-west Scotland. Before the campaign Glasgow
attracted some 700,000 visitors. By 1988, the year of the Garden

Festival on the city centre banks of the Clyde, that number had risen to 2.2 million. Estimates for 1990 are 3 million.

But the Miles Better slogan was also a runaway success in the city's own backyard where it became very difficult to locate a homebred vehicle that failed to sport a multilingual version loyally affixed to the rear windscreen. The more overt Glasgow nationalists among the hackney cabbies even had their vehicles remodelled in yellow and white with the new symbol writ large on the doors. Here was a city that badly wanted to reinvent itself; here was a town its residents were desperate to love.

But the reasons for Glasgow being awarded the 1990 crown were based, it transpired, on a piece of political pragmatism. Those members of the Office of Arts and Libraries who made the initial reconnaissance were not immediately convinced that this essentially gritty city was the ideal candidate. What convinced them at the second inspection was a detailed financial paper provided by the informal but well-established network of arts workers and administrators. Together they had been able to identify an annual arts budget in Glasgow of £24 million. Together they were able to remind their official visitors that all the major national arts companies were Glasgow-based and that, in addition to the obvious attractions of Scottish Opera, Scottish Ballet, the Royal Scottish National Orchestra and the annual Mayfest arts festival, the city could boast seventeen major museums, twenty-five arts galleries and nine major theatres including the renowned Citizens, whose European reputation was already secure.

Thus began the great adventure: a year of many thousands of events both modest and glittering, and a year that prompted an agonizing and still raging debate. The core of it is this: are the arts, 'culture', and participation in the hype of a 1990-style promotion a vital tool in urban regeneration and civic rebirth or have they very little meaning to those many thousands still disenfranchised by unemployment, poor housing and the lack of any obvious escape route from endemic poverty? Indeed, many of those who thought 1990 an extravagant irrelevance themselves came from the creative community. The author James Kelman wrote uncompromisingly about his own standpoint in a collection of essays published early in 1991 by the self-styled 'Workers City' group, who had spent much of the previous year in loud condemnation of the celebrations. Kelman wrote: 'In this past year in Glasgow concentional myths to do with art and public funding have been given full rein. The concept itself of "city of culture" was always hazy, extremely dubious indeed. It had more to do with etiquette than anything else. But if boldness is one essential ingredient of entrepreneurial activity, then those who decided to go for it are champions of the new realism which nowadays seems to cross not only national but party-political boundaries. What becomes clearer by the day is that both the adoption and application of the concept derived from another heady mixture: intellectual poverty, moral bankruptcy and political cowardice.' Kelman goes on to suggest that the 1990 celebrations were actually an assault on the real cultural life of the city and continues, contemptuously, to allege that 'cash investments in the city and environs was the primary motivation as the politicians have confirmed publicly.' That viewpoint was echoed by academic Sean Damer in yet another sceptical lament: 'Glasgow, Going for A Song': 'What the image builders were trying to do was sell the city's investment potential. This was and is the underlying rationale.'

That is an assertion with which the city's ruling Labour group is unlikely to disagree. Where they might find difficulty is in wondering why they should feel guilty about it. Jean McFadden, erstwhile leader of the group, now City Treasurer and current President of the Convention of Scottish Local Authorities, finds no political contradiction in marrying public and private enterprise in the cause of attempting to revitalize the city. 'A lot of what we've achieved has been through the willingness of the public and private sectors to cooperate. Around £2.4 billion has been invested in the city over the past few years in housing, shops, hotels and offices.' McFadden was one of the political representatives on a committee known as Glasgow Action, which also involved some of the major industrialists and financiers. Their joint intention was to make Glasgow an attractive destination for inward investment in both jobs and finance whilst maximizing the benefits of the relatively new phenomenon of arts-based tourism.

It was Glasgow Action that found the money for a specifically Glaswegian addition to the Policy Studies Institute report on the

Economic Importance of the Arts in Britain. Its author, John Myerscough, has again been put to work quantifying the precise benefits of the 1990 exercise. But even in his 1988 research, he found considerable grounds for optimism: 'There was good evidence that Glasgow had tapped new markets through the influence of the arts. In Glasgow 71 per cent of cultural tourists were first-time visitors. The rise of the new market was all the more impressive because there had been little marketing from a cultural angle ... The response of visitors to Glasgow's cultural facilities was especially strong ... a total of 79 per cent of all visitors considered Glasgow was either a very or extremely interesting and enjoyable place.' Myerscough goes on to argue that there are major development opportunities and that the arts sector can have a very real impact in terms of local employment. In Glasgow, he argues, the arts were shown to be 'a major source of economic activity', with each job in the arts giving rise to another 2.7 elsewhere in the region.

Yet even the statistically precise Myerscough cuts little ice with the Workers City group determined, as they see it, to rescue Glasgow's past from sanitization and Glasgow's future from the alleged 'cowboys'. Damer writes at length about the numbers still living on income support in greater Glasgow and located in the euphemistically designated 'areas of priority treatment'. 'What has happened in Glasgow,' he writes, 'is that the managers of the service sector, the restaurateurs and disco proprietors, the yuppies in finance, the civil servants fleeing from the south east of England, the residents and patrons of the "Merchant City", are able to enjoy their enhanced lifestyle at the expense of the thousands of unemployed and low-paid workers living in the aptly named peripheral estates.'

There are some essential flaws in Damer's analysis of what Glasgow is, and should be, about and an inherent arrogance in the collective assertion of the Workers City group that only they are qualified to be keepers of the city's socialist conscience and working-class tradition. There is an arrogance too in their becoming the self-appointed voice of the people in Glasgow on whom, they argue, the regeneration of Glasgow and its refurbished image have never truly impinged.

That Glasgow still has immense problems, some of which stem from a well-motivated but ill-thought-out post-war housing policy, is self-evident. That this error was compounded by a public housing policy somewhere between a lottery and a long-running farce is not in doubt either. Certainly not by anyone who watched or participated in the Byzantine form of bureaucratic snakes and ladders that masqueraded as a housing-eligibility points system. But an acknowledgement of these policy failures and an appreciation of the scale of the task still to hand should not be mutually exclusive from applauding the very real transformation that has been wrought in various sectors of the city. It is simplistic to ridicule the efforts of those involved in the mammoth East End renewal process, or to mock the social aspirations of those who have set up home in the remodelled warehouses now marketed as the Merchant City just a few blocks from George Square and the City Centre.

Would it have been idealogically more sound to leave the scars of industrial decline as ugly, mocking symbols of the heyday of heavy engineering, rather than landscape the gap sites? Were the near-derelict warehouses morally more acceptable to the socialist soul than the bright new apartments? It is evidence of some rather sloppy research to suggest, as many members of the amalgamated union of pamphleteering operatives consistently do, that this inner-city housing project has fallen to the yuppies. In the first place to be a yuppie and a Glaswegian is an obvious contradiction in terms. With the possible exception of Liverpool, no other British city is more adept at putting down, by withering verbal assault, the would-be social mountaineer. In Glasgow, acquiring ideas above your station is not a sport for the faint-hearted. But, paradoxically, realizing 'pipe-dreams' is a well-established habit, of which the 1990 extravaganza is merely the latest manifestation.

Glaswegian innovators from James Watt and Henry Bell through the shipping magnates like Alexander Stephen, David Elder and William Burrell and the early store giants like Thomas Lipton, the tobacco and cotton barons and the architects Charles Rennie Mackintosh and Alexander 'Greek' Thomson, were people of vision who unhesitatingly placed Glasgow within an inter-

national context. In a different, but equally persuasive way, the
deserve nomination to the civic hall of fame alongside the socialis
heroes – the Gallaghers, Macleans, Maxtons and McShanes.

Examined against that backdrop, the current collaboratio
between major corporate figures like Lord Macfarlane and th
Labour leadership of the city ought not to be characterized as i
dereliction of political duty, but rather as a clear-sighted attemp
to achieve a commonly desired goal of urban regeneration and
more broadly based prosperity. These, of course, qualify as hereti
cal assumptions to the ideologically pure in heart, for whom th
longest of spoons guarantees no protection from contaminatio
when supping with the capitalist devils.

Many of those who have most recently put Glasgow under th
microscope during what is, rather chillingly, referred to as th
post-industrial age have made telling comparisons with the socio
logical mix in Liverpool. And indeed the 50,000 souls who fle
famine-struck Ireland for the west of Scotland were irretrievabl
to alter the culture of their adopted habitat, in much the sam
manner as Liverpudlian immigrants. The comparisons continu
with the ready self-deprecating wit, the reputation for hospitality
and the healthy disregard for authority and all its works. Glas
wegian children do not dream of becoming traffic wardens. Bu
there is another point of contact between those spiritually twinne
cities that deserves closer examination than it often commands
Both cities produced dominant Labour administrations tha
wielded considerable power. The Liverpool battles with its Mili
tant wing were to prove a significant distraction from the busines
of effecting urban renewal. There were, of course, many brave
initiatives designed to bring improvements to run-down housing
estates. Scaling down the size of the blocks, renovating and
landscaping, all helped to transform many pockets of housing
Yet until very recently the regeneration of the very heart o
Liverpool had not been a discernible priority. Visitors to the city
are startled still by areas of boarded-up neglect just minutes from
the main shopping centre and by the utter dereliction of what
had once been fine inner-city Georgian terraces.

Yet there is no escape from the harsh reality that people
coming to a city with the power to decide on job-creating

investment will inevitably be seeking an acceptable quality of life for themselves and their employees. City-centre development is invariably an influential factor in that judgement. The largely pedestrianized Glasgow city centre with two major shopping developments, one housing expensive designer-label boutiques, has been pilloried as the worst kind of advertisement for rampant consumerism and a shopping irrelevance to the majority of the indigenous population.

There are two problems with that assertion. First, that kind of development consistently appears in the lists of priorities of incoming investors. Second, thousands of Glaswegians whose own budgets operate on an altogether different level to these emporia have not been deterred from visiting them as a constant and free cabaret. I would imagine much the same may apply to many of the outlets surrounding the fine new Tate Gallery in the Albert Dock development in Liverpool, a project which very clearly took on board the possibilities inherent in arts-led inner-city development.

There is another strand to the argument, and it's loosely encapsulated in what the director of Glasgow's 1990 Festivals Unit, now enshrined as a full-time director of the performing arts in the city, has called the 'Whose culture is it anyway?' debate. One of the accusations which haunted Bob Palmer's festival year was that events such as Pavarotti and Sinatra concerts with their maximum ticket prices of £75 were once again irrelevant to the poorer sections of Glaswegian society. It was a particular frustration for Palmer, whose major 1990 promotions with these two stars, the Van Gogh retrospective, the Peter Brook productions and several world-class orchestras, were but a handful of performances amongst literally thousands of community-based events. He was caught in the media trap sprung by journalists wishing only to chronicle the doings of the megastars and then unblushingly complaining that the community enterprises had been neglected and unheralded. It became an extension of the annual argument over the content of Glasgow's Mayfest, which has to find ways of reconciling a desire to import international product and a need to nourish and sustain a commitment to local initiatives.

Yet many of the most memorable moments throughout the

1990 programme involved the community at large: the hundred thousand plus teenagers in George Square and Glasgow Green for a pop marathon, The Big Day, 10,000 children marching with their homemade lanterns through the worst the October weather could throw at them. (And in Glasgow the worst can be downright nasty.) Palmer asserts that he sees his role for the rest of the 1990s as building on the spirit engendered by events such as these, and continuing to fund, where possible, the theatre groups and small community enterprises. One of the first questions that faced anyone seeking funding from the Festivals Unit before 1990 was how they saw their event or project prospering in the years beyond. For Palmer the year of culture was seen always as a springboard, never as a self-contained, finite project. Neil Wallace, Bob Palmer's deputy in the 1990 Festivals Office and now working on the development of the Tramway theatre, points to the fact that some community-based events scheduled for that year have found sustained and continuing leases of life. He cites the popular 'Call That Singing' choir which has now placed dates all over Scotland, and the fact that 'Street Biz', the annual festival of street theatre and buskers is now four years old and stands comparison with several longer-established events internationally. 'I think sometimes when people talk about whether or not community developed work has a long-term future they're a bit lazy about looking hard enough. The fact that the Glasgow Film Theatre now has a second screen is going to be very important in the community field and so far as using the Tramway as a focus for new and challenging work for local groups in the south side is concerned, well we haven't even begun to sniff the possibilities in that space. The problem is that some of the very real spin-off can seem intangible and is undoubtedly difficult to sustain unless the political will continues to be there.'

The difficulty faced by Palmer and Wallace, and that John Myerscough will also encounter in his new research, is that many of the benefits have proved intangible. How do you quantify the improvement in self-confidence that may result from a single parent being involved for the first time in a local arts project – confidence which may later prove crucial in attempts to improve the domestic situation. It would be crazily optimistic to view that kind of 'culture' as a potential cure for intractable social ills, but equally it would be perversely pessimistic to deny the potential for increasing a sense of self worth that involvement with the arts can demonstrably bring. Long-standing projects such as Glasgow's Easterhouse Festival and the quite remarkable Craigmillar Festival in a similarly deprived housing estate in Edinburgh serve as reminders of the folly of dismissing arts-based community projects rather than seeing them as the potent, ennabling experiences they can be.

Some of the legacies of those 1980s ambitions married to the 1990 aspirations have proved very tangible indeed, however. It's doubtful if the stone-cleaning project that allowed some fine Victorian architecture to emerge in its multicoloured glory from sooty imprisonment would have been accelerated without the deadline imposed by 1990. Neither would the Transport Museum have metamorphosed into the Tramway theatre – a venue which has become second home to Peter Brook – whose spatial flexibility has produced many imaginative and challenging works. The McLellan galleries would not have received such a stunning facelift and significant funds would not have been invested for the purpose of purchasing contemporary Scottish art.

But perhaps the project that most neatly encapsulates the modern Glasgow with its aspirations, its political paradoxes, and its 'chutzpah' is the new international concert hall. People who examine the mechanics of this deal tend to emerge ashen faced since there is little doubt that the vast project was undertaken at a time when the city had something less than a firm idea of who would pay for it. It was, according to taste, the ultimate act of faith or the ultimate piece of political skulduggery. The man who pulled a significant number of the strings involved was Pat Lally, current leader of the Labour group and a man much accused of what we might uncharitably call the 'Mayor Daley approach' to local government, which is to say that too many decisions about Glasgow were thought to have been taken by too few people on the basis of too little information in a process lacking both democracy and glasnost.

It would be iniquitous for an onlooker to pass judgement, but it is probably true to say that without a robust pursuit of the

project, and the consummate game of economic chess played b
Lally and his senior colleagues with the Scottish Office, the ne
concert hall might still be an artist's impression rather than th
recent home of the Berlin and Israeli Philharmonics, the Leipzi
Gewandhaus, the Orchestre de Paris, and other musical lumina
ies. Not for nothing has the new concert space been irreverentl
dubbed 'Lally's Palais'.

There were other legacies of 1990 the city would rather forge
The much criticized Glasgow's Glasgow exhibition, modelled o
Berlin, Berlin, swallowed up almost a third of the reserve fund o
£15 million earmarked as the city's guaranteed contribution t
the £40 million budget for the year. It was the main target als
of those critics concerned that history had been rewritten i
order, retrospectively, to erase some of Glasgow's more colourfu
past. A world-theatre season, inexplicably scheduled for mid
summer, attracted widespread acclaim and tiny audiences.

The greatest danger now is that Glasgow begins to believe tha
the job is even half done. Over the last seven years man
influential figures, not least the Prince of Wales, have held Glas
gow up as a model of urban regeneration within the UK. It ha
in the oddest way, become a 'fashionable' city, and those wh
come to examine its inner workings pronounce it exciting, spea
of the perennial 'buzz' to be found there and compare it to
small-scale New York – a comparison increasingly less flattering
Glasgow, pronounce its visiting gurus, is a 'can-do' city. That's
hard-won accolade, given that the raw material of Glasgow'
previous reputation was less than promising. But it is an accolad
that has constantly to be set in the context of a city where there i
still a prodigious amount to be done. Perhaps that progress ma
be accelerated when those who persist in constantly re-examinin
their city's historical navel invest similar levels of intellectua
energy in helping to fashion its future.

DAVID LISTER

The Transformation of a City:
Birmingham

In the final analysis the test of a civilized city is not the extent of its municipal spending on cultural provision, nor the international eminence of its key arts activities, nor its wealth of locally based creative talent, though all those are important indicators. The test of a civilized city is the liveliness and pervasiveness of the relationship between the arts and the daily lives of all the people living and working within the city.

– Internal report by the chief executive and other department heads of Birmingham city council on An Arts Strategy for Birmingham, March 1990.

In his 1984 novel *Small World*, set in the university city of Rummidge, David Lodge describes how a group of academics go out for a night to see *King Lear* at The Rep. When they arrive they find that *Puss in Boots* is on instead. It turns out that the run of the Christmas pantomime has been extended as 'it's the only production in the whole year that makes a profit'.

As most of the group moan, one person defends the city. 'It's very central,' he says. 'Central to what?' demand the others.

'Well, since they opened the M 50 I can get to Tintern Abbey, door to door in 95 minutes.'

Enough clues there to know that the fictional city was Birmingham. Its reputation as a sprawling, blighted, industrial zoo whose citizens sported a collective inferiority complex dates back more than three hundred years. The entry for Brummagem in the *Shorter Oxford Dictionary* reads: '(contemptuously) an article

53

made in Birmingham . . . with allusion to counterfeit groats, plate etc; counterfeit, sham; cheap and showy, 1681'.

The transformation in barely a few years of Birmingham's image from cultural wasteland to England's most dynamic concentration of cultural activity outside London is a remarkable story of local-authority commitment and imagination. The achievements that have put the city on the international stage have been detailed many times, but are worth repeating to give a context to the next round of challenges the Labour authority must meet to satisfy the aspiration boldly stated in the extract from the strategy document quoted above.

The arts renaissance almost certainly had its roots in the arrival just over ten years ago of Simon Rattle as Music Director of the City of Birmingham Symphony Orchestra. Anthony Sargent, the city's arts officer, says: 'He has been a critical factor, making it credible for the orchestra to demand a new concert hall; and the international regard for the orchestra has given members of the council confidence in the benefit of culture. They can feel a relationship with the benefit of their policies, which an avant-garde gallery wouldn't have.'

And so the purpose-built Symphony Hall, acoustically one of the best of its kind in the world, entered the Birmingham landscape this year, shortly followed by the International Convention Centre and, in Centenary Square in front of the two buildings an £800,000 public art programme of decorative arts and sculpture involving artists of the calibre of Tess Jarry.

In the three years preceding this, the Sadler's Wells Royal Ballet was wooed from London to become the Birmingham Royal Ballet at the Hippodrome; the D'Oyly Carte opera moved to the city and a new home at the Alexandra Theatre; the City of Birmingham Touring Opera developed swiftly in its first three years, recently premièring a radical new version of Wagner's *The Ring* to widespread acclaim; the two principal arts centres began to offer increasingly ambitious programmes; free open-air performances were presented in the city centre and in Cannon Hill Park; the Arts Council awarded Birmingham the title UK City of Culture; and the city's three large-scale festivals (covering between them jazz, film and television, and literature) have grown over the last five years into events of national importance.

In addition, among a welter of less than interesting Millennium initiatives, a rather interesting one has arisen in Birmingham, again partly at the initiative of Simon Rattle. Towards The Millennium is a cross-arts festival lasting until the end of the century that highlights the artistic achievements of successive decades.

In conjunction with the South Bank Centre in London, the festival examines cultural history. Events so far have included debates on the influence of imperialism on the visual arts, a stage production by the Birmingham Rep of Robert Tressell's *The Ragged Trousered Philanthropists*, which provoked great interest in the Labour movement as it toured Britain, and a performance of popular music by one of Europe's liveliest all women's orchestras: The Hot Strings.

It seems almost perverse to conjecture that one of the factors responsible for such an impressive catalogue of artistic achievement was a bureaucratic reshaping of council committees. Yet this is the case. In January 1989 the council decided to set up the arts, culture and economy sub-committee to cement cross-departmental links, ending the system of council departments being virtually independent baronies.

For the arts, the implications were enormous. For a start, and most unusually, the leader of the council now sat on an arts committee. A single committee could now talk to libraries, museums and education about, for example, staging the Millennium festival, could take decisions about public art programmes on behalf of the planning committee and decisions on grants to the CBSO on behalf of finance and management. The granting of such executive powers to a committee whose main business was in reality the arts demonstrated an extraordinary commitment from the council.

Surprisingly, as opposed to, say, Glasgow, the new faith in the arts did not seem to spring from their ability to act as a catalyst in regenerating the economy. After the collapse of the shipbuilding industry Glasgow built up what it refers to as an 'arts industry' and produces figures on how much it earns per year. Birmingham has no such figures.

Anthony Sargent says: 'Our arts strategy most emphatically does not say we value the arts for the money they bring in. The city has a very clear sense that it values cultural investment in the quality of life. Trying to make Birmingham a civilized place to live is something the city takes very seriously. There is a danger of using the arts to sell the city. For people here to feel their achievements are being used to sell an image of the city as a business exercise would be demeaning.' With only the faintest sense of irony one might add that a look at the weekend hotel-visitor figures would show the council that even with its artistic renaissance Birmingham is not going to bring in the tourists. Its arts initiative must be for its own citizens.

And so Birmingham's achievements must be judged on those terms – the terms the city's own leaders have set, equalling what it has achieved nationally and internationally in involving its own citizens, twenty-five per cent of whom are of the ethnic minorities. 'There isn't a problem with the local community,' says Anthony Sargent, citing the adventurous education programmes by the CBSO that put plays into schools, and the Birmingham Royal Ballet which has brought schoolchildren on to the stage of the Hippodrome.

He also cites plans to make available ethnic arts to different ethnic groups, so that Irish communities can see Chinese theatre and so forth. In addition, the city boasts the Cave Arts Centre, a renowned venue for black and Asian arts. An integral part of the city's development as a major dance centre is the national regard won by Kokuma, one of Britain's finest black performing ensembles and eloquent exponents of the relationship between contemporary dance and traditional black culture.

Most of all, the city council emphasizes its five-year plan for the Heartlands project, the artistic regeneration of a particularly deprived and blighted area to the east of the city where sculpture parks and community arts work will, according to the council 'give the area a sense of place, a quality of life and a range of cultural facilities unique in inner city renewal programmes'.

Citywide, there are already examples showing that the art planners are striving to widen the catchment area for arts events. The Birmingham Readers and Writers Festival is a notable even on the city's calendar, with high-profile international figures attending. But it now also spreads into libraries, community centres and youth clubs, with sessions on fanzines for young people, and elderly residents coming into local centres to record their own memories.

Kate Organ, the festival organizer, says: 'Birmingham people come in to tell their stories because, apart from the city's notion of making Birmingham an international venue, it is important that the arts are a part of people's ordinary lives. So, as well as Gore Vidal flying in, we have an 83 year old from Small Heath coming in to tell her story.'

But for all the ventures of that nature and the undoubted success of the last few years, satisfaction within the city is not universal, and the qualms are most evident among the deprived sections of the community. The Theatre of the Unemployed is an interesting community venture in Highgate, near the city centre, and has done commendable work over the years, through both training schemes and less formal contacts, in encouraging unemployed people to put on their own shows and, in some cases, make a career in theatre. Yet in 1989, as the city was planning to spend millions on the arts, it cut this organization's £10,000 grant.

Chris Rozanski, company coordinator, says: 'The city's policy shifted around then from providing growth locally to top-shelf stuff they can advertise in the international arena. There are only about four fringe theatre companies left in Birmingham. Five years ago there were twenty-five. There hasn't been confidence in the work produced locally so they bring it in, as with Sadler's Wells and the D'Oyly Carte. There were good ballet companies in Birmingham but they didn't put the seed money in. There are more touring companies coming in now than local companies performing. I'm not against high-quality international work, but investing in local people has got to be a priority.

'Everyone is screaming about the quality of the international work, but a quarter of a mile from the convention centre are run down areas like Ladywood Springhill, where there is really no provision. Here in Highgate a lot of people get mugged; the lifts don't work in the high rise flats, and when you talk to local people about the arts they don't want to know. They look at the millions spent on the convention centre and they say they would prefer to have the lifts working.'

Birmingham's arts officers will justifiably respond that they cannot cure all the ills of the inner cities. But Mr Rozanski's point remains a valid one. The arts do improve the quality of life, but the arts can become an irrelevance for those whose daily life is needlessly fatiguing, frustrating and dangerous. Birmingham is not unique in having inner-city problems, but as a recent important report, funded by the Gulbenkian Foundation, on cultural life in Britain's towns and cities showed, fears of going out, particularly among women and the elderly, were inhibiting people from taking advantage of arts initiatives. And so, while Birmingham's radical council committee structure is a model for other councils to follow in giving the arts a higher profile, still more radical structures might be necessary.

Without a successful education system, too, even the best arts provision will be targeting an unresponsive audience. Birmingham's does give cause for concern. Government statistics show that in the city's seventy-six secondary schools only 23 per cent of pupils achieved five or more GCSEs at grades A, B or C. When the seven grammar schools were omitted the figure fell to 16.7 per cent, about half the national average. Birmingham's community education adviser recently resigned in protest at what he saw as a bureaucracy unable to tackle the problems in the city's schools, citing reading ages below the expected level of 87 per cent of eight year olds in parts of the city.

A problem that might be easier to tackle in the shorter term, and one which is absolutely vital in showing that arts provision reaches and enriches the local community, is the alienation felt by some of the 250,000 citizens of Asian origin. The arts strategy document talks of 'the need to respond to the wide diversity of ethnic cultural backgrounds that exists in the city, by nourishing self-expression within all those communities; by the encouragement and development of mutual sharing amongst Birmingham's different cultural communities of their individual artistic traditions and heritage, and by welcoming to Birmingham high-quality arts provision of all cultural ethnicities.'

But the extent to which this aim has been fulfilled remains

unclear. Fazlul Khalid, now a race and management consultant in Birmingham, was on the Commission for Racial Equality for twenty-five years. Not enough, he says, is being done to recognize non-European art. The Asian community is not seen as, and does not see itself as, part of the whole scene. That can be said quite confidently. Minority art is seen as a fringe activity although many in the Asian community are not interested in the majority art. It is culturally anathema to them. Art is closely intertwined with people's value systems, and the Western value system has no value to them, particularly the older ones.

'For a start they would like more facilities for their music. One hears a lot about steel-band music because it has been adopted by the Western pop scene. Asian music generally is not to be found, apart from the odd cultish teacher taking up the cudgels. The same is true of Asian dance. Although 50 per cent of the Asian population is Muslim and not overtly interested in dance, the Hindus are.

'Even at the Cave Arts Centre in the heart of the Asian community Afro-Caribbean arts can take precedence. The community has not felt included enough. The council must invest in Asian arts in a big way. The way the arts are handled and presented does not recognize that there is a substantial Asian community here that is culturally minded. We have the odd import from the subcontinent but no belief in the local community. There is one Indian classical-music society operating from Wolverhampton, but interestingly nothing similar in Birmingham.'

It may well be that not all of Mr Khalid's and Mr Rozanski's perceptions are correct, but what is important is that these perceptions exist among sections of the community. And while one can and perhaps should argue that the assertion that a minority community is only interested in art forms produced from that ethnic background is one that should be challenged, nevertheless the perception clearly exists that the minority has not yet been included in the arts renaissance. On their larger worries it is clear that Birmingham cannot be expected to change decades of planning blight, inner-city decay, increasing violence and increasing concern over education standards overnight. But the city, and all cities, must acknowledge that all these seemingly unrelated aspects of urban life do affect people's attitudes towards participation in arts. The arts will either uplift their audiences, giving them greater insights into the way they live or, less pompously, just provide a welcome escape; but neither is possible if those audiences feel they cannot relate to that provision or cannot physically get to it.

With that in mind, one might question whether the arts strategy for the city fully made those connections. The section headed Implications for Women says: 'There are no implications specific to women in this report, but implicit in the issue of equal access to arts provision is the requirement that organizers of arts activities should do all within their power in terms of childcare to facilitate access by women, and in terms of physical security, to facilitate access by women and other vulnerable groups.'

It needs a sterner diktat for this to be realized. The council itself, rather than just the venues, must ensure that the streets and approaches to arts venues, car-parks and transport facilities, are welcoming. The strategy document also states: 'There are no implications specific to people with disabilities in this report, but implicit in the issue of equal access to arts provision is the requirement that organizers of arts activities should do all within their power to facilitate access by people with disabilities.' Again it has to be noted that arts venues nationally, most notably cinemas, have been extremely lax at doing 'all within their power' to help disabled people gain access.

A further problem for the council, and most certainly not one of its own making, is whether it will control any of its arts flagships in two years' time. The Arts Minister has approved a policy, broadly supported by the Labour Party, of devolving the funding of most arts organizations to new regional arts boards, the successors to the regional arts associations. In the case of Birmingham, its main companies are likely to be devolved to West Midlands Arts, whose budget – yet to be determined – will also have to cater for the many competing claims of numerous other organizations, large and small, in the district.

The city council remains to be convinced that this arrangement will work. One of Birmingham's most senior arts officials says: 'We have a very good relationship with the Arts Council (the present national funders) and have discussed our strategic plans to the background of other cities. It simply isn't possible to have those sorts of discussions with West Midlands Arts because intellectually the scope of vision hasn't made it possible. The city would be very unhappy about a situation in which clients of national importance were handed over to a board which didn't seem to have intellectually or culturally the experience to deal with them.'

New appointments still being made at the top of West Midlands Arts could allay those fears, but both Government and Opposition must ensure that Birmingham's achievements are not undermined by allowing companies to be devolved to new funding bodies unless those bodies can first show that there will be an improvement for both the companies and their audiences.

There are, as has been shown, problems, both short- and long-term, which threaten to cast shadows over the arts renaissance in Birmingham. But these should not be allowed to detract from the real, and in recent years unequalled, civic achievements in the arts. The challenge facing the city now is to demonstrate that, having achieved international stature for its cultural output, it can also, uniquely in Britain, convince all sections of the community that they are part of this renaissance, can enjoy it and profit from it.

RICHARD BURNS

The City as Not London

It is an unlikely spot for a city, a place of slopes and inclines where the cyclists are children or daft. Three centuries ago this was a region of hilltop settlements, villages separated by wide valleys and insignificant rivers. Then came industry. The valleys were tamed; the rivers were channelled through mill-races or converted to muscular steam; the hillsides ferrous as well as feral, were quarried and mined. Factories filled the hollows and linked the settlements. The industry grew and flourished. Sheffield was not founded, it was forged. Vulcan, the god of metal workers, was perched on the town-hall roof, and by that mythical period when the sun never set on the Empire, when each page of the atlas bore expanses of comfortable pink, Sheffield and steel had become synonymous. Steel explained Sheffield, justified siting a city among such recalcitrant hills. From the monumental factories of the east end, across the parks and museums that bore the names of ambitiously philanthropic steel magnates, through to the dank sprawling slums of Park Hill and Attercliffe where the workers lived or the leafy suburbs upwind of the smoke that Betjeman loved so well, the steel industry and the hills conspired to shape the city. Even the lovely and characteristic silver birches that plate hillsides too steep for building were planted because birch twigs were part of the steel process. You don't need to study the history. You need only study the landscape. Steel made Sheffield.

But though steel filled the valleys, the obdurate hills remained. The buildings grew around the hills; the city seemed to incorporate them. But the incorporation was incomplete. Sheffield is what it always was, a series of villages linked by an industry.

The industry has collapsed now. The name on the knife blade reads 'Korea' or 'Singapore'. The Little Mesters' workshops, where self-employed craftsmen applied the beauty and finish to cutlery blanks, have all closed. The terrifying buffer girls, cutlery polishers who – still wrapped like parcels in protective brown paper and string – marched arm-in-arm down the Wicker when work was done, are gone. The endless black steelworks, each an inferno of molten metal and noise, are demolished. Our industry was our identity, and now we have lost both.

Such a past, such a present, is hardly unique. Northern England is full of towns and cities that have lost their purpose. The looms are still, the shipyards silent. Built in an ugly age, hewn out of red brick and smoke, such places have little to recommend them beyond their grainy accents and a certain stoical resignation. What distinguishes Sheffield is not the rise and fall of its industrial fortunes. It is the rise and fall of its landscape, the inescapable hills and valleys that give the city its character. At night this city could be anywhere. The stars – man's oldest guide to navigation – are lost behind a sulphur mist, a sodium glow. The shop signs are ubiquitous, the shadowed buildings neutral, the pedestrians evasive. Police cars crawl the kerbs, ambulances rush. Mini-cab drivers read tomorrow's news while, in the day-and-night funeral parlours, the dead are preened for disposal. At night the hills and valleys are flattened into a pattern of streetlights that has neither form nor texture. Darkness insists that Sheffield is a city, a metropolis; daylight reduces it to its component parts, to a series of bloated villages, unfolding across the undulations, separated by valleys and superfluous stockyards, linked only by sewers and roads.

Perhaps this is all Sheffield has become: an infrastructure in search of a city, a system of services and administrative units sprawling across an intractable landscape. It's certainly true that the administration is the prime mover here, and it's certainly true that they, more than anyone, are concerned with Sheffield's identity. The city council, having somehow assumed or had thrust upon it the paternalistic role of the old steel magnates, has spent the last forty years looking to replace the old 'Steel City' tag with some new designation. For a while, making a virtue of factories forced to close and modern techniques in domestic heating, Sheffield was 'The Cleanest Industrial City in Europe'. It was a bold and honourable claim, if difficult to prove. Later, when the bomb sites and the horizontal Victorian slums were being replaced by vertical tower blocks and the city centre was transformed by dual carriageways and concrete, we became 'Sheffield – City on the Move'; by the 1970s, while I put lotion on my spots and stood in front of mirrors playing an imaginary guitar, civic confidence had been replaced by stagnation and the only movement was subsidence. The slogan changed again: unofficially, but with a certain pride, we were the 'Socialist Republic of South Yorkshire'; by the 1980s – socialist republics having lost their clout – we became the self-styled 'Sporting Capital of Europe', our most expensive reincarnation.

There are various theories to explain why Sheffield chose sport to fill the gaps left by our damaged industry. Sober historians emphasize the growth of the leisure industry, the fashion for health and fitness, and the fact that by the 1980s Sheffield's only claim to national fame was that it hosted the World Snooker Championship. Personally, I put the finger on Sebastian Coe: not his running, fabulous though it was, but his tongue. Seb was fluent in the language of sports commentators – 'I was running backwards, Brian' – and, speaking their tongue, he won their hearts. He became 'Sheffield's Most Famous Son', and a title bestowed by the press was endorsed by the city council. Had we produced a Pavarotti or a Picasso we might yet have become a City of Culture, though many Sheffielders would wince at the notion; instead, athletics was presented to the city as the ideal replacement for our lost industry, and new stadia sprung up along the Don Valley, literally on the rubble of the demolished steelworks. For this year Sheffield is host to the World Student Games – 'Sheffield 1991: It's Our Year' says a sticker on my neighbour's Datsun, though she also has a sticker claiming 'My other car's a Porsche' – and new hotels, sports complexes, and accommodation for the athletes are being rapidly completed on schedule if over budget. The World Student Games is second only to the Olympics in the number of competitors it attracts, though 'If t'Student Games are so bloody important,' the dourly smug in Sheffield's pubs ask, 'then who hosted the last bugger?'

And, though we're not a City of Culture, and are never likely to be, already the Student Games has produced benefits. The most important of these has been to make Sheffield a destination, a place people go to for its own sake. Alongside the Student Games, Sheffield hosts the Universiade Festival, the 'Spirit of Ninety One'. The festival, which has attracted acts from all over the world, is a genuinely impressive achievement: even I, Yorkshire-thrifty and worried about having to fork out for the thing, am genuinely impressed. Major sporting events are hard to attract regularly: it may well be that the cultural festival, which could easily become annual, might be the real achievement of this busy year.

It would be good to think so. The arts are not prominent in Sheffield. Although culture is a word with many meanings, conversationally at least it refers mainly to that grand tradition of achievement that reaches back through Renaissance Italy to Classical Greece. And although Sheffield people have supported that culture with no less than average enthusiasm, it is a tradition from which Sheffield feels excluded. The grand tradition visits, in the form of the Hallé Orchestra, touring theatre companies and the like, but it does not really reside here. Sheffield is not London. Nor is it Oxford or York. Its history is neither glorious nor inspiring. Legend has it that Sheffield is built on seven hills (I'm not sure which seven: there are dozens of hills round here) but that is all we share with Rome. And though the city has a proud culture of producing miracles in metal, metallurgy has generally been regarded as a grubby sort of pursuit in comparison with the arts. Apollo is radiant, Vulcan a cripple. The grand tradition misses us out; our clectic, multicultural Universiade Festival suits us. It's true that there's a production of *A Midsummer Night's Dream*, but it's in Romanian. The focus of the festival, in this city that is not London, is not Edinburgh, is on the home-grown or the truly exotic.

The council are the only significant sponsors of art in the region, and they have proved imaginative if eccentric patrons.

They built the Crucible Theatre – and they finance the Redtape Studios. The notion behind Redtape was that local musicians should be given the chance to produce professionally recorded demo discs, and, though there isn't a 'Sheffield sound' to compete with the Manchester bands or the Mersey Beat, enough Sheffield groups have signed with large studios to make the venture look a success. Another council-supported success has been the Leadmill, a converted set of industrial buildings, now a useful focus for the local arts, while the reopening of the elegant Lyceum Theatre means that the touring productions are coming back. The Arena, meanwhile, which was built to house the indoor parts of the Student Games, attracts different sorts of touring production: as I write we've had Paul Simon and Rod Stewart, and whilst sceptics might doubt whether Rod Stewart contributes much culture to the city, at least the big acts are coming now. Previously the only venue was the City Hall, too small for the stars, so the most famous bands we used to get were groups like Hawkwind and Gentle Giant. Like the festival, the Arena suggests that the lasting legacy of the Student Games will be cultural rather than sporting.

Perhaps that was the intention all along. There was certainly something unconvincing about our claim for sporting hegemony. The irony of Sheffield preening itself as a city where sport flourishes has not been lost on those who mourn the passing of first-class cricket from Bramall Lane. Nor has it been lost on those who mourn the victims of the Hillsborough football-ground disaster. In fact, reaction to the disaster at Hillsborough reveals more about Sheffield than any of the new identities imposed on the city. I was away when the disaster happened, teaching in an American college. From there it seemed Sheffield must become a place of tragedy, like Lockerbie or Aberfan. But Sheffield is a series of villages, and the disaster became localized at Hillsborough; Sheffield is a large city, and the disaster became absorbed; most importantly, Sheffield is not Liverpool, and the events at Hillsborough became a Liverpudlian affair. The differences between the two cities are profound. Liverpool takes pride in its emotions, whereas Sheffield prefers self-effacement. Liverpool presumes the world is interested in its affairs, and Sheffield hopes the world isn't. Liverpool's identity – perhaps because it would rather forget that its early prosperity came from slavery – lies with its people, its accent, its humour. Such things are portable and assertive. Sheffield's identity comes from its industry and its landscape. These count for little beyond the city's boundaries.

To compensate, Sheffield scorns the things that those beyond the boundaries rate highly. Celebrity, for instance. Famous Sheffielders are not particularly uncommon, but they are rarely lionized in the city. It is an interesting place for a writer to live. I am not better known in Sheffield than in Bangor or Aberdeen: Margaret Drabble, Bruce Chatwin and Malcolm Bradbury come from the city, but as far as the city recognizes this they might as well come from the moon. Sportsmen do a little better – not only Sebastian Coe but also Herrol Graham, the boxer who became a local hero – which of course encouraged the council to make us a City of Sport. Actually, it seems the Sheffielder the local paper esteems most is London nightclub owner Peter Stringfellow, though his achievements are somewhat limited and he has not lived in the city for twenty-five years. A local paper is not, perhaps, an entirely reliable guide to local opinion but if it is to keep its readership it must reflect local priorities. The *Sheffield Star* generally manages this rather well. It is an unashamedly parochial evening paper; its more sedate and serious sister-paper, the *Morning Telegraph*, went out of business some years ago, though the title has reappeared on a colourful weekly wrapper to the property advertisements. But perhaps the most revealing local paper is *Westside*, a free but glossy magazine delivered to the eponymous executive suburbs.

Westside is a child of the Thatcher years. Both its origins – two journalists unemployed with the collapse of the *Morning Telegraph* used their initiative and demonstrated their enterprise – and its contents reflect the concerns of the 1980s. Yet it is also very much a Sheffield product. Its restricted distribution reflects the curiously abrupt distinctions between one neighbourhood and the next, while its concerns, which reach as far as the posh folks' play-grounds in Derbyshire but rarely beyond, are utterly provincial. On the face of it this should be surprising. The very rich – the magazine's ostensible audience – travel frequently to London, yet

London is rarely mentioned. But the magazine's real audience is not the very rich, but the people who would like to be very rich, and their horizons, like those of their magazine, remain close to home: the aspiring, in a city which is not London, have always had to content themselves with local success or be overawed.

Times change, of course. Perhaps the insularity of the past is being eroded. The Student Games certainly attracted visitors; Meadowhall, a vast and impressive shopping complex built on the site of a vast and impressive steelworks, has attracted far more. Meadowhall is *Westside* made tangible: it is a cathedral to consumerism, a tribute to the joys of shopping and, though its architecture of vaults and galleries is a little like that of a Victorian prison, none the less when there you feel – Goddamnit – wealthy, pampered and as though all the world's riches are within reach. If it isn't quite Bond Street it's not for want of trying; certainly it has more in common with Mayfair than with the standard provincial shopping centre. Many Sheffielders resent it – as they resent all that is conspicuous and has what the city calls 'side' – because it draws attention away from the established centre of the city, but they cannot ignore it. Nor can I. I have no affection for this temple to Mammon, but I acknowledge a certain admiration. At least its builders tried.

This is more than can be granted to those who built most of Sheffield. Not only was most of the development either Victorian or Modernist – neither among architecture's most pleasing periods – but it seems our builders were content to leave grandeur to the landscape. Or maybe the smog-laden atmosphere made architectural niceties seem wasted? Whatever the reason, architecturally Sheffield is drab. Only a handful of buildings achieve any degree of distinction, and of these only the Town Hall is prominent. If Sheffield pleases the eye – which it does often – it is because of its situation, not its buildings. Even those buildings which universally act as the focus of civic pride seem in Sheffield to suggest only our distaste for display. Our cathedral is a converted parish church, and looks it; our railway station is even worse. At one end of the LMS line is St Pancras, that mighty arc of glass fronted by Scott's Gothic hotel; at the other end is Sheffield Midland, dowdy, undistinguished, unambitious. It is as if the architects and engineers of this city that is not London have been overawed. To make a noble attempt and fail is not the Sheffield way.

For we should not be too modest. Sheffield may produce little in the way of grand culture but each of its many villages has its own choirs and theatre groups: several hundred amateur productions are produced here annually. Thatcherism's biggest mistake was not to champion competition but to confuse competition with avarice. The amateur groups are intensely competitive: the financial gains are nil but artistic excellence is often the result. We don't want to compete with London but we do compete with one another; our horizons may be reduced by our hills but within their compass our ambitions are intact. For the key to this city – its limitations, its triumphs, its quiet competitiveness – is Sheffield's tradition of craftsmanship. We are not London, and refuse to pretend we are; we are no Steel City any more, but we used to be. It was not luck or sunspots that caused Renaissance Florence, a city no bigger than modern Wakefield, to produce so many great artists. Neither was it luck that caused Sheffield to produce so many less celebrated but equally gifted artisans. A city defies definition. It is not seamless, as an essay should be, nor homogenous. Sheffield is less homogenous than most. But at its best a city is a thriving place where excellence is encouraged and where proximity means each achievement is soon copied, soon bettered. In crowded workshops by the Don anonymous craftsmen developed techniques for polishing, plating, sharpening and finishing cutlery, the process was less exalted but otherwise no different from that by which, in equally crowded workshops along the Arno, Botticelli learnt from Fra Lippo, Ghirlandaio borrowed from Botticelli, Michelangelo studied under Ghirlandaio. It is a noble history and, though we who are young may never see so much nor live so long, we have no need for shame.

I have little faith in prediction, none in my ability to predict. Sheffield, a series of villages linked by a vanished industry, a city disinherited could become no more than a place where people live, distinguished from other conurbations only by its landscape. But I don't think it too optimistic to hope for more than that: Sheffield may have lost its identity but it still has its character; perhaps it is not too late for Sheffield to develop its tradition of craftsmanship, albeit necessarily adapted to new skills. There are certainly worse places for a writer to come from than a city that is not London, a city that mistrusts celebrity but prizes craft and graft.

Not that it's ever been a matter of choice for me. Willy-nilly, Sheffield is what I've got. Maybe I too am a city that isn't London, a place of familiar byways and unexplored memories, peopled by the stories I've told and those I've yet to tell. For Sheffield lives in me every bit as thoroughly as I live in Sheffield. This is my city and my home; it is my conscience, my measure, my touchstone. One day it will be my tomb. So here's to Sheffield: I wish us well.

II

PERSONAL VIEWS

ALISON FELL

Penthesilea, Perhaps

ACHILLES:

I certainly know what the divine woman holds against me. She sends me through the air enough feathery kisses that come and whisper their sound of death – and her desire – in my ear.

– Kleist, *Penthesilea*

11.30 p.m. in Hackney, Thursday 7 February. The night of the great snows, the night when frost flowers returned to the windows of the city. The thermometer plunging. Gina comes home from her first ever night at the opera and heads to the bagel bakery on the corner of the market feeling, yes, a little vulnerable, but not more than a little, not enough to stop her. Elated, too, by *Madam Butterfly*, by the opera crowd, so unfamiliarly bourgeois in furs and smooth suits. Mildly disoriented but not yet unpleasantly: that requires an opposite, the other pole of the contradiction even now beginning to take shape, unseen, in a doorway, or behind a stack of cardboard boxes discarded by the market stalls. For the moment, hungry, Gina is thinking of smoked-salmon and cream-cheese bagels, hot. Simple.

Entering the shop she's conscious of a man behind her, a man who, curiously, doesn't buy anything, a man who (paranoia?) seems to follow her out. Later, trying to make sense of nonsense, she'll think that she was the one he selected, specifically. (Why? What is it about her? What messages did she transmit? Didn't she catch his eye as she waited at the counter? She shouldn't have, shouldn't.) Later, when she probes for patterns, the day will

73

reveal itself as chaotic – rockets fired at the Cabinet, one of her friends hospitalized after a psychotic episode, frozen traffic, heaped snowbanks. The madman who took her space away and the weather which did the same. Everything linked up.

Gina turns out of the market and into the crescent, clutching her warm bag of bagels.

What does she remember? It's hard to say. Frosty leeks in the gutter, perhaps. Slatted fruit-boxes, oranges rolled loose and squashed, rotting. A shadow in the corner of her eye telling her that the man's still there, some way behind her. Hearing the war-whoop and turning to see him coming at her, arm raised to strike, face inexplicably streaming with sweat on that bitter night, eyes burning like beacons.

Crack, he's on crack, she thinks, as he hits her, the blow falling on the side of her neck. Later she'll recall that his face was weather-beaten, recall (self-critically) the conclusion she jumped to: *Gypsy*. A word standing in for all the homeless and the hopeless and displaced. But at that moment she freezes, can't run: running would be more frightening, somehow, than this eye contact; if she ran he would be behind her. He's staring at her, sweating; they're staring at each other; he's obsessed with something. Gina, blotted out, assumes rape but can't scream it. (Better to scream 'Fire' anyway, or so people say, if you want to be sure of a response.) Snowy gardens, gates, steps; doors she can't run to, doorbells she can't ring on: the chilly codes of the unneighbourly city are graven deep. She's totally alone, then, while this man blazes at her, desperate for something, incoherent. His arm raised to strike again but poised in mid-air.

Do you want my money? says a clogged whisper in Gina's throat as she thrusts her purse at him; and he takes the money and glares at it as if wondering if that is what he wants, if that is what will pacify him: this man not yet thirty in a suede jacket, this maddened dog confused by the proffered bone.

And then he turns and runs. Runs yelling, she thinks later, as she walks home dazed by tension, the bagel bag still gripped in her gloved hand. In her purse possessed by him is her British Library card with the photograph. She thinks of countless films in which a man like this might pin a woman's photo to his wall, lurid, cursing, making dangerous magic with her stolen soul.

Indoors, safe, Gina notices in the waste-bin the chain-letter sent by a superstitious friend, the letter she'd thrown away; and only now does she burst into tears, primitive. *If you break the chain ill-luck will befall you.* Cause and effect: the brutal chain of undoing. At that moment in the realm of magic anything is preferable to the random, even the wildest rationale, self-punishing. Self-recriminations: she should have done this, she should have done that. (Years ago, when Gina's friend was raped the police's first question was: 'What were you wearing?' After that Gina's entire women's group gave up wearing make-up, high heels, dresses. To think that it's one's own fault at least allows the illusion of having some control over the situation.)

And now the police come with notebooks and commiserations, and treat Gina to five minutes of racist jokes about how it's the first white mugger they've had round here in ages. In the bagel shop no one saw anything and no one remembers: evidently this is going to be another unsolved case. What the police don't tell Gina is that if a prosecution isn't brought, victims are entitled to apply for compensation to the Criminal Injuries Compensation Board. And so I tell her: A. got £2,000, M. got over £1,000. In fact Gina had already heard of the scheme but had thought it for people who had suffered worse attacks, who were more entitled.

Next day, passing Dalston Station in the astonishing snows, Gina sees police and ambulancemen bringing out someone who's collapsed, and she the liberal-left-feminist hopes shockingly that it's her attacker: frozen or starved or overdosed, but definitively dead. That day also, a police mobile unit appears outside the bagel shop and remains for three reassuring weeks. Then it disappears.

Meanwhile in the relative security of her shared third-floor flat Gina dreams uneasily not about the face of her attacker but again and again about the window, its glass pressed thin by the outside air. Night after night strangers transform themselves into moths or liquid and slither in.

Gina doesn't walk home at night from the tube now, not ever. Gina takes cabs she can't afford. Gina plans her week in detail, liaising with her brother and his girlfriend. Gina borrows bikes from the men in the house. She thinks: one option, which is really no option at all, is to get rich, buy a car, move to a place where things like this don't happen. Protect yourself. Another option is to take on board the fact that you can never protect yourself entirely, for there are some people who have no stake in making the city a safe place to be. Understand your enemy. Drama-trained, Gina investigates helping out with a theatre group whose work involves the young homeless, the displaced. Week by week the fear subsides a little more, the fear she can't afford. One day she *will* walk home alone again, this is her minimum demand, she insists on this.

> It is common for women to absorb into themselves the pain of violent, degrading and undermining assaults. Women's ability to survive, and not only to survive but to carry on working, caring for children, responding to others' needs, says a great deal about human resilience. The tragedy is that this courage is often used against us, to say that we have not really been harmed.
> – Ruth Hall, *A London Inquiry into Rape and Sexual Assault*

In Stuttgart the underpasses are swept clean, posters go un-defaced, telephone kiosks unvandalized. On every street corner there's a cigarette machine miraculously intact. Canada geese swim on the lake in front of the *Neue Schloss*, and on the steps of the Opera House someone's busking, a clear tenor, laughter echoing over the lake.

In Stuttgart – for the moment at least – there's full employment. Mugging is not a crime one hears much about. In Germany there's rivalry between cities, a striving to make each city a showpiece. Spending on culture, transport and amenities isn't seen merely as the moral duty of an administration, but has the muscular function of attracting investment to the city: the quality of life is, above all, a selling point.

In Stuttgart women go out alone at night, they dress as they choose. They carry handbags, money. As in Paris, Lyon, Bordeaux, they eat alone in restaurants, a book propped up in front of them, cigarettes beside them on the table. In Stuttgart – also in Heidelberg and Essen and spreading – underground carparks have places nearest the exit reserved for women. Such a simple policy, requiring no more than a bunch of feminists and greens in public office and a slap of red paint: *Frauen*. It's so obvious: that women should park their cars by the exit, not five floors up or down, far from an escape route.

Yet the initial thrill (guilty) when I saw the red word is a clear measure of how colonized we are in our British cities, and how few initiatives are taken to limit the free play of male territoriality. There's no doubt that the Reclaim the Night marches of the late 1970s and early 1980s had mass appeal, with their symbolic taking of 'male' space. Women refused to be barred from the streets at night, to be cowed by harassment. But where has our militancy gone? The spaces women inhabit are no less circumscribed now than they were then, and the streets are unarguably more hazardous. All women have imprinted in them the basic politics of male territoriality, all women know instinctively what transgresses. And the incredulity of men when women do!

I'm not talking about *criminal* violence here, although I could: numbers of women attacked, street robbery, sexual assaults, etc. (The Islington Crime Survey estimated that only 21 per cent of sexual assaults were reported to the police and due to the peculiarities of recording procedures only around 9 per cent end up in police statistics. As opposed to, say, bicycle thefts. Rapes, for instance, are often 'down-crimed': that is, the police do not record them as a crime because they don't believe they have sufficient evidence to bring a successful prosecution.) I'm talking, rather, about the so-called non-criminal street violence, the street harassment that defines the parameters of women's lives in the city and keeps them under siege, controlled by fear.

> 72 per cent of women feared for their safety after dark, as opposed to 27 per cent of men. Women generally, and particularly older women and black and Asian women who are subject to racial attack, feel they must restrict their behaviour as a precaution against crime. For example, 37 per cent of women in the borough *never* go out unaccompanied after dark, and 50 per cent usually or always went out with someone rather than alone. 60 per cent of young white women and 72 per cent of young black women experience street harassment – kerb crawling, lewd suggestions, threats etc.
>
> – *The Islington Crime Survey*

And for those of us who insist, like Gina, on our right to move freely around the city, for those of us who refuse what's effectively a curfew, what are our strategies? When approaching a man on an empty street, even in daylight, P. looks at her watch, S. pretends to fumble in her pocket for a handkerchief, L. frowns to herself, directs her gaze *inward*. B. strides purposefully, never lingering – certainly not standing and staring – never taking out an *A-Z* in case she appears lost or uncertain or vulnerable. Countless intricate manoeuvres enacted daily, exhaustingly. And at night, well, at night the strong lace-ups, the butch leather jacket, the handbag left at home, the ear alert for footsteps. If it's a man then the footsteps should walk faster and pass by . . . but why *doesn't* he cross the road, show some awareness? Or else you pace yourself to walk near a couple or a group of women, stick close . . .

Men, ask your wives, your women friends! I know you're incredulous: What, me? A threat? Does this really happen? These stares, suggestions, threats, these hisses and kisses? Do women really look anywhere and everywhere – at pavements, blinds, daffodils – in order to avoid the level gaze, the eye-to-eye encounter which may be interpreted as invitation or provocation? (Uppity nigger: like black men, we know the strategy of sunglasses, we know it's safer to camouflage our gaze. Better not look levelly, for that implies equality. Better look *up* to him, so that he can see himself as he'd like to be.)

Men, lovers, husbands! Do you imagine (as sometimes you seem to) that your protection extends invisibly to us, even when we're out of your sight? Do you find it hard to believe that women – even a lone woman on an empty street – could see you as anything other than chivalrous, protective? Men, ask your wives, your women friends. Let them tell you about these strategies, about the daily million-fold inventiveness of women. Ask them about the spaces they inhabit and who defines them.

> 30 per cent of women across the country said that they were 'very worried' about being raped, a figure which rose to 41 per cent for women aged thirty or less and to 64 per cent for this age group on the poorest council estates.
> – *Taking Account of Crime: Key Findings from the British Crime Survey*

Be sensibly shod, say the sensible self-defence manuals, and so we are, some of us – those of us who aren't obliged to work in banks or offices or law courts or estate agents or department stores, where dress codes demand a fragile and appealing femininity. It's yet another restriction, yet another manoeuvre we must make in our efforts to be safe in an unsafe city. To take responsibility where society won't.

No such accommodations are demanded of men. Think about feminine dress with its emphasis on risk, tottering, display. Among men, the drag queens know this, playing as they do on submission, seduction, the perilous feminine position. Politicians, perhaps, privately in their bedrooms play with it, but it takes a Quentin Crisp to take it on to the streets, to openly and dangerously subvert masculine stereotypes.

A drag queen on every street corner! Imagine it! Demand it!

Drag queens are carnival, laughter puncturing the pompous spaces of the city, a beautiful relief. A float of silks and satins cruising down Piccadilly on the Clause 28 demonstration while I, respectable, giving a respectable poetry reading, stand on a podium in the forecourt of the Royal Academy. Shrieks drowning out the PA system, hoots, warbles, cat-calls – we must all go and *look*, enjoy this pantomime of primly crossed nyloned knees, lipsticks, simpers, preening. The lid of the city lifts off; the sky is larger, suddenly, and not grey. Everything classical on porticoes and pediments, everything stultifyingly allegorical, everything patriarchal recoils and shivers a little and shrinks back, and the streets lie open to new possibilities.

The feeling a city gives you, like the difference between being loved or not being loved.

> This much is ours: to touch one another like this.
> – Rilke, *Duino Elegies*

An image: April, apple blossom blowing out across the streets. A man's bare arm rests casually on the open window of his car, saying: it's natural, I claim, I am, I have rights, I'm a citizen. I drive alone through this sunny city. Now think of a woman's arm, similarly bare, resting as casually. Heads turn – it's an open invitation (she's available) or else a provocation. Who does she think she is? To display, to spread herself, to occupy? (If she spreads herself – publicly – it invokes . . . what? Split beaver, the secret lips of the vagina which must spread apart for men's eyes only. The vagina which threatens to escape their control?)

Think of a city in which women could spread themselves and men would not be afraid.

> We believe it is important that the reduction in staff numbers be accompanied by measures to increase the visibility and availability of the Staff who remain.
> – Department of Transport, *Crime on the London Underground*

A golden day hangs over the city, beautiful pollution. I want to talk about the spaces we might live in but don't. I want to talk about that woman there . . . and there. Black patent shoes pressed tightly together, black-trousered knees too, though this isn't a matter of modesty, of short skirts and stockings: this is the unwritten Law of the Underground.

Penthesilea, perhaps, being Queen of the Amazons and one who never knew restriction, would spread her elbows, wedging them on the arm-rests. And collide. And maybe, having captured one arm-rest or even two, wonder at the angry discomfort that comes off men in waves. Ousted, they can't settle, can't sit still, for it's traditional – this business of the male occupation of the arm-rests while women pin their elbows to their sides.

Undeterred, Penthesilea spreads her knees comfortably apart. And collides. Again the transmitted displeasure, dismay – although this time there's also a frisson of surprise: it's a tease, it's a transgression. Meanwhile men spread their knees wide and slouch, feet rooted and apart, thighs like trees, growing. And Penthesilea wonders: Do the women of this city dress like flowers because they can't open like them? Is this substitution, metaphor, simulation?

What Penthesilea thinks

about the man opposite, the look the reflexive look that turns always back to itself: an anxious male narcissism defending itself against . . . what? The secret desire to be possessed, open, vulnerable – this dangerous poetic position, this permeability, inflow, overflow; this dissolve of boundaries which he perceives only as subjugation, annihilation, calls passive, feminine? Feminine being by definition what he is not. Acts of severance. Not only the distribution of wealth but the distribution of definitions is maintained by violence, by oppositions: master/slave, white/black, masculine/feminine.

And thus the guilty contempt of the look, the hissed suggestion, the invasion of this space defined as not-him, as female, as female and therefore to be entered. (Don't think for a moment that Penthesilea and the rest of us can't distinguish between this gaze and that other one, the casual glance, faintly neutral, faintly appreciative.) We're entered, then. The word, the gesture working overtime to conceal from the man his chaos of love and fear, awe and envy?

Penthesilea wonders: so it's all about control, of self and other, a madness for control, monarchic, despotic?

In the crush of the city spatial politics are heightened.

Pinned to the surface of our bodies by the gaze, paradoxically we can't live in them: they're yet another place we're not free to go. Distanced from ourselves, we become not only men's dark continent but our own, a labyrinth we fear to explore.

> Action isn't the pilots' concern. They have their eyes
> fixed on defence posts, and spread out on their knees
> the map of a world to which nothing can be added.
> Ingeborg Bachmann, *In the Storm of Roses*

Imagine the Euston Road at 1 a.m., not a taxi in sight. Imagine that the only other woman around is the woman on the Morgan's Rum ad., thirty feet high, glossy, air-brushed, seamless, phallic. Offering herself. Imagine seeing your pale hand lying open on the black plastic seat of the taxi that has at last rescued you from kerb-crawlers and whose driver has listened sympathetically to your fear and disgust (the driver who later, dropping you at the door of your visibly empty house, will make identical suggestions); imagine hating your soft belly, soft breasts, jelly knees. How to value at that moment any manifestation of the feminine, of a rich and rhythmic flesh that bleeds, gestates? Wouldn't you prefer to trade it all in for (and this is the heartbreaking exchange) boots, mailed fists, the body made seamless and aesthetic by weight-training? Monumental, like the fascist body beautiful, which was always modelled on the male, the godlike, the Classical. And if we *master* ourselves like this, construct a carapace of muscle with which to repel these claustrophobic sorties into our space – don't we then beg the question of what will happen to the others: the too young and the not young enough, the shy and the halt and the lame?

Streetwise, street cred, street-sussed. The hysteria of the patriarchal city drives us all to wage war on the vulnerable.

Because the London Regional Transport bus lighting contract is currently placed in the hands of an advertising agency, priority is given to lighting the ads. If there is no ad at a bus stop, there is no light.

– Security and Safety: A Borough Plan for Islington Women

Oh, easy enough to say that women have an exaggerated fear of the risk of crime, to tell ourselves this. Hysterical women, over-reacting. But to live in the city is to live with the decay of the city, with unemployment, overcrowding, homelessness, a run-down public transport system: an embattled zone in which degraded attitudes like sexism, racism and machismo flourish. Behaviour which is at the very least *uncitizenly*. (In Germany, giving the Nazi salute is classed – rightly – as an uncitizenly act, and you can be arrested for it.)

Crimewatch, the national TV advertising campaign which was launched with £4½ million this spring, focuses almost entirely on crimes against property: 60,000 Neighbourhood Watch schemes across the country encourage people to guard each others' homes; but what price the Quality of Life for women? Shouldn't we be demanding mass television campaigns, community responsibility, public consciousness-raising? And would we get them?

Initiatives around issues of safety and security for women are small, local, and practical: transport or lighting campaigns, consultations with local women, self-defence classes, seminars on rape and domestic violence attended by local police, conferences on safer design in housing. Some may receive part-funding from the Home Office Safer Cities Project, some from hard-pressed local authorities through their Women's and Equalities Units. An organization like Camden Women's Safe Transport, for instance, receives money from Camden Council for one salaried worker but relies entirely on volunteer drivers; running costs must be met through fund-raising or private trusts. At the deliberately low rate of 75p for journeys within the borough and £1.30 outside, CWST provides door-to-door lifts for individual women – although occasionally there's a shared lift – and average 7–10 journeys nightly. They ferry girls to youth clubs, Asian women to evening meetings, agoraphobic women to support groups – and pick up from Sainsbury's, the theatre, etc. All the drivers are women, and all have a woman escort, for sociability as well as safety. 'We started slowly,' organizer Kathleen Lyons recalls. 'Women in the borough thought it was a very good idea but not necessarily for them. You know – "I'm not deserving enough." Now they say they just feel more comfortable with women drivers.' She believes strongly in the principle of women doing it for themselves, and being seen to do so. 'Transport isn't a field women are very visible in,' she explains. 'It's male-dominated and that's what's got to change.'

Men look *at* women: but is it entirely up to us to force them to *see* us instead?

Imagine a city. Imagine a city in which the Politics of the Gaze would be a matter for everyday consciousness. Imagine a city in which women would not be cowed or denied, controlled or sequestered.

> It is unhelpful to simply portray women as the most vulnerable and fearful in the population, as there is a sense in which this further victimises women. Amazingly, women survive against all the odds. To stop victimising women, attention must be turned on men, in the community *and* in the police. The emphasis on the real problem, how men are to be controlled, rather than how to make women safer, will make the struggle for women less victimising.
> – Jalna Hanmer, *Women and Policing in Britain*

Imagine a city in which women could spread themselves . . .

And so, Penthesilea, with her two elbows insisting – if gently – on her half of two arm-rests, makes her journey through dark tunnels, aware of the puzzled discomfort of the two men adjacent to her, yet even more aware of her task to reclaim the sealed-in territories of body and will, spirit and desire. Easing them back into no more or less than an equal space, a democratic space, Penthesilea senses that these neighbours of hers – itching and twitching as if from the sting of a bee, frothing with unspoken accusations of trespass, of boundaries punctured – are experiencing somewhere in themselves the scandalous eruption of the feared feminine, the permeable, the penetrable ... the very basis, (Penthesilea wonders) of homophobia? Imagine a city in which women could spread themselves, and men would not be afraid.

PENTHESILEA:

Come now, sweet friend, come, put yourself at my feet. Come nearer – even nearer, very close to me. You are afraid of me? You don't hate me, though I was able to conquer you? Tell me, are you afraid of the one who threw you in the dust?

ACHILLES:

As flowers fear a sunbeam.

– Kleist, *Penthesilea*

With thanks to Islington Women's Unit, Lewisham Equalities Development Unit, Safer Cities, StateWatch, Camden Women's Safe Transport, Camden Community Transport, Sheila Rowbotham, and Sophie Gardener.

ACKNOWLEDGEMENTS

Ingeborg Bachmann, *In the Storm of Roses: Selected Poems by Ingeborg Bachmann*, trans. Mark Anderson, Lockert Library of Poetry, Port Townsend, WA, 1986.

Ruth Hall, *Ask Any Woman: London Inquiry into Rape and Sexual Assault*, Falling Wall Press, Bristol, 1985.

H. von Kleist quotations are taken from Hélène Cixous and Catherine Clement, eds., *The Newly-born Woman*, trans. Betty Wing, Theory and History of Literature, vol. 24, Manchester University Press, Manchester, 1987.

R. M. Rilke, *Duino Elegies*, Second Elegy, trans. Stephen Cohn, Carcanet, Manchester, 1989.

RUTH RENDELL

Underworld

There are things you love because you don't know them very well. I am fond of going down mines but I might not be if I were a miner. Which of us would long for the heat of the sun and cloudless skies if we depended on rain for our very existence?

It has never been my lot to travel to work in London on the tube. I have never, even for a week or two, had to use it every day. If I have been on it in the rush hours it has been because I have started too early or overstayed my time at some engagement. I feel a little shy and more than a little cautious when I tell tube commuters I love the Underground. I half expect them – with some justification – to rise up in a body and fall upon me with rage and resentment. I can only say to them that I love it in a sort of abstract way, as a concept. I admire something so ambitious. In any case, unusually I believe for a woman, I enjoy being in tunnels. I love the idea of an Underground, the way Chesterton's hero does in *The Man Who Was Thursday*:

> I tell you that every time a train comes in I feel that it has broken past batteries of besiegers and that man has won a battle against chaos. you say contemptuously that when one has left Sloane Square one must come to Victoria. I say that one might do a thousand things instead, and that whenever I really come there I have the sense of hair-breadth escape. And when I hear the guard shout out the word 'Victoria', it is not an unmeaning word. It is to me the cry of a herald announcing conquest. It is to me indeed 'Victoria'; it is the victory of Adam.

Most people accept it as something that is *there*, as immemorially there as Buckingham Palace or the Bank of England. It is almost as if it were not constructed but discovered. An archaeologist began digging under the city and lo! – a complexity of passages waiting for a train to wriggle through and surface like a glistening red earthworm.

Before the middle of the nineteenth century the only tunnels under London were the sewers. There were 369 of them, emptying their putrid, cholera-bearing contents into the Thames. And there were, or there were said to be, secret passages. One was reputedly for the use of that Duke of Portland who had some sort of facial deformity and always wore a veil. This noble Phantom of the Opera used his passage to travel unseen by human eye from his house in Hyde Park Gardens, now the headquarters of the Sri Lankan High Commission, to Baker Street.

I once lived in Hyde Park Gardens – the other end, the less posh end, though not exactly the wrong side of the tracks. While there I had an idea of writing a history of that pretty terrace where the Royal Society of Literature, as well as the Sri Lankans, have their headquarters. Instead, years later, I decided to write a novel set in the London Underground. Though a work of fiction and I hope an exciting work, it is at the same time a history of the tube. No one is murdered in the tube and no one throws himself under a train, but apart from that I have been free to play with the Underground system. It has been an interesting subject to research.

I started by looking at what happened before. Of course the tube is much older than most people think. Our great-great-grandparents could have ridden in it and probably did. *Their* grandparents walked to work. They walked miles through streets congested with other walkers, with horses and carriages, through the rookeries and in a reek of human and equine ordure. Others came by river or in coaches and drays or on omnibuses.

We are accustomed to the idea of commuting. In a time when people commute to work here by air from Europe and going to London by train each day from York or Norwich is feasible, is constantly done, it is hard to imagine a period when people wanted to work but couldn't get to the work-place. In the first half of the nineteenth century a quarter of a million swarmed into London each day, but still there were those who lived too far away to come at all.

Someone had the monstrous vision of a gaslit subway of streets through which horse-drawn traffic could pass. The very words conjure up a horror: the close atmosphere, the stench, the darkness and the dim still lamps; the loneliness and silence, broken at last by the distant sound of hooves on cobbles; the rush hours when horses and carriages would crush upon each other and the air become unbreathable. That these gloomy conduits would become a lurking place for thieves and footpads was the reason the notion stayed a vision and was never a plan.

Another enterprise was so much more ambitious, so wildly innovative, that it is no wonder Henry Mayhew, the founder of *Punch*, wrote of it that it was a plan to send people 'like so many parcels in a pneumatic tube' and spoke of girdling London round with one long drain. Mayhew had written a book in four volumes called *London Labour and the London Poor* and thought he knew all about it.

Punch laboured the irony: 'We understand that a survey has already been made and that many of the inhabitants along the line have expressed their readiness to place their coal cellars at the disposal of the company. It is believed that much expense may be saved by taking advantage of areas, kitchens and coal holes already made, through which the train may run without much inconvenience to the owners . . .'

Anyone investigating the tube must start with Charles Pearson. He was the Solicitor to the City of London, a liberal reformer as well as an anti-racialist, and must have been a brave man. He campaigned against the ban on the admission of Jews to the freedom of the city and helped to have removed those lines on the Monument which accused Roman Catholics of starting the Great Fire of London. And he was the Father of the Underground.

Curiously, the *Dictionary of National Biography* has left him out. Charles Buchanan Pearson, who published a Latin translation of English hymns, is there and so is Charles Henry Pearson, a history don at Cambridge and educationist in Australia, but the man who envisaged subterranean transport is conspicuous by his absence.

The idea of an underground railway running through a 'spacious archway' came to Pearson in the 1840s along with other visions of creating garden suburbs and bringing London a gas supply, and he first put it forward as part of his by-election campaign in *An Address to the Electors of Lambeth*. Pearson's campaign, like his previous attempts, was a failure and he was not elected. The voters no more wanted him than they wanted his trains in a drain, and his proposal was treated with scorn. Nearly two decades passed before it began to be taken seriously. The tunnel builders diverted the course of three rivers and threw many thousands of poor people living in the Fleet Valley out of their homes, but eventually the first line of the London Underground was built.

The Metropolitan Company offered Pearson a reward for his efforts. He refused it in words that sound antediluvian to us, so out of tune are they with modern attitudes. 'I am the servant of the Corporation of London; they are my masters and are entitled to all my time and service. If you have any return to make you must make it to them.' No one says things like that any more.

The line from Farringdon to Paddington opened on 9 January, 1863. Mr and Mrs Gladstone and other Victorian luminaries travelled on the first train to pass through the tunnel. At their destination a brass band was playing and in the evening a banquet was held for 700 people, but Pearson was not there. He had died six months before.

Few people using the tube today know that the first trains were drawn by steam engines. Then, of course, it was not a tube at all but a trough or cutting just below the surface. Ventilation was a problem from the outset. The tunnels and the trains themselves were so engulfed with steam and smoke that a civil servant home on furlough from Egypt said the murk smelt like a crocodile's breath. To remedy this the Metropolitan Company began using a locomotive which diverted the steam into tanks behind the engine by means of a ducted exhaust. When the train emerged, puffing and blowing, from the tunnel – Pearson's spacious archway – the tanks were opened and the steam released in cumulative clouds.

If you walk down the Bayswater Road in the direction of

Notting Hill, pass Lancaster Gate and turn right into Leinster Terrace, you will find the place where once the engine tanks spewed forth their load of steam. It is a little way past where the Terrace becomes Leinster Gardens. The houses here, like most of the houses in the neighbourhood, are Victorian classical, rendered with white stucco, fronted with pillared porticoes and four or five floors high. Numbers 23 and 24, situated on the western side, have no door knockers or letter boxes, their windows contain not glass but plaster, painted a dull blue. Look at them more closely and you will see they are no more than façades, built that way to avoid spoiling the appearance of the terrace. Behind them, in a great brick-lined shaft, the locomotives stopped and the steam was set free, belching forth no doubt like the effluent from a modern cooling tower, to mask the sky in cumulus and cause appalling nuisance to the neighbours.

Electricity put an end to all that. The passengers who sat facing each other in a light too dim to read by could at least breathe. The days of fear of a subterranean death from suffocation were past. It had perhaps not been a well-founded fear but it must have been real enough in the minds of those who travelled the 'sardine-box railway'.

An American came into control of the District Underground in 1900, by which time extensions had been built all over London: out to Hammersmith and Ealing, down under the river to Stockwell and eastwards to Whitechapel. The first Underground lines were of the sub-surface 'cut-and-cover' kind, but by 1890 a tube had been tunnelled through the green and yellow clay, providing material for those millions of bricks that built long ribbons of little brown houses throughout that decade.

The man who electrified the London Underground was a monopoly capitalist and crook from Chicago, Charles Tyson Yerkes. Yerkes had no particular interest in trains nor the tracks they ran on. He was interested in making money. In the United States he had been an embezzler and had been sent to prison. He was thrown out of Chicago and fled to New York where he built himself a palace and filled it with Old Masters. In London he gradually took over the Underground system and came to control every line except the Metropolitan. He built his own power station at Lots Road in Chelsea from which London Underground still draws its electric power. Yerkes died in the Waldorf-Astoria hotel and his empire passed to the son of a Derbyshire coach-maker, Albert Henry Stanley, who was later created Lord Ashfield. He was godfather to a child born in a Bakerloo Line train and gave her a silver christening mug when she was baptized Thelma Ursula Beatrice Eleanor: T. U. B. E. 'I hope people won't make a habit of this,' said Lord Ashfield, 'as I am a busy man.'

The London Underground is very large but not the largest metro system in the world. Its length of 422 kilometres is just exceeded by New York's, some eleven kilometres longer. Tianjin has the shortest with just 7.8 kilometres, though Istanbul's is not much longer and the earthquake-proof metro in Erevan is only a little over eight kilometres long.

The world has about ninety systems, more somehow than one would expect. If you ask people to guess they will usually answer twenty and then be afraid they have overestimated. The United States has at least ten, mostly with useful acronyms to distinguish them: BART and MART and SEPTA. Moscow's is thought to be the most beautiful, with marble-clad walls and chandeliers in its concourses, and it carries more passengers than any other in the world. When they built it in the 1930s and 40s the tunnellers encountered a quicksand in their path and much of the excavation was by pick and shovel, ruthlessly carried out under the direction of Nikita Khrushchev.

Stations on the Paris metro have the most romantic names, Pasteur and Pablo Picasso, Babylone and Pyramides. On Rome's ACOTRAL you can go from Lepanto to Cinecittà. Tokyo has a line called Ginza and another called Marunouchi. In Stockholm the living rock can be seen revealed as dark and craggy outcroppings above your head in its caverns, and the San Francisco trains, clean as a whistle and with carpet on the floor, travel through tunnels which dive steeply under the Bay. Keeping the trains clean would be impossible in Philadelphia where, on the subway to surface system, every vehicle and every station is hideously defaced with meaningless hieroglyphs. Graffitists have never triumphed in quite the same way here. For all that,

London Transport Underground spends several thousand pounds a week cleaning aerosol paint art off its tube-train cars.

An example of true art is the map of the London Underground. It was designed by Henry Beck and first used on posters in 1933, though the last copy to carry his signature was issued in 1959. They paid him five guineas for it, or £5·25. It was reproduced in millions and has served as a model for metro maps all over the world. London Transport has taken to calling it a 'journey planner', as if 'plan' or 'map' were not words readily understood by travellers. It presents the network as a geometric grid, as the heart of an American city might be. The tube lines do not, of course, lie at right angles to each other like the streets of Manhattan. Nor do they branch off at acute angles or form perfect oblongs. A true map of the London Underground would show the central complex in the shape of a swimming dolphin, its snout Aldgate, its forehead Old Street, the crown of its head King's Cross, its spine Paddington, White City and Acton, its tail Ealing Broadway and its underbelly the stations of Kensington. The outer configurations branch out in graceful tentacles, for the dolphin has become a jellyfish, its extremities touching Middlesex and Hertfordshire. A claw penetrates Heathrow.

On Beck's plan a dark purplish-red or burgundy is the colour by which the Metropolitan Line is distinguished, green for the District, yellow for the Circle, scarlet for the Central, brown for the Bakerloo, dark blue for the Piccadilly and black for the Northern. The Victoria line was built in 1968 and appeared on the map coloured in light blue. When the Jubilee was nearly finished there was some speculation as to what colour would be used for it. Possibilities remaining included pink, lime green, orange and mauve. London Transport Underground chose grey. An ancient line not otherwise much renovated, the Hammersmith branch of the Metropolitan, suddenly appeared in pink, like a decrepit dowager rouged-up and feather-hatted for a wedding.

Conan-Doyle wrote one Sherlock Holmes story about the London Underground: 'The Adventure of the Bruce-Partington Plans'. From a window overlooking the District Line in West London, Oberstein and Colonel Walter put a dead man on the roof of a train waiting near the station at Gloucester Road. The train carrying the body of Cadogan West gave a lurch as it passed over the points and the curve in the rails just before Aldgate Station. The body was thrown off on to the track and investigators were deceived into believing it had fallen from a carriage. Sherlock Holmes alone realized the truth of the matter. It couldn't happen today. The buildings are very close to the line but they are not the buildings that were there in 1895 and they are not close enough for anyone inside to reach or even touch a passing train.

The Underground is not an enclosed complex, accessible only from the stations. Apart from the close on three hundred stations, there are means of access and egress. If it looks as if a train is going to be trapped too long in a tunnel for reason of a power failure – 'in the unlikely event of', as they say in an aircraft when teaching you the emergency drill – then passengers can be rescued. It gets hot down there, hot as a summer's day in Delhi, and the air gets bad. But escape is at hand. The ways out, mostly, are ventilation shafts to let out bad air and let in good. But some of them have staircases inside. In the long stretch of the Central Line between Mile End and Stratford, the Old Ford Fan shaft has a spiral stair winding up in its interior, usable if the power failed. These two stations are more than usually far apart and if the current ceased the distance might be too great for a train to coast to the next platform. Late one night in 1969 sixty people escaped up the shaft and out into the street when the power failed. The round tower at Regent's Park on the Bakerloo is the top of an escape shaft. On another long stretch, the Victoria Line between Tottenham Hale and Seven Sisters, is the Nelson Road fan shaft, also with a spiral staircase inside.

Travellers would feel like passengers in an aircraft when their ears pop if there were no vents in the tunnel to release pressure. Blowholes covered with a grating were once a way of providing relief from sulphurous air. The Central Line put in 'ozonizers' that sucked air into the stations, but the resulting salty tang clung to travellers' clothes and made them smell as if they had come from Southend instead of Oxford Circus.

If there were no fan shaft at Bond Street the wind generated in the tunnels would be a ten-force gale at the best of times and when two trains passed one another enough to blow passengers off the platforms. As a train approaches, before you can hear or see it, your blood pressure drops a very little. But you have no way of testing it. Unlike New York, where a sphygmomanometer was long available to passengers at Grand Central Station, none has been installed in the London tube concourses.

Even in the early 1970s a public address system in San Francisco's BART was scolding passengers into putting out their cigarettes, but the ban on smoking did not come to London Underground until 1985. It was not soon enough to prevent one of the worst tube disasters: the King's Cross Fire. This was in the autumn of catastrophe, 1987. On 16 October the first hurricane for three hundred years destroyed fifteen million trees in southern England. Just over a month later the tube caught fire.

It began when a lighted match fell through an escalator leading from the Piccadilly Line platforms to the main ticket-hall concourse under the mainline station forecourt. The time was 7.25 in the evening, the date 18 November. Dense obliterating smoke filled the tunnels. People later described it as a black hell. Passengers arriving by train smelt the smoke and tried to crush back into the cars but there was no room and they were left stranded. Other trains went through without stopping, though trapped people on the platform hammered on the windows in desperation. 'There was plenty of room in the train,' one man said, 'but we couldn't get in.'

Thirty-one died in the King's Cross Fire. The worst accident before this was on 28 February 1975 when a train hit the end of a tunnel at Moorgate, killing forty-three people. There have always been accidents and no doubt, in spite of safety precautions, there always will be. The wonder is perhaps that there are not more.

There have always been fires. A fire in an escalator shaft at Paddington on Christmas Eve 1944 caused damage but killed no one. Stonebridge Park station burned down in 1917 and again 28 years later. A passenger died of suffocation when fire broke out in a train at Holland Park in 1958. A man was shot in an Underground train between Baker Street and Swiss Cottage one day in August, 1910. The shot was not fatal and he recovered, but the result was to install safety communication devices for passengers in all trains.

Arsenal were playing at home one evening when a bomb, taped to the underside of seats, went off in a tube-train car. It exploded at nine sharp at Wood Green on the Piccadilly Line where the train terminated, blowing out the sides of the car but not utterly destroying it. The car had been quite empty. The bomber had forgotten that most people using the line would get out at Arsenal for the football, as they did. Shortly before this, smoke coming out of the duffle bag on his shoulder betrayed a terrorist entering a train at West Ham. No one but he was hurt and he was shot while trying to escape.

A 73-year-old Polish Countess called Teresa Lubienska was stabbed while in a descending lift at Gloucester Road. In the pages of Agatha Christie that would be enough to strain any reader's credulity but late one Friday night in the summer of 1957 it really happened. In 1983 a booking clerk at Balham was murdered with a sawn-off shotgun. It was not shot or cartridge which killed him but wadding propelled from the gun barrel. In the same year a vagrant called Kiernan Kelly tried to push someone under a train. He was charged with attempted murder and while locked in a police cell at Clapham with two other men, garrotted one of his companions with the man's own shoelaces. Kelly claimed he was guilty of many murders and was sentenced to life imprisonment in 1984.

No one has ever been murdered inside a London Underground train and if any woman has been raped, it is not known. Most assaults on the Underground are caused as a result of drinking.

Brixton Police deal with three times as many robberies as London Transport Police. The commonest crime is 'dipping', another name for stealing wallets and handbags and for picking pockets. It happens all the time. Perhaps it may happen less now London Transport is installing television cameras on all its stations and television screens in its observation rooms. People take their own lives by throwing themselves in front of oncoming trains at an average rate of two a week. Few of us who use the tube, regularly or occasionally, have not heard the public address system announcing a train delayed or taken out of service on account of 'an incident' on the line. Curiously, suicides dive on to the line even though they may never have done so into water, even though they may never have learned how. They dive to their deaths and they do it close up by the portal where the train comes through.

The Underground is always a means of transport, sometimes a means of death, a fruitful ground for pickpockets, a place for the homeless to sleep and be warm in, a concert hall for musicians. London Transport dislikes the pop groups and the jazz bands, classical musicians and the mini-Palm Court orchestras, but passengers, for the most part, like them very much. The warning notice prohibiting music in the station walkways has an escape clause all buskers pin their faith to: 'No person while upon the railway shall, *to the annoyance of any other person*, sing, perform on any musical or other instrument, or use any gramophone, record player, tape recorder or portable wireless apparatus.' It is that 'to the annoyance of any other person' that has let in unrestrictedly the singers, the paper and comb performers, the saxophonists with sophisticated amplifying equipment and the serious musicians who can find nowhere else to play their fiddles.

Perhaps the tube is now seldom looked on as a refuge. But in the Second World War thousands took shelter in it. Heavy air raids began on 7 September, 1940. People bought low-value tickets and refused to leave the Underground until the all-clear had sounded. During that October an average of 138,000 people took shelter in the system and sheltering was finally allowed in all seventy-nine tube stations. Passengers rushing through non-stop from Archway to East Finchley saw whole families sleeping on the platform at the new station that would one day be opened as Highgate. At Russell Square people waking in the night on their makeshift beds heard a soft continuous roar coming through the tunnel. It was the sound made by snoring sleepers on the platforms at Holborn, next station down the line. The British Museum, nervous of the bombs which threatened its treasures, hid them for safety in the tunnel between Holborn and Aldwych.

Naturally, the Underground is haunted. A porter at Covent Garden saw a ghost in the station in 1955. This apparition was six feet tall, slim and wore a light-grey suit and white gloves.

Others confirmed the sighting. It is not known what made them believe this was not a living man in a grey suit and white gloves, on his way home from the theatre.

During the building of the Victoria Line the diggers sometimes saw a black shape in the tunnel. Their descriptions make what they saw sound like a Balrog. Although the complete *Lord of the Rings* trilogy was not published in paperback until 1968, the year of the opening of the line, the three separate parts had been in hardcover in bookshops and libraries for more than a decade. Did they see a Balrog? Or was it because one of them had been reading J. R. R. Tolkien that they imagined they saw a Balrog? According to Tolkien, this monstrous black shape appears in subterranean places when disturbed by mortal men.

Miles of deserted disused tunnels still exist under London. They are the passages that once led to and from exits and entrances no longer used, from above ground to old stations now abandoned, to staircases that have been dismantled and lift shafts from which the lifts have gone. Forty 'ghost' stations lie down there, railway fossils under London: British Museum, Tower of London, Lord's, St Mary's, King William Street and many others. I went down there on a guided tour when I was doing my research, walked through the disused passages, looked up the defunct fan shafts and saw the brown and yellow Edwardian tiling spiralling the vertical cylinders where staircases once went up to the street. Some of the tunnels still have posters on their walls put up before the Second World war.

I rode the tube quite a lot, more concentratedly and more often than I had ever done before. I was the one who wanted to, among all those others who didn't want to but had no choice. They watched me curiously while I made notes. Their eyes followed me as I walked up and down the car and peered out of the windows at the tunnel roof. I wonder if some of them will read my book and, if they do, remember me.

DAVID DABYDEEN

On Cultural Diversity

<hr/>

I am sitting quietly at Frankfurt Airport's departure lounge waiting for my British Airways plane to London. There are about fourteen other passengers. I am reading Salman Rushdie's exciting new essay 'Minority Literatures in a Multi-Cultural Society' in a book called *Displaced Persons*. The book, published in Denmark by an Australian Press (the Dangaroo Press), is a collection of prose and poetry, some of it delivered at a symposium in Stockholm hosted by the Royal Academy of Sweden in 1986. The writers include a Jamaican living on the coast of Sussex, a Trinidadian living in Canada, a Canadian of Dutch parents, a Romanian of Greek parents who lived in Australia and a Pakistani who worked in Birmingham.

By a miracle of timing, a hand touches my shoulder exactly as I alight on this line in Rushdie's essay: 'it has been an important aspect of what it means to be a work of art that the work will cross frontiers'. The line is so compelling that I have to reread it. When I look up, two heavily armed German guards are standing over me. They address me in German, and whilst I don't understand a word of their inquiry, I reach automatically into my bag and hand over my passport. I immediately resume reading the Rushdie essay with a sense of elation and expectation: the generous and humane prose is arguing a dangerous case – that the business of the writer is to break through the confines of narrowness, whether it be the political narrowness of nationalism or the cultural narrowness of localism or the imaginative narrowness

97

of social realism or even the existential narrowness of reality itself.

> Defence of walls which are erected around the culture can have the effect of crushing the literature inside it as well as keeping hostile forces out. This internal marginalization also seeks implicitly to control the writer's choice of subject matter. He must choose to write about the great public issues, that is to say there is pressure to write politically or he is not important, not, if I may use the term, pure. The use of ideas of homogeneity and purity by the majority white culture can easily create such mirror images in the beleaguered minority groups ... I remember when I was twenty-one and beginning to write - I was in Pakistan then, having just left the University – I found it more or less impossible to write there because of the existence of total censorship. My problem with censorship was not so much ideological, although it was there too, it was more that I could never get a straight response to my work. I could never properly evaluate what I was doing ... I came back to England to try to overcome this problem, and although I would agree that England is by no means Paradise, the situation there did not seem to me to be comparable to the one I had left.

How was he to foresee the hatred soon to be unleashed against him by British-based Pakistanis? And how was I to understand the German interrogation that followed?

The guards take away my British passport and return after ten minutes or so. They signal that I must get up and follow them. I am led to an immigration desk.

'How long, what you do Germany?' the man asks in broken English, scanning my passport.

I pause, wondering whether to answer him in my native Creole. ('Three, four day me bin ya' – on reflection, sounding partly German.) Instead, I put on my best official English and inform him that I had been invited to read poetry at a Commonwealth Literature Festival organized by some distinguished German Professors at Berlin and Frankfurt.

'What you do England?' he wants to know, his polite smile masking an aggressiveness.

I reply that I am based at Wolfson College, Oxford. As soon as

I utter the name of the College its Jewishness makes me feel un-comfortable. I remember my Hindu roots with a sudden sense of relief. I throw my mind back to the Second World War, trying to figure out whether the Germans had any grudges against Hindus. I can't think of any. Instead, the word 'Aryan' and the figure of the Swastika, shared by both Germans and Indians, enter my mind forcibly and remain there throughout the interrogation.

'What "PLN.Zealand"?' he asks, pointing to the entry in the passport under 'Place of Birth'. 'You New Zealand? Maori?'

'No, it's Plantation Zealand,' I tell him. 'It's a sugar plantation in Guyana, which the Dutch used to own until the British conquered them.'

A few of the passengers stare in my direction making me feel foolish and guilty. The possession of a British passport by a Guyanese born of Indian parents in an old Dutch slave plantation was obvious cause for scepticism. And they would doubt *me*, rather than the colonial history which created my condition.

'Which year you leave Ghana?' he continues.

'Not *Ghana*. Ghana is in Africa. I come from *Guyana*, in the West Indies, or rather the coast of South America.'

Although a country on the continent of South America, Guyana shares an identical history with the West Indies, a history of British colonization, slavery and indentureship, and is considered a West Indian island. It is, in a sense, an island, being the only English-speaking country in South America. To have to explain all this rich cultural diversity to an immigration officer would be intolerable.

'Spell,' he orders, and I write GUYANA in bold letters on a piece of paper. He looks at it and is perplexed.

'On top of Brazil, next to Venezuela,' I offer, hoping that the names of these bigger, more familiar countries would convince him that my little Guyana actually exists.

A few days before I had stood before the Berlin Wall, filled with the sense of the stupidity of Europeans and suddenly feeling proud that I came from a country of under a million people that had never fought a war, had never contributed substantially to the world economy or to world history, and had never boasted of this or that scientific or technological invention. Its insignificance was its significance. But not now, standing before a hostile immigration officer. The feeling of pride becomes one of guilt and shame, and so the word 'Jonestown' escapes from my mouth automatically.

'What?'

'Jonestown,' I repeat, slowly and emphatically.

It makes no sense to him either. A few years previously, nine hundred black American men, women and children belonging to a Christian cult led by a white American, had committed suicide in the green jungles of Guyana. The news was flashed around the world, Hollywood rushed out a film, a few cheap paperbacks appeared, and Guyana was put on the world's map for a few months. Other obscenities in other countries replaced ours and the world soon forgot us.

He picks up the phone, spells GUYANA to the person at the other end and waits. Several minutes later, he receives a reply. He turns to me and asks, 'Which Guyana?'

'Just Guyana,' I say, confused for a moment, before my sense of geography returns. 'British Guyana.'

The South American coast had been colonized by different Europeans, so that there became a French Guiana, a Dutch Guiana, and a British Guiana. Travel between the three parts, in which the native Amerindians had roamed freely for centuries, then became a physical and bureaucratic nightmare.

Half an hour elapses. British Airways makes its final call. I am growing desperate, but the immigration officer is cool. The phone rings at last, he speaks into it, listens, speaks again, puts it down.

'What papers you carry, other identification?'

I willingly fish out a letter from the University of Berlin inviting me to Germany. He looks at it briefly and hands it back, as if it could easily be a forgery. British Airways calls for remaining passengers to board immediately. I am getting angry. I rummage through my wallet, show him my university card and British Library card. He pays no attention to them. I show him my American Express credit card, the only other piece of plastic in my wallet bearing my name. His mood changes, as in the television advertisement. He takes it from me, inspects it carefully.

'You from Sri Lanka?' he asks. The question suddenly explains everything. Sri Lankans, fleeing from a civil war, were entering Britain without visas, or with forged British passports. Airlines which brought them in were being fined. I looked like a Sri Lankan: small-built and dark-skinned. (I *was* in all probability a Sri Lankan: my forefathers shipped from the south of India in the middle of the nineteenth century to Guyana.)

'No, I am not a Sri Lankan,' I reply. He takes my word for it, gives me back my passport and American Express card, and points to the British Airways gate. I rush towards the plane, only to be delayed at the security point by one of the original guards. Methodically and maliciously he goes through my bag. 'C-a-s-s-e-t-t-e,' I say slowly as he looks puzzlingly at a tape of Calypso, as if teaching language to a child or barbarian. He picks up a box and looks into it. 'C-o-n-d-o-m-s,' I inform him.

When I eventually enter the plane, it is my misfortune to be wedged between two white youths. If either of them speaks to me or if their elbows touch mine by accident I swear I will kill them.

'Cultural diversity' can be a cosy term, evolved out of a blend of European post-colonial guilt and enlightenment, to justify tolerance of our presence in the metropolis. Justification is sought by the white intelligentsia, because deep down they know that a sizeable segment of the British people of a certain generation, those above forty, say, would prefer it if we went away and never came back.

How we got to Britain in the first place still puzzles and upsets most of these people: as Salman Rushdie once said, the British don't know their history because most of it took place overseas. Rushdie was being wicked though, for you can't be scornful of the British for not knowing – most of them in their involvement with Empire merely followed orders and took on the scraps of prejudice handed down by their social and intellectual superiors.

They didn't make the Empire (the politicians, merchants, poets, intellectuals and the like did this), they only made the Empire work. And they worked for the Empire without knowing what it was, what it meant, what it would lead to (immigration to the motherland, for a start). They were happy to feel superior to the rest of the world – who wouldn't, especially when there was little personal gain from the Empire? At the height of the extremely profitable (for whom?) slave trade, the mortality rate of white sailors on board ship was sometimes higher than that of slaves. All they had were intangibles fed to them by their superiors: the belief that they were an economically, culturally, intellectually and theologically superior race, the Master Race. They were even made to fight the Germans in two World Wars to settle the point.

The West Indians who arrived in British cities after the Second World War were brought here to serve the Master Race, on the buses, trains, in restaurants and hospitals. Before long however, some of the children of the Master Race were dancing to reggae and steel band, shopping for plantains in Brixton market and mingling with the West Indians in pubs, meeting houses and bedrooms. This seeming disruption of the master–servant relationship came about quickly. The West Indians soon lost their awe for the Motherland (an awe bred into them through a colonial education which asserted the glory of English customs, manners, history and language), when they quickly realized the levels of basic ignorance in the society. Samuel Selvon, who worked as a toilet cleaner in London bars whilst writing novels, spoke of the 'abysmal darkness' he encountered in England: 'This was the country whose geography and history and literature I had been educated upon long before I knew that Port-of-Spain was the capital of Trinidad. So why did they ask questions like if the people lived in trees, are there many lions, tigers and elephants: and of course, their amazement that I spoke English: How well you speak *our* language! Where did you learn . . .? The stories – the actualities – are manifest, but I'll only say this: not Buckingham Palace, not the West End or the Tower of London or the glitter of Piccadilly Circus, not even white men performing menial labour as porters or road-sweepers, not the fact that there were so many whites who could not read or write, struck me as forcibly, or rather impressionably, as this appalling ignorance about my part of the world, when I had been led to believe that I was coming to the fountain-head of knowledge. Though I was from a small island that might be flicked off the map like a speck of dirt from a jacket, I felt ten feet tall.'

The British, as described by Selvon, were ignorant of the way their economic appetites refashioned the personality of the African and Indian shipped to the West Indies. They were unaware of the trauma of loss (especially of ancestral languages, which still afflicts the living West Indian). They were unaware of how the West Indian created anew out of this void: how they took on the English language, altered it so that it could bear the weight of their personal and communal experiences in the shape of a novel by V. S. Naipaul or a poem by Derek Walcott. Or how they took the quintessentially English game of cricket, mastering its conventions but also inventing new stroke-play (Kanhai's sweep shot) or forms of spin (Valentine and Ramadhin) to delight British spectators.

Unlettered as many of them were, the West Indians who arrived in the 1940s were a highly complex people, containing traces and amalgams of Africa, India and Europe, survival skills nurtured over centuries, a huge curiosity for the world outside their islands, and a desire to give and take and be generous in the New World of Britain. The best aspect of the West Indian is this willingness to take, transform and give back. We only pelt stones or start fires when the British seek to wall us in, cut us off, from the possibilities of social and cultural exchange, social and cultural growth. The main lesson that the British can learn from the West Indian is how to give and take. When Naipaul wrote that 'nothing was created in the West Indies' he was pointing to the absence of British gifts to the place. They built a few fortifications, a few neo-Palladian mansions, a few churches, a few schools, and little else. When they gave, they did so sparingly and out of self-interest. Shakespeare, Milton and Newton were made accessible to a select few who were to be fashioned into mimic men, slavishly obeying the dictates of the metropolis.

The greater self-confidence brought about by the loss of awe at things British enabled the West Indian migrants quickly to put down their cultural baggage. Black-led churches, reggae bands, restaurants, publishing houses, bookshops and community centres, sprang up, many of which survive today in spite of financial difficulties and attempted vandalism by hostile white people.

The city, by its very nature, seemed to encourage West Indian culture to take root. Mandeville's enduring image of the hive to describe London betokens the city's capacity to allow for the growth of new cells. Brixton and other parts of south London became such cells. West Indians who moved in soon refashioned them into Jamaican or Barbadian villages (as far as possible), complete with bars selling Red Stripe beer and grocery stores selling coconut, patties and pepper sauce. They also gave new names to places, altering English words in the process: Bayswater became 'The Water' (or more correctly 'de wata'); Notting Hill Gate became 'The Gate'. Every Easter they organized a huge carnival, just like back home. They put on masks and costumes and road-marched behind floats ringing with steel band music. Hundreds of thousands of white people came for the spectacle, music and spicy food.

A city packs people in. They live on top of each other, alongside each other, sideways to each other. The city is a hive in this sense, but there are no inevitable passageways between one cell and another. And this has been the problem for West Indian culture in London – the white people who come to the West Indian cells for a while, to attend a carnival or to taste curried goat, return afterwards to their own cells. They don't spend long enough in the West Indian cells to appreciate the syntax, metre, chords, daubs, noises and smells created in these cells.

And they don't invite West Indians to visit *their* cells (called universities, banks, concert halls, theatres, arts councils, art galleries, Houses of Parliament, television studios) for a prolonged period either, or in any great numbers. The city is culturally diverse, but there is little cross-fertilization of cultures taking place. White people remain incarcerated in their own cells, afraid to venture out in case they are mugged by West Indians.

It has always been so in the Metropolis. Black people arrived in London in significant numbers two centuries ago as servants to the British aristocratic and mercantile classes. These black immigrants were the most culturally diverse and widely travelled people in the world. Some were born in Africa, then shipped to the West Indies, perhaps to several islands, then sometimes to America before being brought to Britain. They set up cells in parts of London, like St Giles; those not employed in households ustled a living by street, fairground or circus entertainments. As long as they remained colourful entertainers, they were tolerated by the populace. Those with economic or educational ambition were liable to be shipped back to the West Indies and sold into slavery. A few, like Olaudah Equiano and Ignatius Sancho, were befriended by enlightened white people, who gave them access to schools and books. It was only when the Anti-Slavery Movement got into full swing at the end of the eighteenth century that public sympathy for the plight of black people grew substantially.

The black presence was only barely tolerated. Influential voices kept calling for stricter immigration controls and for deportation of those already settled in Britain. Philip Thicknesse, writing in the 1770s, complained that 'London abounds with an incredible number of these black men . . . a mixture of negro blood with the natives of this country is big with great and mighty mischief . . . if they are to live among us, they ought by some severe law to be compelled to marry only among themselves . . .'. In the 1970s Enoch Powell was saying the same thing, albeit with more eloquence and classical erudition ('mischief' was also one of his favourite words, cropping up in speech after speech on the immigration/repatriation theme). As to the need for cultural purity, Margaret Thatcher's infamous speech on the 'swamping' of Britain by immigrant cultures finds echoes in dozens of eighteenth- and nineteenth-century pronouncements:

'Tis said there is a great number of Blacks come daily into this city, so that 'tis thought in a short Time, if they be not suppress'd, the City will swarm with them.

– *Daily Journal*, April, 1723

In the anniversary year of Columbus's journey to the Americas, and the subsequent profound alteration of boundaries and cultures, Britain will enter into an integrated Europe. Over time, Britain's own cultural boundaries will be altered and the Old World will become a New World. The New World values in Britain will not be those derived from its West Indian citizens, but from white Europeans. We'll all be eating more pizzas, downing more lager, spraying more French perfumes, driving more German cars and exchanging more footballers. My limited

and symbolic experience of European immigration controls make
me fear that British blacks, the original New World folk, will be
largely excluded from the new New World jamboree. Our ca
lypso, reggae, Creole poetry, art of cricket and the like, already
only of minority interest in Britain, will compete for attention
against German folk songs, dissident writings of Eastern Europe
the French passion for cycling, and so on. If 1492 created us
1992 could possibly kill us. Perhaps West Indians will eventually
slip their cultural moorings and get lost in the swamps of New
World Europe. Or perhaps we will be able to adapt, modify and
enrich our culture in the new environments. Perhaps new excite-
ments will arise when we encounter the Dutch blacks, the French
blacks, the German blacks, and discover what we share that
transcends colonial boundaries.

PAUL BAILEY

'Tears in the motley Strand'

In my third year at school, I was encouraged by my favourite English teacher to learn poems by heart. One of the first I committed to memory was Edmund Spenser's 'Prothalamion'. The word is of Spenser's own coining, and has passed into our literary language with the definition 'a song sung before a marriage'. Each stanza ends with the line:

Sweet Thames, run softly, till I end my song.

'Sweet Thames'? I lived by the river then, in Battersea, and saw it every day, and 'sweet' was not how it seemed to me. Cans and bottles and sinister pieces of wood floated on its brownish surface. It stank. Sometimes, it stank horribly. Why did it smell so foul? 'Sewage,' a knowledgeable friend told me. 'They don't realize what they're swimming in,' he said, pointing at the boys from even poorer homes than ours who were bathing in the infested water. 'If they did, they'd be sick.'

With that same friend, I once stood on Westminster Bridge, marvelling at what we saw below us – a mass of used contraceptives, or 'French letters', as we called them. ('Trust the French to have their name attached to an object like *that*,' observed a relative in the course of a man-to-man conversation about Life. 'They've no shame – that's their trouble.') We both agreed that William Wordsworth, while composing his sonnet on 3 September, 1802, would not have seen such shameful objects beneath him, since they hadn't been invented. (We were not to know, diligent students of history as we were, that there was a market in sheaths throughout the eighteenth century. In 1705, the Duke of Argyll displayed a 'quondam', purchased in London, before the Scottish parliament: it was, he announced, an 'instrument which occasioned the debauching of a great number of Ladies of quality, and other young gentlewomen'.) We reckoned that there were more than fifty of them in the river and for the rest of that day we wondered why they had suddenly appeared to us in such an abundance. Unusual experiments involving the staff at St Thomas's Hospital, perhaps? An orgy in the House of Commons? Was there a brothel – the word that always suggested soup to me – in the neighbourhood?

We returned to Westminster Bridge on successive Sundays and noticed more contraceptives in the murky Thames, but not so many, certainly not a shoal of them, as on that first, extraordinary occasion.

The London of my boyhood was a city scarred by war. A bomb had disposed of the house I was born in, and a prefab stood in its place. A prefabricated dwelling, as the term indicated, did not have to be built on the spot: it was put together in a factory, and conveniently deposited wherever it was needed. There was a certain odd glamour attached to living in these fragile-looking temporary residences, so reminiscent of cardboard boxes with windows: they were *new*, they were modern, and they had every convenience inside, which was considered the ultimate in luxury by the poor citizens of Battersea. The occupants of prefabs – and this was an optical illusion – actually seemed to be younger, to appear more youthful, than their neighbours in the remaining Victorian terraced houses, 'the ones that Jerry missed'.

The bomb sites, those grim reminders of the Blitz, vanished gradually and the prefabs went too. In the early 1950s, after years of necessary austerity, strange buildings began to rise – most notably, the Royal Festival Hall, which was accounted an 'eyesore' then, and now forms part of what has become known as the South Bank Gulag. Ugly as it is – and one does not have to share Prince Charles's vacuous taste for the neo-Georgian to consider it ugly – I am still fond of it, for it was there, night after enchanted night, that I saw and heard Guido Cantelli, Bruno

Walter, David Oistrakh, Clifford Curzon, Elizabeth Schwarzkopf: reasons enough for fondness. How fortunate I was to be a Londoner, I used to think; and think so today, recalling those concerts and recitals and, afterwards, the long walks back to Battersea, my head full of Mozart and Schubert and Brahms. If no one was around, I sang the tunes aloud and occasionally 'conducted' them.

London was vast, and vastly different – the perfect city for a boy given to wandering, as I was. It had its forbidden areas, I was warned – the East End, where the poor weren't respectably poor and criminals flourished, and Soho, which was the prostitutes' paradise. One Saturday evening – Saturday was always the day for wickedness – I went with the same friend who had witnessed the Westminster condoms to Soho 'to stare at the tarts'. We stared at them – and they glared back at us giggling, prurient schoolboys, and swore at us in French. Such danger, such excitement, and all from the safe distance of pre-adolescence. We were struck by the *age* of them. They were old – ancient, even – beneath their lurid make-up. They might have been grannies, else. In Florence, in Piazza Santa Maria Novella, elderly women still ply their trade – seated, rather than standing, in doorways, to give their feet a rest.

There was an Act to clean London's air, and then there was an Act to clean London's streets. The story goes that a rich and influential American, staying at a swish hotel in Park Lane, was so distressed by the sight and sound of the prostitutes soliciting business that he persuaded an English politician to bring the subject up in Parliament, with the result that the 'girls' were sent underground. In 1646, the metaphysical poet, Henry Vaughan, had witnessed similar, upsetting, physical displays:

> Should we go now a-wand'ring, we should meet
> With catchpoles, whores, and tarts in ev'ry street:
> Now when each narrow lane, each nook and cave,
> Signposts, and shop doors, pimp for ev'ry knave . . .

London now has beggars and derelicts and people made homeless from want of the kind of ambition our society favours, to give offence to visiting American puritans and Welsh poets with their eyes on eternity.

The London I encountered in poems seldom resembled the city
I had been born and raised in. William Dunbar's 'flour of Citie
all', his 'New Troy', his 'Pryncesse of Townes' was not what I
espied (poets were an *espying* bunch) from the windows, back and
front, of our terraced house. I had a choice of two dispiriting
views: the soot-stained chimneys looming above the Gas Works
or a junk-encumbered stretch of railway embankment where
stray cats cohabited shrilly amidst a quasi-host of dandelions. I
was ignorant at that time of William Blake's 'London', with its
'charter'd Thames' and its 'midnight streets' in which the 'youthful Harlot' contracts a plague that is clearly syphilis, although it
isn't stated. Until I read those terrible little masterpieces in
Blake's *Songs of Experience*, I think I believed that great poetry
was concerned only with the sublime, despite the enormous
quantities of evidence to the contrary in Shakespeare's plays.
The London of Spenser's 'Prothalamion', of Dunbar's 'In
Honour of the City of London' and Wordsworth's sonnet was
magical, merry, sunlit – an enchanted place 'all bright and
glittering in the smokeless air'. On certain fine spring or
summer mornings, walking up Ludgate Hill, with its then unob-
structed view of St Paul's, I found I could share something of
their sense of wonder. Theirs was a recognizable heaven on
earth, after all.

But the air wasn't smokeless for much of the year. When I was
a boy, London was as famous for the fog that enveloped it each
November as for the rain that descended on it regardless of
the season. I experienced that 'implacable November weather'
Dickens describes in the opening chapter of *Bleak House*, and
can say that I was one of those 'Chance people on the bridges
peeping over the parapets into a nether sky of fog, with fog all
round them, as if they were up in a balloon, and hanging in the
misty clouds'.

London's fame as a fog-bound metropolis persists. The George
and Ira Gershwin standard, 'A Foggy Day', in which the singer
declares that 'The British Museum had lost its charm' and
wonders 'How long . . . would this thing last?', may aid and abet
the legend. And in the countless adaptations of Conan Doyle's
Sherlock Holmes stories, the 'pea-souper' – as it used to be called

– is an important element, a necessary handicap to the quick detection of a crime or criminal. Films set in London and made in Hollywood invariably had their 'fog sequence', unlike those set in a sunny or rainy Paris. Where London was concerned, 'local atmosphere' tended to mean 'fog'.

It still does, and not just in fiction. Two years ago I was stranded in Florence in *un mare di nebbia*, a sea of fog. Italian friends and acquaintances remarked that it was *come Londra*. No, I insisted, it wasn't like London in the least. I tried to explain that there hadn't been *un mare di nebbia* in London since the introduction of the Clean Air Act in the 1950s. Some of them knew otherwise, and smiled at me as if I were harmlessly insane. They had gained their knowledge from the cinema, from television, from books both good and bad – unimpeachable sources.

Fog isn't pleasant like sunshine or light summer rain. It constricts breathing; it affects the lungs; it causes the eyes to smart and impedes the vision. Fog is suggestive of concealed malevolence, of evil doings perpetrated under its murky aegis. And it's this particular kind of fog – the fog that descended on Whitechapel when Jack the Ripper was going about his diabolical business – that has become synonymous with London. Milan is probably Europe's foggiest city now, yet it is our unfoggy capital that continues to inspire purveyors of fictional mist.

Loving descriptions of London are comparatively rare in English literature in the last two hundred years. Dickens's city is, by and large, a horrifying place – a 'great oven' in summer, and a fogbound, freezing hell in late autumn and winter, when even the hardy sparrows hop arthritically and chirp asthmatically. In Dickens's countryside, that often near-impossible Eden with its shortage of serpents, the birds have healthier constitutions – they strut and fly and sing with ease in the clear, blue air. They haven't been citified.

Only Virginia Woolf, accounting for Clarissa Dalloway's morning walk in St James's Park, comes close to expressing that sense of contentment with London and Londoners we find in Robert Herrick's poetry:

> From the dull confines of the drooping West,
> To see the day spring from the pregnant East,
> Ravished in spirit, I come, nay more, I fly
> To thee, blest place of my nativity!

In that same poem, celebrating his return to the 'fruitful Genius' that is London, he exhorts:

> O Place! O People! Manners! framed to please
> All nations, customs, kindreds, languages!

Herrick was writing in the early 1600s. Three and a half centuries later, the West Indians resident in Notting Hill encountered a place, a people and a set of manners that did not seem 'framed to please' them. Perhaps Herrick's 'nations' were entirely European, unlike those noticed by the young Wordsworth and recorded in Book VII of *The Prelude*:

> Among the crowd, conspicuous less or more,
> As we proceed, all specimens of Man
> Through all the colours which the sun bestows,
> And every character of form and face,
> The Swede, the Russian; from the genial South,
> The Frenchman and the Spaniard; from remote
> America, the Hunter-Indian; Moors,
> Malays, Lascars, the Tartar and Chinese,
> And Negro Ladies in white muslin gowns . . .

But these were, mostly, itinerants, and itinerants with means. They came, were marvelled at, and went. They weren't – like the Huguenots, the Jews, the West Indians, the Indians, the Pakistanis and others who would settle in the ever-expanding city – fleeing from tyranny and pogroms, from the sometimes dreadful consequences of British possession.

More than fifty years ago, the great Danish writer on architecture, Steen Eiler Rasmussen, fell in love with London and stayed faithful to the city for the remainder of his long life. What distinguished London from the other European capitals, he recognized, was its acknowledgement of, and respect for, the space human beings need in which to live. Rasmussen was particularly impressed by the humble dwellings he saw in the humbler boroughs – little houses with little gardens, but spacious by comparison with the tenement blocks in which the poor were usually accommodated. In the 1960s, we flew in the face of Rasmussen's enthusiasm and unlearned the lesson he was trying to teach Scandinavia, and constructed huge towers of concrete where once we had provided homes. 'Let them eat cake in the sky' was the inhuman, and unspoken, idea that motivated this cynical piece of civic planning.

Extolling the virtues of the countryside, writers and journalists point out that London is filthy and overcrowded and noisy. John Berger is a recent convert to pastoral bliss – in his case, to community life in the French outdoors. I am more persuaded by the novels of Mauriac, Bernanos and Simenon, among many others, that provincial existence à la française, or indeed anywhere, isn't all that it's cracked up to be – that there's rotten weather just the same, and rustic narrow-mindedness and its concomitant meanness of spirit. We talk, and Berger certainly does, of urban squalor as if squalor were entirely created by cities and their citizens. No one has argued more convincingly against this sentimental and ever-prevalent notion than Charles Lamb, who responded to an invitation from William and Dorothy Wordsworth to join them in Cumberland with the following, unforgettable letter:

With you and your Sister I could gang any where. But I am afraid whether I shall ever be able to afford so desperate a journey. Separate from the pleasure of your company, I don't much care if I never see a mountain in my life. I have passed all my days in London, until I have formed as many and intense local attachments, as any of your mountaineers can have done with dead nature. The lighted shops of the Strand and Fleet Street, the innumerable trades, tradesmen and customers, coaches, waggons, playhouses, all the bustle and wickedness round about Covent Garden, the very women of the Town, the watchmen, drunken scenes, rattles, – life awake, if you awake, at all hours of the night, the impossibility of being dull in Fleet Street, the crowds, the very dirt and mud, the Sun shining upon houses and pavements, the print shops, the old book stalls, parsons cheap'ning books, coffee houses, steams of soup from kitchens, the pantomimes, London itself a pantomime and a masquerade, – all these things work themselves into my mind and feed me without a power of satiating me. The wonder of these sights impells me into nightwalks about the crowded streets, and I often shed tears in the motley Strand from fulness of joy at so much Life . . .

He goes on to say that he has 'no passion . . . to groves and vallies'. His is the most heartfelt, the wisest appreciation of London's varied beauty that I know of – and it is, surely, still applicable. It is not sentimental, for Lamb had lived with uncommon horrors. I think he would have glowed with pleasure at the sight of contraceptives floating on the Thames.

MIKE PHILLIPS

London: Time Machine

The number 36 from Queen's Park skirts Maida Vale, trundles through Paddington, and up Edgware Road into Marble Arch and Park Lane. Between five and six in the morning the bus is more or less full, and the passengers are mostly black. They're African, Caribbean, with a few Spaniards and Asians mixed in. Cleaners, porters, waiters, workers in the essential services. These are the people who clean the offices, empty the dustbins, service the machines, and are gone by the time most people arrive to start their day's work. At this time of day the streets are empty, and you can hear the sounds of the city waking up from a long way off. Sometimes the driver sees a man running, and slows down half-way between stops so he can get on. Nobody talks much. It's as if they're reluctant to disturb the silence. Let the city sleep. At Marble Arch the hotel people begin to get off the bus. When I used to take this route regularly, I'd huddle up in a seat next to the window wishing I was still in bed; but later on, whenever I paused to think about London and my life in it, this is one of the memories that comes to me unbidden. Crossing the city in the 36 before dawn, trundling down to the West End, quiet, companionable and domestic in the lull before the day begins.

London is my city. There was a time when feeling this sense of ownership and belonging used to seem incongruous and even a little shameful, but nowadays it's a fact that gives me pleasure and security, and I've come to see the process that altered my feelings about it as part of the essential character of the city, any city, but in my case London's the one.

I first saw the place in the January of 1956, and the first impressions I can recall were sensual. My eyes and ears had been trained and nurtured on the colour and texture of a tropical landscape. Primary reds, the murmuring sea, wind rustling through the trees, the shrieking of bird-song. In my memory the buildings hardly feature. Perhaps the cathedral, and the tower that housed the market clock, standing out against the sky.

In contrast, London was a maze of buildings: damp, grey-brick corridors, through which I could only catch glimpses of a swirling, sulphurous sky. And the sights and sounds that affected me most powerfully were all by-products of some aspect of the city's functioning; artificial. For instance, the light from the street lamps gave my skin a strange grey tinge and, caught in a circle of this same light, the leaves of trees glowed a translucent, tender green, a colour I've never seen anywhere else, before or since.

But this was nothing in comparison to the shock of encountering so many strangers. Up to that time I had lived among people who were more than familiar. In my street I had known every twist of every family's lives, as they knew every twist of mine. Now everywhere I looked I saw people about whom I knew nothing at all. It was like an ant-heap of strangers: crowds of them on the pavements, at the bus stop, in the tube, in the cinema, in the pubs. And all of these seemed to repeat themselves endlessly, stretching further and into more districts than I could imagine. Yet, they seemed to be as much strangers to each other as they were to me. Instead of meeting and greeting each other openly on the street, they lived enclosed behind their walls, shrouded and veiled by curtains that concealed the hidden mysteries of their private worlds.

In hindsight, it seems obvious that everyone coming from a village or a small town to a big city must feel something similar. These first impressions must be shared by huge numbers of Londoners, probably a majority, who are all migrants, the children of migrants, or have their origins elsewhere, in other parts of Britain. Nothing new about this. Big cities have always been a magnet for the population surrounding them as well as the first port of call for travellers. But in the second half of the twentieth century internal migration has simply reinforced existing trends. On the other hand, the continuing movement of people from the poorest areas of the world into the industrialized countries gives the cities to which they come a new role and a new meaning.

There's a consensus reading of what's been happening to London since the 1960s. Not the one about the running down and neglect of services: that comes out of a different, more rational, network of ideas. At one extreme though, the debate elides into a kind of city dwellers' paranoia, which New Yorkers and Angelenos have down to a fine art and which started to become a part of the mythological baggage about London a couple of decades ago. It's a familiar litany: the noise, the dirt, the mess, the high prices, the bad schools, the assaults on the street, the drugs, the no-go areas, the ethnic strife, the crime. The nuisances and dangers of city life are exemplified in these things and, although the myth far outstrips any conceivable reality, it's not hard to believe. One stage further and the city becomes a synonym for fear and violence, a symbol of the nation's decline, a sort of madhouse where chaos threatens and loonies rule.

Along with this visceral terror goes an idealized portrait of life before the fall. The sacred prelapsarian word is community, which usually means something like village life, the population coherent and integrated only bigger, more colourful and with easy access to theatres, art galleries and concerts. Even those people who like the city and feel comfortable in its many currents tend to justify its future in terms of this ideal. The result is a slow drift towards the creation of enclaves, within which the better off Londoners look outwards and lament the state of the city.

Reinventing the past is one of the strategies in this process. Step forward the wartime propagandists and the image-makers of Ealing Studios. *Passport to Pimlico*, plucky London, Cockney spar-rers, *Dixon of Dock Green* and all the rest. Not too many people actually believe in the London they invented, full of supportive working-class communities and lovable rogues, but these images provide a constant background to arguments about the city's identity. Everyone talks about getting back to an ideal of urban life, which is to do with safety, community and a stimulating breadth of choice. The myth of the past becomes a goal of the future. But London has always been very different from the place that emerged from the fantasies of nationalists and PR strategists.

A typical experience in my first meeting with the city – I am thinking of an evening in winter near the end of the fifties. 1958 perhaps. I am going towards Finsbury Park with Theo (Theophanides), Papa (Papetrou), Bobby, Geoff and Kenny. We walk in a solid group because it looks more intimidating. Other kids leave you alone. We are dressed in the fashions preferred by fourteen year olds in North London. One or two button drapes. Trousers sewed tight to our legs. Thick soles. Kenny is a dark Burmese with a temper, whose hair falls over his forehead, just like Elvis. He is the only one with a leather jacket. We are going to Hollywood, which is a dancehall near the park. It is a sort of crossroads between various territories, and teenagers from all over the district encounter each other here. The girls dance. The boys lamp each other and fight. Nag's Head, ruled by the legendary Flanagan boys and the other Irish kids, is one point on our compass, Muswell Hill is another. The kids from the Angel and Hoxton, who gather in the Blue Kettle café, only come down here mob-handed. We are taking something of a risk because we are all immigrants except for Bobby.

This is the sort of situation which makes me nervous as a cat, because as usual, Geoff and I are the only West Indians in sight. There are ways of avoiding trouble. Stay away from the bad ones, don't meet their eyes, don't go to the gents. But I know that we'll be lucky to get out without a fight. Inside we meet Maureen and her friends from school. She's second generation Irish, pretty, well known for it, and she likes Kenny. They start dancing, embracing each other sexily, doing the creep. This attracts attention and before long there are little knots of Teds staring at them and following Kenny around. Before long it happens. Turner, a Ted from round the Cally, whose dislike of wogs is famous and who likes Maureen into the bargain, bumps into Kenny and pushes him away angrily. 'Are you screwing me mate?' he says, a conventional signal for starting a confrontation. Kenny, no hesitation, hits him in the face. Turner's friends pile in and surround Kenny. We pile in to rescue him. The place erupts with people screaming and running. Everyone seems to be hitting us. I hit back but mostly my efforts are devoted to getting out, although I'm keeping my eyes open for knives. Eventually we're out and I'm running down past the park gates with the rest of the boys. They've stopped chasing us and we go towards Kenny's house in one of the streets opposite the park. We stand outside waiting for him. Theo and Papa are bleeding, and I'm not sure what we're doing but I don't want to go off on my own. Suddenly Kenny reappears. 'Come on,' he says. We look at each other, and then Kenny opens his jacket and shows us the hatchet tucked into his belt. He turns and walks back down the road, moving fast. Theo is the first to react. Ten years later he'll be a doctor, and even now he's the most sensible of us. 'Grab him,' he shouts and together we surround Kenny, talking to him, telling him to calm down, it's not worth it, the police will be around, anything we could think of. For myself I know that I'm never going back in that place.

The memory is of an arena crawling with conflict, unease and confrontations over territory. Newcomers are obliged to establish and protect a space within which they can feel safe. Those already in possession fight back in a number of ways. This is the engine, both inevitable and necessary, that drives change in the city and makes it more than a collection of villages, or a museum of communities.

Walking through Islington the landscape is almost unrecognizable. I go past the house where we lived when I first arrived, crumbling, no bathroom, each floor packed with families. Now it is gentrified and expensive, blazing with new paint and smart railings. Four people live in it, occupying the space which used to be home to a clothing factory and more than a dozen tenants. In the maze of streets between the Cally and Holloway Road I look for Bride Street, where Geoff used to live, but everything looks so different that I can't find it. Or perhaps it's gone.

In London the buildings, the streets, the monuments, the solid things are actually ephemeral, although they are always there because it is in the nature of the city that they should decay and die and be rebuilt again. All these are merely the framework within which the real business of the city takes place.

A wet night in January. Perhaps it's 1972. Somehow it always seems to be winter. I have a streaming cold, and I am trying to sniff and blow my nose unobtrusively, which is difficult because I'm seated cheek by jowl, elbow to elbow with my fellow committee members. Opposite me are Charles Wegg-Prosser and Francis Deutsch. Next to me is Susan Marsden-Smedley and on the other side Gloria Cummins and Pansy Jefferey. We're talking about Paul Boateng who has just been appointed to assist Francis at the law centre. He is young and energetic, Francis says. Just the thing. Francis has been swamped with cases and administration, and Paul's presence will make all the difference. I think of his reputation for vigour and enthusiasm with a little envy. He's not much younger than me, but energetic is the last thing I feel now. I hunch up into my overcoat because it's cold in the room, but I'm already worrying about going out into the freezing wet night. I can't wait to get home. The centre has just opened and I seem to have attended a meeting every night for the last couple of weeks. I think briefly about the number of meetings Francis and Paul are facing. Sooner them than me. Francis talks about the number of cases and the people who are coming. The clients are West Indians, a few Asians; all they have in common is being in trouble and not knowing what to do about it. Charles says we have to run over the budget and I wonder for a moment whether I can get up and go home. Then I decide I can't. It's another couple of hours before we file out into Harrow Road. The rain is dripping down steadily, and I huddle in the doorway for a moment, chatting with Pansy and Gloria. By coincidence they both have husbands named Lionel and I keep getting confused. Suddenly Stedroy calls out from across the road. He's been waiting to tell Gloria that one of her neighbour's kids has been arrested, and she rushes back into the office to phone Paul. Time to go. I say goodnight before anything else happens and run for the 31 down to Notting Hill.

The city is not a monolith. It varies from district to district. Sometimes there's a persuasive core of truth to the oily estate-agent speak that pins a badge of nostalgia on the priciest property. Marylebone Village. Hampstead Village. Little Venice environs. On the other end of the scale are districts whose ugliness and desolation are appalling. But there's nothing new about this. The differences have, in any case, blended perfectly with 'normal'

British patterns of class-based disadvantage. From this perspective the miseries of the East End, and the political drama of Cable Street blurs smoothly into the ersatz 'tradition' peddled by TV soap operas like Eastenders.

Our view of the past tends to be determined by the needs of the present; and so far it's been possible to represent the fragmentation and variety of the city as part of a unified national identity, mimicking on a large scale what occurs in the rest of the country. In this version London's prime function is to be a space in which people work and live; there is nothing unique about it except its 'problems', and only its importance as the capital of the country makes them urgent. Generally the plans of planners are based on this reading, and assume that it is possible to determine and control the patterns and direction of growth.

The view from the other side of the fence is different. Cities like Paris retain control and coherence by dint of banishing dissident and radical population dynamics to its outer fringes and freezing change. But it's a lot easier to level mountains and destroy rain forests than to impose control on the movements of a great city like London, a living machine inside which molecules collide and fuse, spin out and disintegrate so that each stage of the process creates something new and like any good machine London goes about the most efficient way of achieving its functions, creating its own climate, its own ecology, its own internal structures. The product is change: the assembly and remodelling of identity.

In the postwar decades it has become increasingly difficult to maintain the fiction of London as part of a unity whose elements match the features of a national consensus. The arrival and establishment of a large number of racially diverse Londoners had changed all that, however vigorous our attempts to fit the present population into an assimilationist model of 'traditional' immigration. The focus is identity: the mould has been broken and the identity of London and Londoners has now become a major plank in the secret agenda of national anxiety about the future of the country. Underlying this concern is the sure and certain knowledge that London is a time machine determining and living out the next stage of our history.

Scratch the Londoner and you uncover a loony living a British future in which the national project is reassessed, the interpretation of our history is a comparative exercise, citizenship is divorced from racial origins, and you can't tell an Englishman from an Indian or an African or a Chinese.

One of the pleasures the city offers now is to be in it during the bank holidays, when all the commuters have gone home, and the only people walking around are cleaners, waiters, workers in the essential services. The languages are Spanish and African, Urdu and the Caribbean dialects. Except for these voices there's a peaceful hush in the streets and the great buildings are blank and quiet. These are the times when you can look at the city without distraction, like a tourist in an unfamiliar place. Drive around, stop in a few places, and London's beauty takes your breath away. Doesn't matter how often you've seen it. Some bits are obvious. The view from the South Bank. Waterloo Bridge. The perfect curve in Regent Street. For instance.

But sometimes memory determines what I feel. As a child I used to think that the grey-brick tower set in its own grounds along Green Lanes must be a castle. Going past on the bus I used to wonder about its history, until I found out that the lake was a reservoir and the castle was a pumping station. But even that revelation did not totally destroy the illusion, and driving past it now I still wonder. Then there are familiar rutted tracks. From Great Portland Street it takes about fifteen minutes through Camden Town, past Finsbury Park up to Tottenham. That's what I did last Christmas, ending up in the alleyway through Downhills Park, where I used to walk when I was a teenager.

Autumn turns it into an avenue of great golden drifts, but by winter the leaves had become a greasy, wet, brown carpet slipping and sliding under my feet. Halfway down I stopped in my usual place, leaned on the railings, and looked up to see Alexandra Palace hanging in the sky. At that distance I couldn't see how it's shrunk or the decay, and it looked the way its builders intended. Magnificent. Terrible. Somehow the fact that it was never finished and never occupied adds to its appeal. It's been my secret place for thirty years, and if it disappears I'll miss it, but in the end it wouldn't matter that much. Give me time and I'll find another. The city's full of such places.

III

VIEWS FROM THE GROUND

TIM HILTON

Art Schools and Urban Culture

Art schools are vivid places for those who have direct experience of them. To others they are mysterious. Little has been written about the modern British art school. There is no general literature on the subject: art colleges don't produce their own institutional histories, records are erratic and student magazines a rarity. Educationalists ignore art schools (perhaps they would not be especially welcome) and when did you last read anything at all about them in the columns of *The Times Higher Educational Supplement*, or the Tuesday education pages of the *Guardian*, or indeed anywhere else? They are unexplained, unapplauded: yet these colleges are a wonderful source of creative energy in our national life.

How is it that we have them at all, why are they so widely spread, and why are they the best in the world? No other country has a comparable system, probably because art schools in Britain started early, were not modelled on classical academies and answered local needs. The general pattern established by the end of the 1860s is still in place today. Their administration is, of course, modern. Many of the old art schools have been closed, merged or rationalized in one way or another. Practically all of them are now constituent parts of our polytechnics (to their benefit, I should add). But they retain a separate and stubborn identity, not only because they have their own traditions and purposes but also because they often still occupy their original buildings. Furthermore, their geographical distribution follows the growth of nineteenth-century industrial development. The major schools are the oldest, and they are in such places as Manchester, Leeds, Newcastle, Glasgow. Other areas don't have advanced art education: the school at Norwich serves the whole of East Anglia, students from the larger part of Wales find their way to Birmingham and Liverpool. Strangely, perhaps, the first new towns such as Welwyn and Hatfield did not develop a local art education. We need art schools in new centres of population such as Milton Keynes and the upper Thames valley. What a lovely job for someone, to devise a good art school for the 1990s!

Meanwhile, there's no harm in stressing that art colleges have belonged to the Victorian city. In Birmingham, for instance, we find the classic British art school of the nineteenth-century type (I admit to some local patriotism). Though it is now part of Birmingham Polytechnic the School of Art is still in its original home, separated by some miles from other polytechnic departments. It is at the very centre of the city, 100 yards from the Museum, the Council House and the Town Hall, in an early-1880s building that is a pure example of neo-gothic municipal architecture inspired by the ideals that first found expression in Ruskin's *The Stones of Venice*. In Birmingham one hundred years ago this meant good housing, meaningful work and positive leisure. But this was not all: the Ruskinian building proclaimed a belief in art education for all the city's children, an alliance between industry and art, and the hope of a proud municipal culture linked to social regeneration.

Such late Victorian civic optimism may seem dated or impossibly remote but that is no reason why it should be irrelevant to the 1990s. A paradox of art schools is that they are devoted to making new art and yet are conscious of old municipal traditions. The attitudes I describe as typical of Birmingham could be encountered in its studios within the last decade. I think the cities now need to make new partnerships with their art schools. Perhaps the process has already begun. In the mid 1980s a number of colleges started to open in the vacations and offered month-long courses for the unemployed. The results were often remarkable, for you don't need a long apprenticeship to trade secrets to make successful art. Art schools can lead the way with exhibition programmes, as they do at Norwich. If Norwich does indeed become a model city of the next decade as many hope, then it should look to its art school for ideas. It might at least thereby avoid the falsities of the heritage industry. The same is true of two other old cathedral cities: Winchester and Canterbury. Generally, why not revive the architecture departments that in days gone by were part of our art schools? Might not architects benefit from being trained in a more creative environment? And why not devise new departments in art schools devoted to urban planning? Most artists find schemes for public art to be utterly sententious. Let them come up with something else.

The schools at Canterbury and Winchester have gained recent prominence because of, among other reasons, the decline in the London colleges. In London are the grander establishments of art education. The Slade School is part of University College within the University of London. The Royal Academy Schools inherit their own particular tradition. The Royal College of Art is a postgraduate institution with a special interest in design. Its fine art students (recruited from colleges all over the country) are usually poised for professional success. But aspirant artists no longer feel that London is their goal. The main London art schools (Camberwell, the Central, Chelsea, St Martin's) have a leading place simply because they are in the capital; but they have lost that bright edge that once made them a little bit smarter than their provincial counterparts. They are cramped, lack basic facilities and their students can't find anywhere decent to live. Above all, the insensitive amalgamation of these four colleges into the London Institute demoralized staff and students alike.

Much of the excitement of art-school life disappeared during the Thatcher years, and the quality of new art was also, by no means coincidentally, depressed. It is not my task here to lament the education cuts or to criticize the business ethos that was forced on London art students, made to believe that the only point their art had was its immediate commercial viability amidst the young business classes. Recession has terminated that particular capitalist dream. I do want to say that morale in art education is linked with other values in our culture and quotidian lives. It is a myth that youthful art exists in some avant-garde vacuum separated from the rest of the world. Nor does it grow unaided. It is fostered and in its way is artificially maintained – as is literacy. There ought not to be a need to say this, but it is a fact that art education has become undervalued. A curator from – of all places – the Tate Gallery recently told me that there were too many art schools producing too many artists. Since not too many people want to purchase works of art, he reasoned, a whole class was being created whose skills were quite useless. Well, I think the opposite. Art-school education is valuable whatever its graduates do with their lives. It is not narrowly vocational. Sure, very many people have been to art school and have left to pursue other things. And perhaps they are so numerous that they do form something of a 'class', to use the Tate curator's slightly frightened term. We won't find them in the professions (except teaching) but they are all over the place: people who as art students learned to think independently and creatively and who in their maturity are disinclined to be governed, want to make what they will of their own lives, and take a keen, critical interest in the newness of things. If this is indeed a class, then I for one hope that its numbers will increase.

Because of the heavy materials, the sculpture department is always on the ground floor. There will be kilns, plaster, wood, steel, a welding shop, plus any amount of stuff brought in by students mostly, it would appear, from scrap yards. At the end of the day the sculpture tutors like to have things as clean as on a factory floor (whose workshop procedures exert a considerable influence on all fine art departments) but there's a danger in too tidy an art school. People need to kick stuff around. Unformed and inchoate today, this material might become a work of art tomorrow or next term. Visitors to art schools are often taken aback by the seeming chaos, the combination of noise and concentration, a sight of someone naked, bizarre experiments, the informal manners and the absence of intellectual privacy. Often enough there are no separate quarters for members of staff. Tutors visit pupils, not the other way round. Students live and work in spaces of their own, demarcated usually by tallish, temporary, hardboard screens. No space is completely closed:

doors are not part of the ethos. Everything a student does, however personal, finished or unfinished, botched or consummate, is visible to everyone.

Hence, surely, the competition and camaraderie, the frankness, the shared enthusiasms, the exhilarations and occasional depressions, the waves of inspiration and emotion that flow so rapidly through the studios. The tutor in charge of a year may at times feel that he or she is in control of a wild team rather than two dozen individuals. These young people scarcely ever join student societies, being themselves such an exciting society. Yet they are indeed individuals and are encouraged to express their personality. 'In art school you find out what you are', the adage goes. Life in the studios is tremendously demanding even before people start telling you things about your work that you may not like to hear.

By and large, men and women in art school are more committed to their work than any other group of people in higher education. They certainly get up to the things that parents find vexing: sleeping all through one day and working all the next night. But they do have commitment and without their daring and dedication they would not survive their self-imposed course. They discover their own selves and also come to terms with modern art. To some extent you join the avant-garde at art school.

The date at which the provincial colleges became local centres of modern art is uncertain. It varied from place to place and, again, we have no historian to call on. But the tendency was well advanced by the 1930s. By the early 1950s it had become essential to an art school's functioning. It was realized that student art (and the art of the people who taught) had to be of its time or it would be dead. This development was without parallel in higher education of any part of British provincial life. In places where you might least expect to find the new impulses of art – in Chesterfield, say, or Falmouth – there would be a knot of people gathered around the local art school talking about some discovery or other: Tachisme, Abstract Expressionism, concrete poetry, Ionesco's drama, Italian film – all the things that enlivened culture in Britain in the years after the war.

Some say that the great period of British art schools was in the mid 1960s. They point to Pop Art, largely the product of the Royal College of Art, and the emergence of a succession of innovative sculptural styles at St Martin's. But this was a quarter of a century ago, and isn't of much interest to artists who were born in 1970 or later. *They* are the people who are going to form the visual culture of the end of the century, and they want their great art school period now. What can we expect of them, or they of us? The art schools in which they will learn to express themselves are already in place. But they need recognition, revival and expansion. Recognition should come first. We still suffer from a distrust of modern art. However, the old prejudices are not at all shared by the younger generation, and I expect art to have a wide and natural place in the urban culture of the future.

RICHARD CORK

Art in the City

———

Anyone seeking to discover just how ruthlessly art was excluded from the post-war urban environment need look no further than the south bank of the Thames. For here, on an extensive riverside site housing the largest arts complex in the world, artists were given no role to play in the shaping of public spaces. Blank, forbidding and often buffeted by wind, the buildings erected there during the 1960s are as cheerless as the exposed walkways that encircle them like roads coiling around a motorway junction. Everything appears to be marooned in dismal expanses of stained, decaying concrete. The foul-smelling areas underneath seem designed only to deter visitors from penetrating them and mounting the shadowy staircases lodged within their labyrinthine structure. It is ironic that an area containing so many buildings dedicated to the nation's cultural vitality should have become, in many respects, such a wasteland.

The irony multiplies when the present state of the South Bank Centre is compared with the spectacular regeneration it enjoyed in 1951. For a few effervescent months the entry site was transformed into a 'tonic to the nation'. Celebrating the end of war's prolonged ordeal, and counteracting the debilitation and austerity that dogged the country in its aftermath, the Festival affirmed a resilient faith in the ability of artists and architects to create a more imaginative environment. By commissioning monumental paintings and sculpture from Moore, Hepworth, Nicholson, Pasmore and Sutherland, alongside members of the emergent generation like Paolozzi, the organizers implied that art deserved to perform a central part in the creation of the post-war world. Cities throughout Britain needed reconstructing in the wake of the Blitz, and the Festival dared to hope that its sprightly initiative would prove widely influential.

Although attempts were made to build on the event's immense popular success, they were disappointingly sporadic. After most of the Festival was peremptorily swept away by the incoming Conservative government, the whole notion of involving artists in urban renewal began to falter. Architects, some of whom had eagerly invited painters and sculptors to embellish their buildings on the South Bank, now settled for unadorned and dogmatically functional monoliths. The need to economize also militated against any ideas about extending budgets to include works of art in new developments. And so the archetypal post-war city began to assert its bleak identity through the country. Bare, slab-like architecture, combined with a relentless emphasis on multiple road systems that drove pedestrians into a depressing network of subways, dominated these stern territorial assertions. Whenever attempts were made to alleviate the prevailing aridity with a large-scale sculpture or mural, the outcome often seemed arbitrary. The works looked raw and uncomfortable, dumped in locations that remained inimical to their presence. More frequently than not, they were rewarded with indifference, bewilderment or outright anger by those obliged to pass them in the street. By the time that the South Bank was finally given its theatre, gallery and smaller concert halls, all the enthusiasm generated by the Festival had long since evaporated. Brutalism became *de rigueur*, and no hint of celebration could be found in the bunker-like exterior of the Hayward Gallery or the Queen Elizabeth Hall.

Such sterility was bound, eventually, to provoke a reaction. During the 1970s it took the form of community murals, many painted with good intentions but poor judgement on the gable ends of blighted inner-city housing. Lacking any persuasive relationship with the architecture they were supposed to enhance, these stop-gap, makeshift images provided no viable model for the long-term development of an art properly integrated with the environment. But they did at least break the deadlock, and their makers' determination to consult the local population emphasized the importance of escaping from arrogant, token gestures imposed on cities without any real thought for the character of the spaces they occupied.

During the next decade, more sustained and concerted initiatives began to emerge. Industrial decline provided the springboard for a venture at Dundee, where the collapse of a once-thriving textile industry had led to urban stagnation throughout the Blackness area. In October 1981 a joint agreement was signed by the Scottish Development Agency and the two local authorities. It committed them to rehabilitation as well as economic regeneration and within a year a fully-fledged Public Art Programme began in Blackness. Unlike so many previous attempts to invigorate depressed streets, the Dundee enterprise was regarded from the beginning as an integral part of the overall improvement scheme. The needs of the entire area were taken into account and the programme's management group brought together the different skills of (among others) an engineer, a town-planner, an artist working with Dundee District Council and teachers at nearby Duncan of Jordanstone School of Art. They ensured that each work, far from being an isolated afterthought tacked on to an alien surface, was informed by careful consideration of the site's particular requirements.

Such a policy prevented them from adopting a standardized approach. Although they wanted to retain at all times a guiding awareness of the area as a whole, each project was approached on its own terms. Rather than confining themselves solely to painting on gable ends, the commissioned artists adopted a more versatile attitude. Stanley Bonnar employed mosaic on the main elevation of the Indoor Bowls Club, but experimented with white chip in his path-pattern design for the tarmacadam pavement alongside. Brick, ceramics and silk-screened tiles have been used in window-panel reliefs for the outer walls of formerly disused factories. Lizanne Wood carved into a stone block when she produced her free-standing monument on a landscaped street-corner. Modest in themselves, the works of art enlivening Blackness add up to an unpretentious act of faith. They provide a continuous reminder, to visitors and inhabitants alike, that the most dilapidated district can be rejuvenated if sufficient care is devoted to the task. Even the Edwardian public lavatory, at the Westport entrance to Blackness, underwent a surprising metamorphosis when it was rescued from demolition and became an imposing pyramidal landmark.

The strength of the working relationship between the artists and everyone else involved in revitalizing Blackness has now been carried over to the Dundee Public Arts Programme, identifying and developing sites all over the city. But Bob McGilvray, the coordinator of the programme, acknowledges that funding has suffered from cut-backs in recent times. The first three years of the Blackness venture were supported by a budget of £90,000 and produced sixteen completed projects. Now, however, each new work is funded separately, and this scheme-by-scheme approach has led McGilvray to conclude that private sources of patronage must be found in future. Without them the Dundee initiative will never be able to go beyond the limits of its current policy.

Response from the public has, until now, been positive with very little hostility or damage to the work. The programme's existence is known and accepted, largely because it has always consulted local opinion and aimed at becoming part of everyday surroundings rather than an expensive, jewel-like addition. But there is a growing recognition among the team's members of the need to produce something more ambitious and radical. Much of the current work is restricted to fulfilling semi-functional purposes, like John Gray's infill panels at Victoria Bridge, Chris Kelly's gate sculptures marking the entrances to Dunsinane Industrial Estate, or David Wilson's painted fence and display for Captain Scott's research ship *Discovery* at Victoria Dock. The regeneration of run-down council housing on the Whitfield Estate is being accompanied by a whole series of works related to the area, and carried out in concert with the engineers and landscape architects working on the project. There is, nevertheless, no sign of artists collaborating with architects at the inception of a major develop-ment. Nor is there any immediate likelihood that an artist with an international rather than a purely local reputation could be invited to install a monumental work in a prominent location, either in the oddly barren city centre or by the side of the magnificent River Tay. Dundee's natural surroundings are specacular enough to deserve a large-scale manifestation of art's apacity to help furnish a city with its public identity.

Gary Fisher, the chairman of the programme, would certainly ke to realize such an ambition. Having educated the people of)undee to a high level of acceptance, he feels that it is now time) present them with a tougher and more demanding body of work than the projects completed so far. Although it might well rovoke controversy, the result would at last dare to stray beyond ae constraining boundaries of a tame art that tried to be user-iendly. While a certain amount of consultation is clearly neces-ry, artists can dilute and compromise their work if they become verconscious of the obligation to produce instantly acceptable nages. Ronnie Forbes, who runs the Public Art and Design)urse at Duncan of Jordanstone College, is right to insist that 'ood public art grows out of a private vision – it must be real t, not culturally vacuous'. Although his students execute rojects for a diverse range of locations, from a home for the derly to a quarry, to local schools and housing estates, Forbes mains convinced that such work should be fed by the same gour of thought and feeling that informs the best private art.

This central challenge, to ensure that art in public spaces pires to the highest standards rather than settling for mundane cessibility, also confronts the consultative bodies set up to ediate between artists and their potential patrons. In 1983, a ar after the Blackness venture began, Lesley Greene founded e pioneering Public Art Development Trust. Based in London, quickly grew into an indispensable means of guiding the com-ex negotiations that surround the commissioning process. The rust also tried to foster, in the broadest educational sense, an in-rmed awareness of the responsibilities involved, and its initiative s since been extended by no less than eleven other bodies in other rts of Britain. They include Birmingham's Public Art Commis-ns Agency, Edinburgh's Art in Partnership, Cardiff's Welsh ulpture Trust, Sunderland's Artists Agency and, in response to e special needs of art in hospitals, Manchester's Arts for Health d the British Health Care Arts Centre also based in Dundee. aeir rapid proliferation proves that the work they foster is now lourishing part of contemporary art across the nation.

This steadily expanding activity was boosted further by the publication in 1990 of *Percent for Art*, the report of a steering group established by the Arts Council with the Council of Regional Art Associations, the Welsh and Scottish Arts Councils and the Crafts Council. The architect Richard Burton, who chaired the steering group, made his loyalties clear by allowing art to perform a highly visible role in his newly designed St Mary's Hospital at Newport on the Isle of Wight. Fired by the belief that healing can only be enhanced by surroundings far removed from clinical impersonality, Burton deplored the gulf separating artists and architects. 'What is needed,' declared the report, 'is a method whereby the talents of artists can be assured an integrated place in building-design.'

But how can art and architecture play more of a part in the £40 billion that Britain invests each year in the maintenance of buildings and new, mainly urban developments? The report's first and most important recommendation proposed that 'all public building schemes and public works whose contract price is at least £3 million should adopt Percent for Art on a mandatory basis at a level not less than 1 per cent of the total cost'. So far forty local authorities have embraced such a policy on a voluntary basis through the planning system. The country as a whole has, however, not yet committed itself to setting aside a proportion of the capital cost of building and environment schemes for commissioning art. Unlike its French counterpart, the British government sees no need systematically to involve artists in the design stage of public-sector buildings. The report therefore resolved that 'capital spending plans for Departmental Executive Agencies should include Percent for Art on a mandatory basis from 1992, thereby bringing Britain into line with practice elsewhere in Europe'.

Even if these measures were introduced, though, they would be no guarantee of quality. Indeed, if the proposed legislation were extended to private-sector buildings as well, it might lead merely to a rash of banalities commissioned by developers who resented their new responsibilities rather than welcoming them. Without a firm belief in its desirability on the patron's part, collaboration between artists and architects could easily be still-born. Worse still, the results might discredit the entire venture and associate it irredeemably with anodyne, half-hearted work. So the idea of compulsory enforcement should be replaced by a greater emphasis on the importance of fostering a genuine change in attitudes. The alliance of art and architecture could then enjoy a convincing outcome. The report was fully justified in recommending joint courses on a pilot basis for architects, artists and craftspeople in selected areas of higher education.

In the meantime, distinguished work can be produced for urban centres only if it is informed by the requisite amount of energy, resourcefulness and discrimination. In 1988, while Birmingham was finalizing plans to remodel Centenary Square in the middle of the city, a percent-for-art policy was suggested by Vivien Lovell, the indefatigable Director of the Public Art Commissions Agency. The fact that Lovell's proposal was supported by Michael Diamond, Director of the Birmingham Art Gallery, helped to win the day. They both became key members of a working party set up to decide how 1 per cent of the total building costs should be allocated to artists. It was already too late to think in terms of full collaboration with the architects of the new Convention Centre, RHWL and the Percy Thomas Partnership. The exterior of their disconcertingly lumpish building was already finished, but the working party did succeed in choosing a number of strategic sites within the structure. The substantial sum of £800,000 was originally earmarked for artworks; and although that figure remained the same while building costs spiralled, several major projects were commissioned. Deanna Petherbridge was invited to paint a strongly architectonic four-storey mural on the drum wall, while Ron Haselden's neon birds filled the entrance canopy and Alex Beleschenko designed stained glass for the immense end wall overlooking the newly restored canal.

The most felicitous aspect of the venture can be found outside, however, where Tess Jaray was initially invited to design a richly patterned pavement in coloured brick for the square itself. Gradually, and very surprisingly, she was able to assume responsibility for designing all the light-fittings, benches and litter-bins as well. Elegant yet sturdy, these ironwork structures show Jaray's respect for the Victorian street furniture still surviving elsewhere in the city. But they also possess a lightness of touch and a leaning towards simplification that marks them out as late twentieth-century in feeling. They certainly chime with the sensibility of an oriental carpet. Rippling at the edges, the design grows in complexity as it approaches the centre of the square. Alternating between sections alive with zig-zags, and bands filled with hovering lozenges of colour, it pushes forward with a momentum as irresistible as a powerful mosaic floor running up a cathedral nave.

But Jaray never allows the sense of exultation to grow beyond a human scale. This is a pavement subtly attuned to the needs of the individual walker and the figures who traverse it appear reassuringly at home as they negotiate the individual components of the pattern she has devised. The colours accentuate the air of welcome it offers. On a dry, warm day the overall hue is reminiscent of terracotta interspersed with pale mustard, parched ochre, sun-baked orange and a refreshing use of darker, blue-tinged elements. It stirs memories of dusty Renaissance piazzas and Jaray acknowledges that Italy has provided her with an indispensable source of inspiration. Viewed from the upper levels of the Convention Centre, the full extent of her *tour de force* becomes apparent. Glowing softly in the daylight, her limpid design restores sensuous delight to a city that had forgotten how to nourish it.

After suffering the polluted tyranny of the inner ring road ever since it was hatched in the post-war boom period, the citizens of Birmingham now find that the planners are beginning to release them from its grip. The immensity of Centenary Square is dedicated to the pedestrian rather than the car and nearby Victoria Square is soon to follow its example. Traffic will be banished by a plan which involves sculpture by Dhruva Mistry, a grand water-cascade and an open international competition for another sculpture outside the new TSB headquarters. Vivien Lovell, who is arranging the latter, views the future of Birmingham with optimism. She has written a strategy for art in the imminent development of the Bull Ring, proposing that the London and Edinburgh Trust spend 2 per cent of its budget on painting, sculpture and related work. Although that amounts to £2 million, Lovell says that the trust is very sympathetically disposed to the idea of acting as patrons and creating a more civilized setting for shoppers. She will also be briefing the contractors engaged in building Midland Metro, a city-wide tram system with an overall budget of £600 million, on how artists could contribute to the construction of transport fit for the new millennium.

The sheer scale of art's likely involvement in the Birmingham of tomorrow, backed by the commitment of the city's recently appointed Director of Planning and Architecture, Les Sparks, would have seemed impossible a decade ago. Today, by contrast, the precedents established on a localized level in Dundee and with full civic grandeur at the centre of Britain's second largest city may well prove widely influential. Already there are encouraging signs, in the development areas of places as disparate as Cardiff and Wakefield, that artists have come to be regarded as an indispensable part of urban transformation. Even in London, where the growth of art in public spaces has been far more fragmented, a promising experiment is now taking shape in the borough of Lewisham.

In the Orwellian year of 1984, Lewisham Council became one of the first authorities in the country to adopt a formal percent-for-art policy, and the move is about to bear fruit. The crowded and traffic-throttled town centre urgently needs a radical overhaul in order to fulfil its hopes of becoming a focus for shopping and employment. Comprehensive redesigning of the area has commenced under the slogan 'Lewisham 2000' and the eighteen-strong team of engineers, urban designers and landscape architects contains an artist as well. Working from former shop premises in Lewisham High Street, where the glass frontage shudders with vibrations from the incessant surge of traffic while trains clatter past on the railway bridge nearby, the team welcomes inquiries and comments from anyone wanting to study the scale model, seek information or air opinions.

This remarkable open-mindedness led the town centre's principal planning officer, Derek Moore, to take the unusual step of involving the sculptor John Maine at the planning and design stage. According to Mike Jackson, engineer and leader of the team, Maine was chosen from a large field of applicants because 'he thinks in three-dimensional terms, had previous experience of working with design professionals such as landscape architects, and didn't seem likely to have continuous battles with us'. For his part, Maine relishes the opportunity to coordinate all the visual aspects of the project from its inception. Far from 'buying in' work at the end, the Lewisham team wants the art to arise from a carefully researched overview of the entire location. Maine has studied the history of Lewisham, and aims at uncovering some of the lost character of an area that used to be dominated by two rivers, the Quaggy and the Ravensbourne.

For some years they have been sunk in concrete channels to prevent flooding, but he would like them to become more visible again in the town centre. The confluence of the rivers behind the bus station could well be marked by a sculpture in a new park, and removing most of the traffic to Molesworth Street will provide space in the High Street for café tables, seating and carefully contextualized artworks. Having already designed his own set of cast-iron bollards for an improvement scheme in Marishal Road, Maine is now designing an undulating central reservation for the widening of Molesworth Street. Elsewhere, though, his plans are less discreet. If art is too well integrated, it runs the risk of going unnoticed. Maine believes that it should challenge people as well, and envisages a grand columnar gateway at the southern end of the road. At the other end, a large roundabout offers the site for an even more arresting structure, so Lewisham may be furnished with monumental images once its transformation is complete.

Even though his work will not be finished for several years, Maine's involvement with the project has attracted a great deal of interest from city-planners elsewhere in the country. He hopes, however, that the example set by Lewisham 2000 is never lavishly imitated. 'We want others to do what is appropriate for them,' he insists, 'not copy us with a doggedness that devalues our ideas and turns them into clichés. It's always important to think freshly.' Only then will the danger of degenerating into a knee-jerk implementation of percent for art be avoided. Mediocrity remains an ever-present threat, and no one wants cities to become repositories for a torrent of third-rate work. Stale formulae will always flourish without the participation of truly imaginative artists, who may not have received a public commission before. Lack of previous experience could even be an advantage in this context, enabling them to take on new challenges with minds unclouded by the predictable solutions which seasoned practitioners too often supply.

Brancusi had never been given the opportunity to work on a grand public scale before he was invited, in 1934, to make a monument to the Great War at Tîrgu Jiu in his native Romania. He nevertheless arrived at the most impressive fusion of sculpture and urban setting in the whole of twentieth-century art. Beginning with *The Table of Silence*, a horizontal image of loss, reconciliation and unity by the edge of the river Jiu, he then celebrated a loving and generative embrace on *The Gate of the Kiss* before achieving, just over a mile away, the singleminded vertical thrust of the *Endless Column*, soaring away from the earth with a sublime certitude which would, in Brancusi's own words, 'sustain the vault of heaven'. As well as adding up to a powerful and redemptive ensemble, this tripartite memorial supplies Tîrgu Jiu with an indelible identity. The sculptor William Tucker was particularly moved by the way Brancusi's structures 'sit in the environment, the way they are *used* by people. In fact the monuments are no more regarded by the people of Tîrgu Jiu than is their own cathedral by the people, say, of Peterborough or Durham. Yet in their passing by or through, their waiting or working near, their occasional glance or stare, the citizens acknowledge these things as part of *their* place.'

Brancusi's *tour de force* deserves to be regarded as a talisman by anyone attempting to enliven urban spaces today. His involvement at Tîrgu Jiu shows how much enduring imaginative meaning can be invested in a public setting by someone who shares his ability to remain fully alive to the surroundings he was invited to transform. The precedent created there proves with eloquent authority, that more artists of the first rank should be encouraged to venture beyond the gallery's limits, so that they can enjoy a supple interplay between private and public ways of working. If they are given spaces that stimulate their energies rather than confining them and receive the support of architects, planners and patrons motivated by an informed understanding of the pitfalls as well as the enormous possibilities, our cities will have everything to gain from placing the finest art at the very heart of modern urban life.

KEN WORPOLE

Trading Places:
The City Workshop

For William Morris, art and work were synonymous. A long line of socialist cultural politics has been about bringing art and production back together again, the two having been disastrously separated by the industrial revolution into distinct spheres of human activity: individual works of art and mass production. The industrial revolution drove the poets and the painters to the valleys and mountains in disgust and horror; some novelists such as Dickens, Gaskell and Gissing stayed behind to record the general degradation. The 'sensitive artist' and the 'brutalized worker' went their separate ways; the folk and crafts traditions were pronounced dead. Art was produced and collected in private, and the new mass-produced popular culture – penny dreadfuls, part magazines, cheap reproduction prints, song-sheets – was distributed through the market-place. Only the public library, museum and municipal gallery attempted to cross the great divide. The city became a showcase rather than a workshop.

Urban popular culture developed through commercial forms, and the crafts movement became associated with an arcadian countryside or the sequestered lives of a privileged élite. Was there ever anything sadder in the history of English socialist self-remonstration than C. R. Ashbee's valediction for the Arts and Crafts Movement, when he wrote to Morris saying that, 'We have made of a great social movement a narrow and tiresome little aristocracy working with great skill for the very rich.' The country and the city became associated with radically different cultural traditions.

Occasionally even an artist as private as T. S. Eliot would acknowledge some degree of shared or collaborative creation when he dedicated *The Wasteland* in 1922 to Ezra Pound, '*il miglior fabbro*', the better workman. In more recent times collaborative work, group endeavour, artistic creation as a form of collective production, have emerged once again, using the vocabulary of 'the workshop' as a metaphor for something rooted in shared experience, in the development of a common cultural form, the point of view of a group of people rather than a single individual. Joan Littlewood's Theatre Workshop established at Stratford East in the late 1950s revived the use of the word; many others have followed since. The history workshop (largely associated with reclaiming past histories and traditions), the writers' workshop, the music workshop and the dance workshop have become familiar features of the contemporary urban cultural scene. They have often been forcing houses of talent.

In addition to the performance-based arts, small-scale workshop production is back on the agenda again both in handicrafts and hi-tech cultural forms such as video animation, computer graphics, electronic music, desk-top publishing. 'Flexible specialization', the name given to the more individualized forms of manufacturing now replacing standardized mass-production in many industrial processes, and involving small-batch production using computer-aided design and computerized stock-control systems, is today one of the hallmarks of industrial success in advanced economies.

Urban policy in the late twentieth century is now inseparable from cultural policy. The one informs the other. Both will depend on creating a working economic base. In any programme of urban and civic renewal, getting the economic base right is going to be a key ingredient. Here the arts and cultural industries have a key part to play. As Ralf Dahrendorf recently argued, 'Civic pride and good government are probably intertwined. Both have a great deal to do with economic vitality. In Europe, a new dynamism has taken the place of the Eurogloom and Eurosclerosis of the 1970s. However, the dynamism is not universal. It is strongest where inventiveness and industry combine, as they do in Milan, in Frankfurt, in Paris.'[1]

The new urban mix, the successful city core, requires all kinds of activities – residential accommodation, a decent transport infrastructure, facilities for leisure and recreation, and above all, places in which to work. Urban policy is now a matter of some urgency, as the French socialists have belatedly discovered after nearly a decade in power. In December 1990 Prime Minister Rocard announced the appointment of a Minister of Towns inspired, as the *Guardian*'s French correspondent, Paul Webster, has written, 'by a general recognition that urban policy has been the biggest single failure of the past decade'. It is to be hoped that a Labour Government will not make the same mistake. Over the past decade cities have been demonized, seen as a source of insoluble problems, their local authorities castigated, their populations denied, with the 'inner cities' being anathematized as one of the last circles of a Dante-esque descent into hell. Labour should celebrate cities – and many Labour councils have, of course, been doing this for decades – and see them as great creative melting points for the future, each with its own distinctive character.

The history of cities and the history of markets are inextricably linked. The story of cities is the story of the rights of urban self-government, of the right to hold markets, regulate trade and even, historically, to coin money. As Lewis Mumford argued in *The Culture of Cities*,[2] the determination by urban settlements to secure city status was in large measure a determination to attract permanent groups of craftsmen and traders and to establish an indigenous local economy. In many places this was often determined by specific topographical factors – steel-making, ship-building, fishing, pottery, chemicals, engineering – but increasingly these local and regional factors no longer exert the same influence and towns and cities are seeking to establish new industries, service-based and even arts-based. Sheffield's 'cultural industries' strategy, as with Liverpool's 'media economy' strategy, can never be seen as replacements for steel, ship-building or dock-work in terms of numbers, but none the less they are both serious economic strategies.

Markets and trading are indisputable features of successful

towns and cities. The higher the degree of local trading and local circulation of goods and services, the more self-reliant an urban economy is likely to be. In recent years the great fear of many urban planners has been the reliance on national or multinational firms as chief sources of local economies – the 'branch economy' syndrome – withdrawal or closure of which has often had devastating effects. A similar pattern has emerged in the 'retail revolution' of the 1980s whereby some town centres, almost wholly dominated by branches of multiples, have little or no local retailing capital, expertise or traditions to fall back on should the multiples start pulling out as they have already begun to do. A town centre in which it is no longer possible to buy a pint of milk, a tin of paint, a fishing rod, a ball of wool, a bicycle tyre, or get a pair of shoes mended – and there are now many such towns in Britain – will be in serious trouble in future, when mobile companies and populations start relocating again and look for self-reliant towns and cities that exhibit an economic and cultural dynamic and its associated 'quality of life'.

The left should stop getting so anxious about the word 'market'; it has a popular and progressive history, as the French historian Ferdinand Braudel has shown. Markets are mechanisms. They do not produce anything themselves. In his 1990 Royal Television Society lecture, BBC Programmer Bill Cotton remarked that '"The market will decide" has become a rallying cry. I personally have never known a market write a sketch, or tell a story or sing a song.' Precisely. Artists and cultural producers who fear markets should disabuse themselves of the notion that markets *per se* will determine artistic content. They are mechanisms of distribution, re-allocation, exchange and trade. If anything the main problems facing cultural producers in recent years – especially independent producers, or creators of new cultural goods – have been problems of distribution and establishing a foothold in the public marketplace. There has been no shortage of young visual artists, black film-makers, women writers, Asian musicians, independent record producers or independent photographers whose work has been challenging but who have failed at the point of distribution rather than production. New networks of cultural distribution and exchange are urgently needed. Urban planning could help.

Post-war British urban planning has been essentially antagonistic to production. As architect Peter Buchanan has argued, 'British planning is predicated upon a desperately impoverished conceptual model of the city. In essence that model (when planning still had some life and credibility) was consumerist rather than civic.'[3] The good life, according to his planning ideal, was suburban housing, plenty of roads and garage space, and a town centre dedicated to shopping. Rigid zoning and land use regimes separated work, housing and leisure into separate and watertight compartments. Spatial separation also became time separation – the town centres and commercial districts were busy between 9 a.m. and 6 p.m. and then they suddenly went quiet. The housing estates were empty of people during the day. Leisure had to be somehow fitted in to the small interstices, or moved out of town into theme parks or suburban complexes only accessible by car.

Streets became roads, and hundreds of years of one of the most tenacious forms of urban culture seemed destined for oblivion. Street life, street credibility, street culture none the less held on in some places. When Dickens was ill in Lucerne during a lecture tour, he attributed his malady to 'an absence of streets'. Streets are places where people live, work and play sometimes all at the same time. And as Judy Hillman has argued, 'People going about their business is one of the keys to the successful street. So is the public nature of the place and the opportunity for casual contact.'[4]

Artists and cultural producers are thankfully moving back into city centres. A number of urban regeneration schemes have demonstrated that the cultural industries and the performance arts are among the best activities and businesses for reviving a run-down area and making best use of empty industrial buildings, shopfronts and warehouses. Developers such as Mike Franks, Nicholas Falk and Bennie Gray have pioneered the revitalization of old London industrial districts through projects such as *Clerkenwell Workshops*, *Rotherhithe Workshops* and *Canalot* in North Kensington. In 1990 Whitechapel Gallery began organizing guided coach tours to enable members of the public and tourists to visit artists in their studios in Tower Hamlets, Hackney and Islington, to view work and even to buy.

In Halifax the Dean Clough mill has been almost wholly turned over to arts activities and businesses; Newcastle's proposed Theatre District' in the West End of the city is intended to be primarily for arts and cultural companies; the Sheffield 'Cultural Industries Quarter' is a linked network of live venues, recording studios, design studios, film and photographic workshops, galleries, record companies and other small businesses; Bradford's 'Little Germany' is a regenerated industrial district largely devoted to crafts and design industries; Brighton Council's new economic development plan speaks of developing the 'Art School economy'; and already supports a number of artists by subsidizing studio space as well as running an 'Art Spaces' scheme which encourages owners of empty buildings to give them over to arts activities at reduced rents as part of the overall development of the town's economic infrastructure; Reading Council supports the excellent Open Hand Studios where some dozen local artists have their own studios open to the public for viewing and selling, and where they run workshops and organize festivals.

In future, cultural policy and funding may well be more closely associated with urban policy, economic development, planning gain, land use development plans, Use Classes legislation, development trusts and public commissions, than with traditional subsidies from dedicated 'arts' public funding. Most of this should be welcomed with just one note of caution.

A graphic lesson in how not to do things comes from New York, and is admirably accounted for in Sharon Zukin's book, *Loft Living*.[5] The extraordinary explosion of artists' studios, galleries and use of old warehouses for artists' living quarters that happened in the 1970s in downtown Manhattan, which was hailed as a model of urban renewal, was subsequently discovered to have been a cleverly coordinated real-estate coup. Artists were encouraged to move into downtown Manhattan, take over shopfronts for galleries and studios, and warehouse lofts for living in, all at cheap rents in order to lever out the remaining old businesses. Having effectively raised land values and real-estate prices, they were themselves then winkled out by the warehouse owners in order to create residential accommodation for stockbrokers, bond salesmen, accountants and city executives.

Unknowingly the artists were used by developers and real estate agents to create an ambience and a buzz in SoHo, Tribeca and other downtown industrial areas, which was then capitalized over their heads through the rise in property values. In short, the artists whose activities had created a desirable place to live in displaced themselves in doing so. They could no longer afford to live in the neighbourhoods they had revitalized.

The lesson is that urban renewal, through the designation and creation of cultural districts or cultural industries quarters, should be firmly regulated by long-term contracts and agreements, the creation of trusts and other management mechanisms, and by long-term planning on behalf of the local authority. Urban renewal is not about gentrification but about new dynamic mixes of activities and uses, based on cultural diversity. It is about cultural production.

THE CLERKENWELL EFFECT: A CASE STUDY

The complex urban ecology that successfully sustains both working and residential communities in city centres is clearly evident in London's Clerkenwell district, a traditional area for craft firms, particularly in printing, bookbinding, costume making and other skilled activities. In 1989 Islington Council commissioned two studies of the cultural industries in the borough, one a general overview of all arts-related employment in Islington, and the other a detailed study of crafts employment in Clerkenwell. A *Study of Arts & Employment in Islington* and *A Study into the Premises Needs and Problems of Crafts Firms in Clerkenwell* were both carried out by the Centre for Leisure and Tourism at the Polytechnic of North London, and to date are the best detailed and quantified analyses we have of just how important the cultural industries are to successful urban economies.

For the purposes of the research, the 'Arts' were defined as including the following: performing arts; visual arts; crafts work; literary work; film, photography, video, TV and radio; graphic and industrial design/printing; and museums. These, in effect, are the cultural industries of the late twentieth century, the burgeoning production and service industries that produce, distribute and disseminate the artefacts, images, performances, styles and meanings that in turn create the material and intellectual currency of our daily lives. Areas of activity which were not included in this survey were: advertising, public relations, architecture, and the borough's own employment in arts, libraries, local government and museum provision.

It would be assumed that employment in these sectors in Islington (a London borough with a higher than average number of theatres, bookshops, publishers, printers, etc.) would be high, but few would have anticipated that the survey would reveal that at least 10,000 employees were to be found in the arts and cultural industries sector; a 'high' estimate put the figure at 5,000. Over 2,000 arts businesses were identified, together with over 700 individual artists. The largest sector proved to be graphic design and printing; the smallest visual arts. More relevant to the argument here was that the majority of companies surveyed were 'independent firms operating only from the address given', that is to say genuinely local companies for which success or failure would be highly sensitive to local conditions and which could most benefit from local infrastructural support. This was no 'branch economy' for which the major decisions were made in boardrooms hundreds or thousands of miles away, but a vital local growth with roots deep in the history and topography of the area – but which remained in need, as do all economies, of continuing strategic support, monitoring and encouragement.

The average number of people employed by each firm was twelve, and 41 per cent of the sample intended to increase staff within the year. In general it was felt the sector was fairly stable with prospects of expansion but some factors created real problems of security, the most important of which was that only 25 per cent of the companies owned their own premises. This issue rises to prominence in the second study. Another factor that may well in the past have inhibited growth was the sheer lack of information the companies surveyed had about new potential markets, sources of private and public finance, training schemes and other services. Many if not all of them could clearly have performed better by simply being better informed. Few had any contacts with local schools and colleges, though many claimed they would have welcomed this.

The second study put the Clerkenwell district under the microscope and found that this one small area supported over 1,000 businesses within the cultural industries sector, of which 25 per cent were specifically crafts firms. Jewellery-making was by far the largest subsector, with silversmithing next followed by metalworking, goldsmithing, weaving and pottery-making, followed finally by engraving and picture framing. The majority of businesses operated as sole traders, with others operating as limited companies or partnerships. There were no cooperatives in the sample, despite the fact that Islington Council has a policy of supporting cooperatives through its economic development programmes, a clear mis-match of principle and practice. Many of these crafts firms were located in two well-known managed work spaces – the Clerkenwell Green Association and the Clerkenwell Workshops. The former is a registered charity and in addition to its main activity of managing some eighty workshops (100 per cent occupancy at the time of the survey) also provides grant-aid to some start-up businesses, training schemes and even bursaries and travelling scholarships – a model for industrial practice if ever there was one. Clerkenwell Workshops are managed by a private limited company, but the premises, which were owned by the GLC, were recently sold by the London Residuary Body (a government quango bereft of any strategic or social responsibilities) to a property development company, putting the long-term future of this invaluable initiative in doubt.

In Clerkenwell, demand for studio and workshop premises has continued to exceed supply even though rents and rates are rising fast as a result of the Unified Business Rate and the impact of the Use Classes Order 1987 which allowed property previously designated as light industrial to be re-designated for 'office' uses, forcing many of the more precarious crafts businesses to move or go into liquidation as their leases came to an end and the premises they were in converted into offices. The outstanding attraction of Clerkenwell is, as the report puts it, 'the synergy created through cross-trading and reliance, the indirect economic impact on suppliers and services and the variety and in some cases arity of job and work skills available for local residents and for new craft practitioners'.

Among the report's main recommendations are that in future Islington Council ensures that in the next Unitary Development Plan full recognition is given to the importance of the cultural industries in the economic and social life of the borough, possibly designating particular areas as zoned quarters for mixed industrial and cultural development. Without strategic planning the opportunistic winds of the market will simply blow through whole historic residential and industrial areas, turning them into office parks and private villages, killing the activities and complex historical and social relationships that make towns and cities vibrant and dynamic.

Successful cities need a strong economic base, preferably based on indigenous skills and manufacturing traditions. The disasters of urban zoning and the rigid separation of the commercial, civic, retailing, manufacturing, entertainment and residential areas have produced fragmented and deracinated urban cultures linked only by ring roads, service roads, daily traffic and local radio bulletins. The return to mixed-use planning, of bringing residential accommodation and environmental-friendly manufacturing back into the city centre should be welcomed. Many of the new, high-quality specialist manufacturing sectors have strong design and cultural features; the cultural-industries sector, including fashion, publishing, sound recording, film and video, photography, crafts and visual arts, is a growing sector in the modern economy, and works best in a city-centre environment where producers and distributors can work in close relationship with each other. 'New collaborations' is more than just the name of an Arts Council fund for work that doesn't fit the traditional genres: it is the name of the cultural and economic future.

These new forms of urban economic development will need planning, financial support and encouragement. Local authorities will have some planning powers left, and the requirement upon all of them to produce Unitary Development Plans should enable them to designate mixed-use districts, cultural industries quarters, and dedicated areas for arts and crafts industries if they so wish.

What local authorities lack today is capital and the powers to raise capital to any large degree, and therefore partnerships will have to be sought with the private sector for the funding of managed work-place schemes and new mixed-use development and urban districts.

The managed workspace has been defined as having three distinct features: small unit size; flexible letting arrangements and shared support services. In many ways these are pre figurative of a new kind of urban manufacturing culture that meets social and environmental concerns of the kind William Morris himself would have approved. They encourage collabora tive work across cultural forms, technological synergy, the harmo nizing of skilled crafts traditions with new technology, a high degree of self-management, local inter-trading and the creation of a stronger indigenous economy, the sharing of common services such as cleaning and security, meeting rooms, photo-copying and design work, marketing, publicity and promotion, as well as common rooms and in-house cafés and restaurants. In turn they create secondary employment in the neighbourhood for suppliers and other services. There will be failures as well as successes in the drive to develop the new urban economies, but a number of local authorities have signalled their commitment to this ap proach, and they should be strongly supported. The culture of cities is essentially the culture of intellectual, artistic and material production. The alternative is increasing formlessness, attenuation exhaustion of variety and, in Italo Calvino's words, the end of cities.

NOTES

1. Ralf Dahrendorf, 'Does London Need to be Governed?' LW London Lecture, 6 December, 1990.
2. Lewis Mumford, *The Culture of Cities*, Secker & Warburg, London 1945.
3. Peter Buchanan, 'What City?' , *Architectural Review*, November 1988.
4. Judy Hillman, 'The Importance of the Street', *Town and Country Planning*, London, 1990.
5. Sharon Zukin, *Loft Living*, Radius Hutchinson, London, 1988.
6. Italo Calvino, *Invisible Cities*, Picador, London 1979.

NASEEM KHAN

Asian Arts

On the face of it, the hanging is a charming piece of work. It's a collection of embroidered pieces stitched together in which peacocks strut, roses bloom, fish ripple along in a gently colourful artefact. But there is more to it – not just the years that have gone into it, nor the scores of hands involved. The hanging is the work of a project that has brought Bedford's Asian women together, that has created an income (as yet modest) and a possible blueprint pattern for other similarly placed women.

Above all, the wall-hanging for North Bedfordshire District Council has done something to fracture the depressing stereotype attached to Asian women. They are popularly supposed to be docile and retiring and utterly lacking in initiative. They miss out on local-authority and other arts-funding provision (as do Asian arts in general, but we'll come back to that). However, the most superficial look at the subcontinent will show how mistaken such a view is. Women have long been a force in political life there, having provided leaders for India, Pakistan, Sri Lanka, Bangladesh and (in opposition) Burma. In India, approximately one third of the considerable female work-force are the providers for their families. So much for passivity.

So how can this formidable energy and talent for organization be tapped in Britain? What will give Asian women access into British social and artistic life? Fears have been voiced in some local authorities about imposing alien structures and ideas. The somewhat blunt instrument of the Arts Council diktat that 4 per cent of its panels' budgets should go to the multicultural arts did not have as much success as it had hoped in transferring resources, changing patterns and increasing integration of funding. However, this should not be taken as an indication that overall policy-making bodies should do nothing until dictated to by communities themselves. There is hardly any substitute for sensitivity at the top.

It is a lesson that can be learned from, for instance, the role of Leeds City Council in getting Hansa's off the ground. Hansa's is a rare venture – a woman-run Indian vegetarian restaurant, in a world of determinedly male endeavour. 'Women feel they can't go into business,' said its young creator, Hansa Dabhi, 'but they don't realize that you're almost a manager doing all the thing that make up housework. It's just a matter of bringing it out.' The thought came to her in the school playground, seeing the enthusiastic reaction of other parents to the Gujarati specialitie she brought in from home to help raise money for the school Cooking, she explains, is a skill that is taken for granted: hardly any Asian woman realizes that it could give her self-respect and independence. 'All it needs is a bit of help and support.'

Leeds City Council's support was crucial. Its start-up gran gave the project the stamp of authority and helped to unloc funding. But it wasn't just a question of money. 'They frequentl rang up to ask if everything was OK. They were very ver helpful.' Hansa Dabhi needed the help: she was new to busines and terrified, when she had time to think in that first hectic year by the responsibility of it all. Training courses were invaluable She learned how to do bookkeeping and to calculate flow-chart and, most importantly, 'what I had let myself in for!' He successful restaurant, which employs only women, will, she hope show other Asian women that given the basic motivation the can do it too.

Harshinder Sirah also got vital help from her local authority i Bristol. As long as she could recall, she'd wanted to work i fashion. Following her basic training at fashion school, her intere became focused on the ways in which traditional Asian fashio could inform and interact with Western styles. A start-up gran from the Business Enterprise Allowance scheme, and skills ac quired through training sessions in accountancy and marketin helped her display her first collection at an adventurous show in a Bristol disco. Her work was picked up by the BBC who featured it in *The Clothes Show*.

There is, of course, a difference between the example of Dabhi and Sirah, and that of the Bedford women responsible for the hanging and other pieces of work. The first two women had clear ideas of what they wanted to achieve; what they needed was help in reaching their objectives. The members of Mehfil-e-Tar had initially no such professional aspirations. In 1988, when the story began, they were merely a number of women of largely Bangladeshi origin who came to an adult-education centre to learn English. At the centre Hameeda Awam encouraged them to bring sewing with them. The staff sensibly took their cue from this, commissioning a survey of other Asian women to see whether embroidery and sewing might be a generally popular area to develop. The response was overwhelmingly in favour.

It was a delicate operation to set up. First, staff from the centre had to visit homes and persuade not so much women as their husbands that such an activity would be no threat to them. 'Some said yes. Some said, "No, who will look after the children?"' recalled Hameeda Awam philosophically. 'Like many men, they don't like women to have the upper hand,' added the lively chairperson of the group, Nasreen Amin. 'It's not just Asian men!'

Transport had to be arranged so that protected women wouldn't be thrown off balance and the husbands' approval lost; childcare needs had to be anticipated. The project had to demonstrate it was totally respectable and responsible. But despite the in-built problems, thirty or so women – now Punjabi and Pakistani as well as Bangladeshi – finally sat down in the Westbourne Centre to learn stem stitch and satin stitch, kantha, mirror-work, appliqué and more besides. Some stitches were very familiar, like the traditional Bangladeshi running stitch: kantha. Other skills were new: training residencies by experts in techniques like Bangladeshi vegetable dyes and painting on silk expanded the possibilities.

But the hangings came about almost by accident. Hameeda Awam had set the women to work on individual bits of material.

What on earth could be done with them, she wondered, as the bright pieces slowly grew in number? Hangings, very much part of the subcontinental tradition, were a happy inspiration. Putting the pieces together, the women remember, was in itself an experience that helped to draw them together. The collective spirit of the enterprise drew other people in. Young women from an Asian youth club in Bedford contributed pieces of embroidery. Asian students from around the country heard about the project on the grapevine and came to Bedford in their holidays, embroidered a bit and wrote about the venture in their dissertations. The scheme became known as 'A Hundred Pairs of Hands'.

There are several morals and principles to be drawn from Mehfil-e-Tar, some of which reinforce lessons already learned. First is the role that the right sort of training can play. The workshops and residencies organized for the women stimulated them and extended their range. But even more important, in this case, has been the involvement of the Bedford Adult Training Group. Its adoption of the scheme has meant that the women qualify to be paid a small weekly honorarium – a modest sum, but enough to convince their families that the venture had a more serious point than mere socializing and frivolity.

Status is also important, connected as it is with self-respect and esteem. Mehfil-e-Tar's success in this has been helped by their recent Working for Cities award given by the Arts Council and British Gas. Not a financial prize, it might still help to guarantee them that other necessity – continuity. Until it was picked up by Bedford Adult Training Group (BATG), the project had progressed in a series of fits and starts: dying down when the money ran out, reviving when more funding was found.

Projects like these are pioneering ones. They carry with them the likelihood – as their families perceive – that the women involved will change. They also have the power to challenge the way that institutions operate, as the new Nia Centre in Manchester demonstrates. Set up as a platform for Afro-Caribbean and African culture, the centre wants its purpose to be carried through into its style of management. Its Cultural Director says the Nia will not follow Western hierarchical styles of organization, but consultative structures drawn from living African roots.

Some cities and institutions accept the importance of a two-way flow of influence. Leicester built it into their museum and art-gallery policy nearly ten years ago. Julia Nicholson's appointment as Assistant Keeper (Indian Arts and Crafts) opened up a new relationship between the gallery and the substantial Asian community. The post was clearly regarded seriously. Nicholson was given a brief and money to build up a collection (something that inevitably requires a long-term maintenance commitment) as well as to stage large-scale exhibitions. From the start she expected the impetus for the exhibitions to come from the community, and so it proved. In 1987, the Jain community pressed for an exhibition. The following year there was a major show on the traditional arts from the Indian state of Gujarat. 'The museum was an enabler to give people their own voice,' Nicholson recalled.

With the exhibitions came ancillary but no less important activities. Some of them took place in the museum: the Gujarati exhibition supported embroidery and block-printing workshops, and a wildly popular fashion show. Some of them took place outside, in schools, community centres, residential homes, libraries and neighbourhood centres. Reminiscence workshops that used some of the rural artefacts from the museum – a toy bullock cart, cooking utensils – unleashed poignant memories in some of the elderly.

But most interesting of all was a move, just starting as Nicholson ended her time in Leicester in 1990, to decentralize the collection. This programme envisages the development of small permanent exhibitions within the community rather than solely in the museum itself. The Jain Centre, for instance, would eagerly cooperate as would the Sikh *gurudwara* (temple) currently planned. 'The institutions have to let go of their power,' Nicholson said. The prospect of small, accessible collections, displayed by communities whose direct ancestors, in many cases, had been responsible for making them, is an exciting one. It also has implications that go far wider than the Asian community alone, suggesting quite a different relationship between museums and 'consumers'.

Such a relationship formed the basis of Nima Smith's immediate response when she was appointed Keeper (Ethnic Arts) in Bradford. Cartwright Hall was, like Leicester's museum, near Asian centres but unvisited by their inhabitants. Smith immediately acted to set up a system of consultation with the city's rich range of ethnic communities. By all accounts, the relationship has prospered. Her exhibition plans are routinely and regularly laid out for community response. Before each exhibition she is careful to consult. Before her large exhibition on gold, for example, she went to the Asian community to ask whether they would support a critical element – a comment on the destructive nature of gold and the dowry system in the subcontinent. Interestingly, she says, the consensus was in favour. Equally interestingly, a similar exercise undertaken by Leicestershire Art Galleries (who shared the exhibition) drew a contrary opinion. As a result, the comment was dropped.

Her latest major exhibition demonstrates how important is the interaction between gallery and community. On Sikh art, and called 'Warm and Rich and Fearless', it was preceded by months of introductory community-based lectures, which generated immense interest among Muslims and Hindus as well as Sikhs. She enlisted specialist Sikh advice for the catalogue and labelling: 'You needed to be of the culture.' And when the exhibition finally opened, it was with volunteer Sikh guides from the community and a large-scale traditional Sikh meal (or *langur*) lined up at Cartwright Hall.

Not surprisingly, the gallery has come to have a different place in the lives of many Asians. Both Smith and Nicholson found the communities placed a similar demand on their respective institutions to be a 'positive showcase', and 'the place in which their various cultures can shine'. The communities wanted them to redress negative stereotypes, to show their own children and their new British society the stuff of which they were made. At its best, a museum can become a source of and expression of pride. Both Smith and Nicholson, however, are careful not to allow exhibitions to be stuck in a reverential past. Their exhibitions have determinedly created contemporary links to show that a culture has an evolving life. Looking back on her years in Leicester, Nicholson now wonders if she shouldn't have gone further and used the exhibitions more directly to make a clearer anti-racist statement.

It is significant that often the best examples of good practice by local authorities are found not in the performing arts but in fine arts and crafts. It is a curious phenomenon, for South Asian communities support a wide range of performing arts: theatre groups and folk dancers, music groups, singers and poets. The festival put on in Birmingham recently by the new SAMPAD organization (a name that conveniently means both 'wealth' in Hindi and is an acronym for South Asian music, performing arts and dance) triumphantly showed the drawing power and quality of the arts – from bhangra rock to classical dance. Yet on the whole they impinge extraordinarily little on the life of the wider community. They have very few buildings in which to perform regularly and develop their own voice. They make few demands on mainstream resources, as the most cursory glance at the records of fund-giving bodies demonstrates.

Why is this? It is not a simple question of racism or indigenous institutional resistance to the new: Afro-Caribbean arts have – to some extent – broken that barrier. The Nia Centre attracted £250,000 of Arts Council money for its national and international centre. Talawa Theatre Company has been given a grant to open their own building, a home for their fine Afro-Caribbean touring-theatre work. This, ironically, occurred as Wandsworth Council removed the grant to the admirable Asian Tara Arts, forcing them to end activities at their modest centre. Why does this cultural disparity exist? If one form of cultural diversity can find its way into the mainstream and enrich it, why not another?

A number of reasons have been suggested – for instance the fragmented nature of Asian communities, broken up into many different language and cultural groupings. Perhaps more relevant is the fact that the ownership of Asian culture is predominantly vested within communities: in religious organizations, Tamil Saturday schools and so on. While British funding institutions can come to terms with an arts product (particularly one with familiar mainstream aspirations) they cannot negotiate unfamiliar societal structures.

The huge potential of Asian arts and culture is absolutely

evident. Some aspects of it touch the British mainstream. Classical dance in particular is engaged in a debate to find forms that will be true to its roots and still be relevant to its new circumstances. However virtually none of the dancers has a base. Only one company has assured revenue funding from the Arts Council. Like dance, Indian classical music enjoys vast respect yet is unimaginatively supported by funding bodies. The same is true of the visual arts – the sole gallery devoted to subcontinental art, the Horizon in Bloomsbury, looks likely to close. It is little wonder, given such disheartening professional horizons, that very few arts administrators have emerged from the South Asian communities – a matter that should surely be addressed.

In order to raise the profile of Asian arts, training, resources and networks all need to be developed, building on the community cohesion and autonomy at their root. It is not a small endeavour, probably best implemented initially through series of locally based strategies, rather than through a single, high-profile national arts centre that would be both a challenge and an opportunity for local government. Leeds and Leicester, Bradford and Bedford have all given an indication of things that can be done to make institutions more responsive to the Asian presence. Until that responsiveness becomes more general and instinctive, the Asian community will continue to be culturally marginalized and the wider community deprived of an extra dimension.

STEVEN BARNETT

Selling Us Short?
Cities, Culture and Economic Development

Ever since Harold Wilson scraped into power on the back of his White Heat of Technology battle-cry in 1964, British politics has been obsessed by the Big Idea. It made little difference that the White Heat slogan was less a Big Idea than a medium-sized afterthought that tripped nicely off the tongue, and that Wilson's narrow victory owed considerably more to a morally and politically exhausted Conservative Party. Like some political holy grail, the Big Idea has been feverishly pursued by both political parties in the intervening years.

But Big Ideas are not the sole preserve of national politics nor even national political election strategies. Smaller versions are evident in company board-rooms, in local politics, in classrooms, in fact in any environment where an individual or group of people are looking for a competitive edge or a creative way forward. In whatever field they occur, BIs that catch the tide have a habit of sweeping all – constructive critics included – before them.

For the past five years, one particular Big Idea seems to have taken Britain's cities by storm: media. Although 'inner cities' have not been a visible feature of national policy initiatives since Margaret Thatcher's empty rhetoric during her 1987 victory speech, urban regeneration has been a major priority for most city councils. And in the politics of urban regeneration, 'media' has become a buzzword. Starting with the GLC in London in the mid 1980s, media initiatives of varying kinds have emerged in many towns and cities throughout the country.

What has been the catalyst for this dash to embrace the media, in its widest possible sense, throughout the country's town halls? What has been the rationale behind this latest Big Idea in urban areas, and how has the idea been translated into strategy? What exactly are the media initiatives currently being pursued? What benefits are they bringing to their local communities? And is the pursuit of this particular holy grail obscuring a potentially grander vision of the cultural and creative role that media initiatives could fulfil in city communities? The rest of this essay falls into three parts. The first asks precisely why the media should suddenly be adopted so unanimously by city elders as a means of regenerating urban areas. The second is an examination of the philosophy behind these initiatives – and how they have been implemented – with special reference to three British cities. And finally it looks at some of the limitations and potential drawbacks of these approaches for the local communities they are supposed to serve.

From the beginning, one abiding feature of British media has been the emphasis on a national dimension. From its earliest days in both television and radio, the BBC has ensured that coverage of its stations and channels should be as close to 100 per cent of the population as possible. The first local radio station was not operational until 1967, and the vast majority of BBC listening is to its four national stations. Although it operates regional television services, the number of hours these contribute to total BBC television hours is tiny.

The model for ITV is ostensibly different, with licences awarded for franchises in fourteen separate regions of the country. In practice, most ITV programming – particularly at peak time – is networked and the regional emphasis falls mostly on news and sports output. Commercial radio is the most 'local' of British broadcast media, with around sixty stations covering 85 per cent of the country. It is easy to forget that commercial radio is still less than twenty years old.

Even a thriving market for local newspapers is dwarfed by the number and popularity of national daily papers. More people read a national daily paper in Britain than in any other European country, a fact which owes more to tradition and long-established distribution networks than any particular preference for national over local news. This is important because it goes to the heart of an intractable sociological problem: the importance of local identity and people's sense of geographical location. If it is true that decisions on Britain's communications infrastructure have been dominated by national considerations and imposed from above by policy-makers, and if it is true that these decisions have failed to reflect a need for more local self-expression, then here lies a serious gap in our broadcasting structure which policy-makers should be seeking to remedy.

Complex arguments, about what evidence there is that some sorts of local cultural expression might be inhibited and what evidence that greater opportunities would be welcomed, are untangled later. But what are the new technological initiatives that could allow far greater access to media at the local level? Within the broadcast media, there are three possibilities. Although home computers and desk-top publishing have breathed new life into opportunities for disseminating the printed word locally – as evidenced by increasing numbers of well-produced neighbourhood-watch and jumble-sale leaflets – it is the broadcast media that afford the more exciting possibilities for local creative initiatives.

First there is Channel Five. Carved out of a part of the spectrum that used to be reserved for radar, Channel Five will eventually cover 65–70 per cent of the UK. Because its coverage is not universal, and because it requires a new transmitter system which need not be configured according to existing transmitter sites, Channel Five offers great potential as a city-based television service. The Independent Television Commission has announced a 32-transmitter system, but is prevented by the Broadcasting Act from giving any preference to a local or network service. As with ITV franchises, the winning licencee will be the one with the fattest cheque in the envelope.

Second is cable. Ever since an early Thatcherite decree proscribed any public subsidy for the cabling of Britain, and thereby condemned an important communications infrastructure to years of inactivity, it has remained an inglorious reminder of the free market's moribund hand. While Germany, thanks to an enlightened government and Bundespost, is moving towards an interactive network covering most of the country, the few (mostly American) investors in British cable have so far brought the potential benefits to fewer than two million homes. In principle, however, 136 local cable franchises have been awarded, covering 70 per cent of the country; and each of them has local programming obligations built into the licence awarded by the old Cable Authority. Albeit slowly, cable should start to take off – mostly because operators are now able to offer telephone services in competition with British Telecom and Mercury, which will give them a vital edge.

Finally there is local radio. Theoretically, the greater availability of frequencies for radio broadcasting should foster a host of different local and community stations serving different interests and different communities. In practice, revenue opportunities will be small (advertising agencies still find it hard to believe that radio can be effective) and the process of achieving a licence via the Radio Authority is still a laborious one. Further down the road, perhaps there are great possibilities for new models of public access and community-type stations.

Given these relatively recent developments, no one can blame local authorities or city councils for getting excited about what the media can offer. There may not be massive riches at the end of the rainbow, but there are economic investment opportunities clearly too good to miss. Some cities have seized on them with more alacrity than others, but the approach has been surprisingly uniform. Unfortunately, local self-expression has not always been at the forefront of new approaches.

A clue to the nature and direction of city media initiatives is the originating agency. In most cases, it has been an Economic Development Unit or similar office within local councils, that has seen the media as an expanding industry with investment and employment opportunities. In all cases, 'media' has been generously interpreted to cover all audio-visual activity. As well as film, television and video, this includes music, photography, animation, design, script-writing and a host of related fields within the creative arts. Economically, however, television has always been seen as the breadwinner.

Cardiff is a case in point. With BBC Wales, HTV and S4C

having a significant presence in Cardiff, and spin-off companies in cinema, film and video, the media industry was already prominent. There was a feeling, though, that this clustering of expertise was too narrowly focused and that Cardiff's skills in the field were not sufficiently widely recognized. Having identified media as a growth area with greater potential for the local economy, South Glamorgan County Council appointed Coopers and Lybrand to undertake a study and advise them on 'a strategy to make the best use of the development potential which media activities offer for the area'.[1]

The upshot of this study was a series of initiatives and the creation in 1987 of a Cardiff 'Media City', with a grant of around £40,000 per annum, to coordinate action. Initiatives included a directory of all media-related companies in the area and their fields of expertise, promotion of the media skills available in Cardiff, exhibitions and festivals to assist the development of media activities, and research and training initiatives to encourage more young people to learn assorted media-related trades. Not surprisingly, given its genesis, the emphasis of this initiative is essentially on marketing Cardiff. Its philosophy is rooted in taking a relatively thriving industry in an area of slow economic growth and stimulating it through wider dissemination of its strengths and attractions, thereby attracting more business for the area and more businesses into the area. As the Coopers report said, 'London is the overwhelmingly dominant focus of UK media activity ... The highest rewards for creative talent and technical expertise are available there, acting as a drain on other regions.' Cardiff's head start, with three major TV outlets already prominent, meant that it could claw back some of this handicap with more aggressive promotion.

Birmingham's initiative also came from the Economic Development Unit of the city council, with Comedia as the beneficiaries of the consultants' silver dollar. Again, Comedia focused on Birmingham's inherent disadvantage in the audio-visual sector through its proximity to London: the concentration of independent producers, facilities houses, ad agencies and decision-makers just 100 miles down the motorway acted as a magnet on Birmingham's creative reservoirs.[2] The room for Birmingham's improvement was summed up in terms of its relative size: 'Although the second-largest city in the UK, it is only the fifth-largest in audio-visual terms.' Linked to this inferiority problem was 'the image problems Birmingham encounters in the outside world'. In other words, the city itself was perceived in an unfavourable light by those it should have been seeking to tempt back into the urban fold.

Comedia recommended the establishment of a Media Development Agency, which is now up and running with four key functions: promotion, consultancy, training and stimulation. Promotion involves both marketing the audio-visual activities within the city to attract investment and employment from outside, and promoting Birmingham's locational qualities for filming and production purposes. Consultancy includes information and advice to assist those working or aspiring to work in the media sector, a directory of relevant companies, and acting as broker between creators and commissioners. Training involves publicizing and coordinating existing opportunities. And stimulation is the fostering of new expansion opportunities: particularly a Media Centre with studios and other creative facilities, and a Media Zone centred on Digbeth to act as a focal point for audio-visual initiatives.

Newcastle's initiatives were already well advanced by the time its city council commissioned a 'sector study' report from the University's Centre for Urban and Regional Development Studies (CURDS).[3] As in Cardiff, the North-East has seen a gradual evolution of independent producers, facilities houses, workshops and the growth of other creative activities centred around Tyne Tees television and regional offices of the BBC and TVam. In 1984 a North East Media Development Council was established to, amongst other things, 'further the development of a new media industry in the North East regions' with a stated emphasis on 'marketing and distribution initiatives' and an explicit brief to 'enhance the region's self-image and its power to communicate both inside and outside its boundaries'. Its special concern for training was rewarded by a large grant from the European Social Fund to set up a Training Centre in 1986, from which it runs two-year training courses. Having lost the European money it is now, according to CURDS, 'increasingly aiming to operate on commercial principles as a facilities house in order to support its training role'. A final, more wide-ranging initiative has been the rn Media Forum, which aims to draw the whole industry in the region together and promote its development.

In the North-East, perhaps more than elsewhere, a perception of industrial decline and the urgent need for areas of expansion has led to a series of initiatives from different agencies, with the attendant risks of what the CURDS study called 'incoherent, unbalanced or uncoordinated development agendas for the sector'. Its recommendations for cultivating a more coordinated strategy included an audio-visual guide to serve as a directory and to 'promote Newcastle and the region to the outside world', establishing Newcastle as a contender for Channel 5 as well as other new services, the appointment of a Film Officer to promote the region as a location for film-makers, support for companies willing to take on trainees, and a media centre to provide audio-visual facilities and act as a focus for media and cultural activities.

Other cities are pursuing similar themes. Examples of established media centres are the Watershed in Bristol and the Cornerhouse in Manchester. Nottingham's media consortium created a Media Centre along the same lines. Liverpool has a film liaison officer to promote the city as a film location. Sheffield has a cultural industries quarter 'to accelerate regeneration of the city centre' and an Audio-Visual Enterprise Centre acting as umbrella for the host of local workshop groups. Several cities have advanced persuasive cases for why they should play host to the new fifth Channel.[4]

These city-based initiatives are not identical clones, but they have similar themes based on similar strategies adjusted to suit individual areas. Given the agenda of urban regeneration and the need to expand local economies, provide local employment opportunities and resuscitate large areas of urban wasteland, the rationale is admirable. It is, however, overwhelmingly economic and competitive, taking an industrialized view of media which might not always do justice to the burgeoning opportunities. While accepting the need and applauding the enterprise, we need also to ask the question: are these initiatives all in the best interests of local communities? And what might they be missing? 'Culture has been mobilized to the marketing cause,' wrote Franco Bianchini recently.[5] Marketing's role should not be dismissed out of hand. There is nothing intrinsically wrong with attempts to burnish a tarnished image or obliterate mental pictures of urban decay and desolation, if such campaigns succeed in attracting new money and raising the self-esteem of indigenous populations.

But marketing is a two-edged concept. In adopting heritage as a promotional tool and applying strictly economic values, cities will sometimes try to repackage the same product in more alluring wrapping paper or – even worse – sell short an intrinsic value that has little purchase in the contemporary market. It may well be true, as Ruth Wishart convincingly argues on page 43, that most Glasgow people were not offended by the city's 'smiley' campaign. But Bianchini quotes a supporter of a recently deposed officer of Glasgow District Council writing in the local press: 'The wish locally to bury the facts of a past which had become inconvenient, and to superimpose a new, sanitized, marketable image of the city required . . . a bland, self-congratulatory hype, which found its true apotheosis in the insultingly patronising "Mr Happy" of "Glasgow's Miles Better".' The danger is clear: that city marketing strategies will deny any voice for or celebration of those elements of their indigenous culture that might impede the competitive search for wealth or jobs or a glossier image.

This is particularly true when applied to local media initiatives. Because their rationale is economic, beneficiaries tend to be either those involved in media occupations or those on the receiving end of a stimulated local economy (by no means all, or even a majority, of local populations). This competitive emphasis potentially distracts attention from pressing non-economic problems, which a different direction or initiative or philosophical approach to local media might help to overcome. How can the media be used to overcome some of the difficulties of inner-city living, or even outer-city living? Are there local cultural requirements, or local informational requirements or local citizenship requirements that local media technology can be adapted to serve? Given the increasing professionalization and inaccessibility of the industry, what sort of access can people be offered at the local level?

Of all these questions, perhaps the most critical is how local media can be harnessed to improve local access, information and accountability of decision-makers. In their recent Channel 5 monograph, the BFI wrote: 'One of the essential functions of communications in a modern democracy is to provide opportunities for citizens to be informed and to be heard.'[6] This is even more fundamental at the local than at the national level. An electorate will cast its vote once every four or five years at the national level, but it is interaction with the local that ultimately dictates the quality of our everyday lives. We may have an increasingly centralized education policy, but it is local schools and teachers that educate our children. Policies on benefits and welfare are disseminated by Whitehall but pensions and allowances are interpreted and distributed at the local level. Even after a decade of burgeoning centralization, local councils and town halls still prescribe policies for leisure facilities, for parks and recreation, for libraries, for the state of our roads. Most people's experience of health policies or law enforcement is through local hospitals and local policemen and women. Even with the vast increase in car ownership and mobility we shop locally, eat locally, go to local places of worship and drink in local pubs.

And yet our commitment to involvement at the local level is pitiful. Most people know little of the local decision-making process and care even less. With turn-outs at local elections rarely exceeding 40 per cent of the electorate, local politics in Britain is characterized by indifference, indolence and impotence. With the means to disseminate more information, to consult with members of local communities, we can start to alleviate some of that sense of apathy and powerlessness. Local cable, in particular, offers real opportunities: an interactive, addressable system through which information can be conveyed and individual members of the community can be consulted and make their voices heard. In fact, cable companies are bound by statute to provide those opportunities. The 1984 Cable and Broadcasting Act obliges operators to include 'programmes in which [local people] are given an opportunity to participate' and 'programmes provided by local voluntary associations'.[7]

Would anyone watch such programmes or are they merely delusions of local grandeur, doomed to defeat by terminal apathy? Research by the Institute of Local Television demonstrated that over 90 per cent of Edinburgh people would like a local news service, and 56 per cent would like to participate in local programmes. Consistently, research has demonstrated an interest in local affairs and an appetite for local programming that is not being fulfilled.[8]

Cynics who dismiss such surveys as unreliable barometers of actual behaviour should look at real-life experiences abroad and in the UK. Rotterdam has a nightly hour-long news programme which 38 per cent of residents watch at least once a week. And in the UK, the residents of a small Lancashire village were introduced to the possibilities of local television when Granada provided them with cable and satellite channels as part of a televised experiment. The locals of Waddington, as well as being introduced to the joys of movie, sport and pop satellite channels, were given a frequency on which to broadcast their own home-grown programmes. Not only did local people, whose only experience of television had been from the living-room armchair, queue up to become involved in programme making; more importantly, virtually everyone watched the daily hour-long programme. Waddington Village Television outrated *Coronation Street* and towards the end of its five-week stint achieved a 97 per cent share of household viewing![9]

Perhaps such a rating success is to be expected in the first few weeks while the novelty survives. The true significance of this foray into local television was the reaction of villagers when they saw what they themselves were capable of creating and how local decision-making could be exposed to public scrutiny. In the words of one onlooker describing the potentially galvanizing effect of local television on parish politics: 'Suddenly those debates and those issues are in their living rooms and it blows the whole thing wide open.'

Apart from encouraging access and a greater awareness of local democracy, local themes can provide a rich seam of programme ideas beyond straightforward news and information. Mainstream programmes like wildlife, history or geography can all have a distinctly local focus which may not be of mass interest outside the immediate area (and will not therefore have much value in the programme commodity market) but will make a valuable contribution to the community's sense of itself. People value local programming; but ITV's 14-region structure cannot possibly emulate the level of localness that could be created through Channel 5's thirty-two stations or cable's 136 areas.

The sense of local identity and mutual support that local media are capable of fostering will be particularly valuable to those groups who rely entirely on their local communities: pensioners, the disabled, single parents are less likely to have the mobility and flexibility to move out of their immediate environments. But even beyond these immediate and demonstrable needs, most citizens would probably appreciate an enhanced sense of the local environment as a counterpoint to the roller-coaster of images they face from unfamiliar lands and unfamiliar places. As one writer has asked, 'How, in the face of all this movement and intermixing, can we retain any sense of a local place and its particularity?' [10] Here is a transparent role for local audio-visual media and technology: to enfranchise and enliven local communities.

This is the time for towns and cities to grasp the policy issues raised by new media and exploit the opportunities for access and information, for consultation and therefore greater integration, via a genuinely local media network. Their objectives should be four-fold: programmes featuring the local environment, relevant information about the local community, access to decision-making bodies and individuals within the local community, and encouragement to individuals to involve themselves at every level of local audio-visual activity. These are not necessarily initiatives which would stimulate local economies. But they might stimulate greater involvement in the institutions and organizations that fashion our everyday experiences. Access and accountability have not been a feature of British broadcasting and they won't make anyone rich. But they might make for a healthier society.

NOTES

1. Coopers and Lybrand, *Media City: Final report to South Glamorgan County Council* [*Executive Summary*], South Glamorgan CC, 1986.

2. Comedia, *Birmingham's Audiovisual Industry*, Birmingham City Council, 1987.

3. James Cornford and Kevin Robins, *Broadcasting and the Audiovisual Industries: A sector study for Newcastle City Council*, CURDS, University of Newcastle upon Tyne, February 1990.

4. For an excellent discussion of Channel 5 and 'Media Cities' see James Cornford and Kevin Robins, 'Questions of Geography' in *The Challenge of Channel Five*, ed. Simon Blanchard, British Film Institute, 1990.

5. Franco Bianchini in *Marxism Today*, June, 1991.

6. Wilf Stevenson and Richard Paterson, 'A channel in the public interest' in *The Challenge of Channel Five*, op. cit.

7. For the full text of section 7 of the Act, and a study of what resources cable operators are devoting to local channels, see Peter Kitchenman, *Survey of Local Channels on UK Cable*, Institute of Local Television, 1989.

8. Dave Rushton, *Making Local Work*, Institute of Local Television, 1990. See also Michael Svennevig, *Audience Reactions to Television Programmes*, Independent Broadcasting Authority, 1989.

9. Luise Nandy and Richard Ellis, *The Television Village*, Broadcasting Support Services, London, 1991.

10. Doreen Massey in *Marxism Today*, June, 1991.

GILLIAN REYNOLDS

Tuning along the Dial:
Local Radio

Listening to unfamiliar radio stations, other people's local radio, can feel like eavesdropping or picking up the telephone on someone else's conversation. What is said may be intelligible but it is not always understood. I sit in strange rooms sometimes, tuning along the dial, waiting for voices between records to tell me by words or even by accent something of the peculiarity of that place. It can be a long wait. There is something wrong with British local radio, something set askew at the start so that no matter what people try to do with it now they never quite prevail against the currents of its old history. Tune along the wavebands. Hear what I mean.

BBC local stations are now charged to pursue a lower ratio of music. In a 'Charter for the 1990s' the Managing Director of Regional Broadcasting, Ronald Neil, said, 'BBC local radio's trade mark is speech: news, information, sport, interview and debate.' But if you listen to the on-air discourse it sounds tinged with unease, the spaces between songs often filled with shivering insecurity lightly layered over with egotism. 'BBC local radio should be the community messenger: a friend, adviser and local champion,' runs the Neil message. The unspoken response below the on-air words is 'Yes, but for how long and on what sort of budget?'

On Independent Local Radio it is the commercials that tell you most about where you are and what is happening. The voices between the records bear only the faintest homoeopathic tinge of local identity. The records themselves are the same records as they play down the road in the next city. A listener will learn about nightlife and shopping and the price of a bargain bus ticket but only the bare outline of what is happening at the town hall. A common ILR argument is that commercials tell you as much about a community as any structured speech programme. It is a shallow and cynical argument that reduces ILR to the status of a freesheet newspaper. While pretending to a free market, libertarian approach it actually reduces the choice, range, diversity and identity of all local radio. Only those who pay for commercials can make their voices heard.

This is why local news, wherever it is broadcast, tends to sound oddly familiar. The voices pursue a style of their own, full of metronomic emphases shoring up sentences for no good reasons of grammar but only because that is how the reader has heard it done. Meaning and significance bleed away. This is the small change of language, the copper coin. Those who trade in it affect to despise any other, dismissing the silver of crafted words as too hard, too big to handle. The listener is kept within a small circle of exchange. Everything beyond is portrayed as funny, peculiar, dubious.

Say this, though, and you will be besieged with claims and counter-claims. BBC Radio X raised Y thousands of pounds in the scanner-appeal last year. In the snow it was Independent Local Radio's Z side who got help to people cut off – and brought in a new sponsor for the weather forecast as a result. The BBC says its local stations, taken together, are now second only to Radio 1 in national popularity. ILR says it beats the BBC locally and nationally. BBC local radio costs the listener a penny a day. ILR says it costs the listener nothing. It does, of course, but the cost of advertising is hidden within the price of goods.

The listener might wonder what all the fuss is about. Why can't they just coexist, get on with it, live with each other, swap the odd disc-jockey, off-load the occasional sports reporter? Why does there have to be all this bickering? The fuss, the claims and counter-claims continue, dear listener, because of the peculiar evolutionary pattern of British radio. Alone among nations west of the old Iron Curtain our commercial radio system arrived last. It did so because of the power (and occasional glory) of the BBC.

In 1926 the Crawford Committee recommended there should be a public corporation, set up by Royal Charter, given authority to operate for fixed periods, non-profit-making, providing public-service broadcasting financed by licence fee, to carry no advertising, to enjoy a monopoly. That is how the BBC was born. It developed into two services, Regional and National, of mixed programming – drama, serials, variety, outside broadcasts, news, dance music, orchestras. On Sundays it was strict and sober. When listeners got the commercial alternatives of Athlone or Normandie or Radio Luxembourg, they tuned away from the Corporation's Sabbatarian gloom.

The 1939–45 war imposed its own agenda on the BBC. The two services became the 'Home' and 'Forces', with a discernible difference in brow level between the two. Home was sober, informational. Forces was lighter, more fun, more of a boost to wartime morale. News was expanded. Everyone listened. Before the war was over Sir William Haley, the Director General, laid plans for change. In addition to the Home Service, there would be a Light Programme (replacing Forces) and joining them would be the Third, the first network in the world wholly dedicated to highbrow music and speech.

Fred Allen, the great American radio comedian, was once asked to describe the experience of listening to the Third Programme. 'It began,' he said, 'with a talk on how to stuff a fieldmouse and went on pretty much like that all day.' He must have missed the programmes of Louis MacNeice and Dylan Thomas and James Joyce, the great new flow of cultural patronage, the Golden Age of the radio feature. So did most listeners. What most tuned to was the Light.

A concerted lobby for commercial radio began in 1951. The arrival of ITV in 1955 both helped and hindered it. If there were to be a commercial television service, why not one for radio too? But by the late 1950s both BBC television and ITV were rapidly contributing to radio's decline. The audience, still listening on those big, non-portable valve sets, was deserting in droves. Radio was dying. We knew it by the utterances of its high priests. 'At the end of the war it had not been unusual,' wrote D. G. Bridson in 'Prospero and Ariel', his memoir of the BBC, 'for Home Service features to attract an audience of ten million listeners or more: a decade later the average feature audience on the Home Service had shrunk to something less than a million. Audiences on the Light Programme continued to be larger, but only a very few features were carried there. As for the Third Programme – though it was never larger than minimal – at least it stayed comparatively constant and compared favourably with the audience of the entire West End theatre or the circulation of the leading weekly reviews.'

Bridson was one of the great radio producers. His ear for language and his capacity for creativity were enlisted in the service of the listener for whom only the brightest and best should be set forth. Imaginative radio was, he believed, what would always draw listeners. It need not be expensive but it ought to challenge. It was not a view that stayed in fashion at the BBC. Radio seems to have been viewed as an expensive and inconvenient inheritance – an old house no one wanted to live in any more with lots of aged retainers to take care of and damp in the attics. But Bridson's description of the mid-1950s BBC turns out to have been curiously prophetic. It stands, more or less, today – even after all the rapid and radical change of the last decade. If that change had its roots anywhere it was not at the BBC but with the pirates.

When Radio Caroline went on the air in 1964 it had no advance publicity, no promotions, no posters. After the first three weeks Gallup found it had seven million listeners. Within the next three years more than a hundred more pirates joined Caroline. Who said radio was dead? The BBC and the government, however, were not thrilled at the rising of this phoenix from the ashes. The pirates, it was claimed, were stealing the copyright of artists and musicians, taking the bread from live bands by playing only records, stealing wavelengths, interfering with foreign stations and endangering shipping. The 1967 Marine Offences Act drove them all (except Caroline) off the air. Disc-jockeys like Kenny Everett and Tony Blackburn transferred overnight from pirate boats to Radio 1, a new network, part of a brand new BBC.

There were now four national services (Radios 1, 2, 3 and 4) all of them offering not mixed output but streamed, generic programming targeted for the first time at specific audiences. With them came eight BBC local stations, the first of a projected network of forty. The BBC's claim to local radio was that this was a return to its own roots. More cynical onlookers detected a certain disingenuousness here. Why, if this was to be a local service, had the BBC planted the first stations in big conurbations? If small was good, then why not site in Kirkby or Moss Side rather than Liverpool or Manchester? It seemed plain that the BBC was staking out a prior right to local-radio territory against the day, growing ever nearer, when local commercial radio would arrive.

Those first local stations were on VHF only. Some had financial assistance from local authorities. 'There's been more on it than listen,' said Arthur Dooley, the Liverpool sculptor after a year of BBC Radio Merseyside. At the time it was true. Not much later, though, it became clear that there was a demand from the audience and that local stations had a real part to play both as a service and as an outpost of BBC empire in training, in supply of news, in direct liaison with the public. Twelve more stations were announced in 1969, with the hope of more to follow later.

On the sidelines in the cities there were nascent entrepreneurs who couldn't believe the BBC was getting away with it. There had been commercial television for a decade and a half; it was popular and profitable. Pirate radio had also been cheap and popular and profitable. Why were British audiences being denied commercial radio?

In December 1969 the House of Commons debated both the BBC's plans and the pattern of the radio future. John Stonehouse, Minister of Posts and Telecommunications in the Labour Government (then the man responsible for broadcasting), spurned the Opposition's proposals for private-enterprise local stations. 'We reject commercialism,' he said, 'because we believe that all experience in other countries demonstrates that it does not provide the local-community service that we feel should be provided.' (Labour cheers.) There were more Labour cheers when Christopher Mayhew (then the Labour MP for Woolwich East) asked how far the Conservative campaign was seriously preoccupied with wanting the BBC to maintain a high standard and how far it was 'interested in clearing the field of popular local broadcasting for the commercial interests which lie behind their party?' The Opposition, he said, were the front: 'the stuffed shirts which concealed the vested interests'.

The general argument at the time was dual: was the BBC jettisoning the best of its tradition to provide quantity over quality, and would commercial radio none the less displace the BBC from its most popular functions. It is odd how familiar it all still sounds today, as does the caution from Christopher Mayhew, that the Conservatives 'wanted to push the BBC out of local radio to make room for their commercial friends'.

The BBC declared roundly in 'Broadcasting in the Seventies' (that radical document for restructuring that caused so much internal strife) that, although it wished to develop local radio as an element of what the BBC offered, it made no claim for monopoly. 'The BBC has matched up to competition in television and, given equal opportunities, it could do so in radio.'

Possibly it was this prim assurance that saved it. The Government of that day set its face against commercial radio. The next one did not. The Sound Broadcasting Act of 1972 changed the Independent Television Authority to the Independent Broadcasting Authority and the following year the first Independent Local Radio stations were born. The IBA regulated their company structures, schedules and transmitters, technical and editorial standards. The stations themselves were to make their living through the sale of nine minutes' advertising in the hour. (ITV was permitted six.)

On 8 October LBC opened, a week later it was joined by Capital. The first stage of ILR development lasted until April, 1976 when Beacon opened in Wolverhampton and the ILR had nineteen local stations compared to the twenty run by the BBC.

It was not, to put it mildly, an easy birth. The last of the boom years was edging into the miners' strike and the three-day week when it all began. It would have been a hard medium to launch anyway but at a time of industrial crisis it was particularly difficult. ILR had other problems too: the requirements of both the Act and the IBA made expensive technical demands; there was very little managerial experience of commercial radio; financial expectations were pitched to television standards. The local nature of the system created petty rivalries, some of which persist to this day.

Competition between several vendors of national advertising meant that radio was never sold properly to agencies as a viable and convenient new national advertising medium – another bitter legacy carried forward to the 1990s. The whole system might well have gone to the wall very early had it not been for the investment of Canadian money and the swift learning of some lessons about the ratios of cost to income.

What the audience was getting was something presented as new but sounding familiar: local news, information and lots of recorded music. Other things were tried too; there were experiments with drama and documentary. When these proved too expensive for the size of the audience they attracted they rapidly dwindled. The IBA system, however, demanded programme diversity. It also obliged ILR to spend 3 per cent of its total net revenue on the employment of live musicians, part of the bargain under which stations could play nine continuous hours (eighteen broadcast hours) of records over a 24-hour period. As the ILR stations started to find their feet and their profits exceeded a certain level they became liable to pay 'secondary rental', a form of Robin Hood cross-subsidy, which redistributed monies for 'exceptional' kinds of programmes or for training from the richer to the poorer stations. The first ten years of ILR were to produce, under the benevolent dictatorship of the IBA's Radio Division, more various and ambitious programming than it ever will again. The ILR of those years was, however, a freak, an aberration.

The pattern from television – make money but put some back into what is on the air – was transposed. The problem was that the amounts of money made were much smaller and more precariously earned. A basic formula of music, news and phone-ins became the pattern, with the strict requirement to broadcast the same output on both the AM and FM frequencies. Yet listeners, after the first couple of faltering years, voted with their ears and began to tune in loyally.

A view commonly stated at the time was that growth in one area of radio was good for all radio, that ILR's advance would mean the parallel progress of the BBC in both local and network radio. It is a view you still hear today. What ILR did do in the late 1970s was boost radio's image. It clearly offered a choice, it certainly brought jobs. Local loyalty from listeners became fierce. At Capital there was even chic. ILRs were by this time not only leaving their BBC rivals behind, they were poaching listeners from Radio 1. As time went by profits started to grow. Only one station, in Leicester, went to the wall. The IBA did all it could to foster as well as regulate the infant business.

The steady expansion of ILR over the years, roughly in parallel with the BBC local system, made it logical that it should provide the pattern for deregulation when, once again, the political wind changed and a government arrived intent on bringing market forces to broadcasting. Enough signals were sent and received before legislation made the IBA of the late 1980s a much altered entity. Gradually controls were eased, requirements lifted. Sponsorship, hitherto held at both arms' length by legislation and regulation, began to be accepted as a means of programme funding.

Then came permission to split frequencies. What Douglas Hurd, then the Home Secretary, gave to ILR was the possibility of operating two stations where they once had one: double the potential audiences, double the advertising, a wonderful rationalization of assets. It was not achieved everywhere without tears. The split into separate AM and FM services at some stations (Radio City in Liverpool, Piccadilly in Manchester and LBC in London) brought terrible financial problems and failure to reach the target audiences. It could be argued that the ambitious and unconventional nature of those three splits held the seeds of failure. Where the twin operation has worked best has been with the simplest and clearest division of programmes into two musical menus: oldies on AM, younger music on FM.

There was still more change ahead. The 1990 Broadcasting Act lifted the public-service requirement from ILR. It was no longer necessary to employ an expensive newsroom, to offer diverse, minority or educational programming. The proposed new national networks would be awarded to the highest bid, with no 'quality threshold'. The requirement that they should add to the listener's choice could equally be read as a protection of the existing ILR's local interests, a bar against competition. This is not – as American, French and German would-be investors at once declared when the Act was in their hands – a free market. A vast amount of discretion over the allocation and regulation of franchises remains in the hands of the new Radio Authority. The Authority itself is less accountable to the public.

A cheering note for big investors was the trend to corporate ownership. Where once local money and local small investors had been stipulated and preferred by the IBA, the effect of stock-market flotation on ILR was to bring about larger radio groups and multiple-station ownership. Radio Clyde, for example, now owns wholly or partly all except one (West Sound) of the Scottish radio stations. The pattern will be repeated.

London, by 1991, had meanwhile acquired more new radio stations than anywhere else. But against expectations the BBC remains in the game. Local radio is no longer the unloved bundle left on successive unhappy managerial steps. Its fate has now been intertwined with that of regional television: staffs are being trained to be 'bi-medial', capable of operating both on radio and TV. In May 1991 the BBC's Chairman, Marmaduke Hussey, gave local radio a ringing endorsement. It was serving a loyal and different audience from ILR, he said. There was room for both.

The listener might well agree. Radio Scotland, for instance, now offers speech of a high quality all morning and a sparkling diversity of new music at night, both quite unmatched by local ILR competition; but Scottish ILR audiences remain much higher and very loyal. Why can't we go on having both? Because, quite simply, despite all the growth and all the success of commercial radio it has not, in seventeen years, grown beyond a 2 per cent share of national advertising. To expand, it needs the BBC to contract. If the BBC were to give up local radio and Radio 1 then ILR and INR could take several immediate monopolistic giant steps forward. As long as the BBC is competing, they cannot.

The two armies have begun to glower at each other again. The Radio Authority accuses the BBC of hoarding frequencies. The BBC says that to cede an inch of territory now could lead to the collapse of its whole radio system. Take away the popular services, runs the argument, and the funding for Radios 3, 4 and 5 will look prohibitive, be shrunk and eventually lost. Somewhere in the middle of this battlefield a small voice is heard. 'What about community radio?' it says. 'What about small-scale, very local neighbourhood stations, run by volunteers, funded by local authorities or sponsorship?' Examples from Australia are cited. The eyes of idealists glow.

Radio pragmatists reply that community radio remains a snare and delusion. Public money invested in the medium has, in past experience, tended to melt away like snow. Private money needs a bigger and safer return on capital. Sponsorship is what makes such stations work in Australia; but everyone in broadcasting is now actively seeking sponsors and so community stations might well wait in vain.

There is a way of changing this. It has to do with money. Why not make it worth ILR's while to help new, tiny stations get started? Now that they have been freed from public-service requirement but obliged to pay heavily for transmitters, research and their licences, help given to community radio could be rewarded by tax advantages or licence-fee concessions or both. My proposal for the BBC would be even more radical. Although it is not the policy of any party I believe it deserves consideration. The time, I think, has come to sever the bond between the licence fee and the government of the day. Now that the shackles have been taken off independent broadcasting, the political chains could be loosed from the Corporation. The licence fee has proved itself to be the cheapest form of subscription, the most effective way of turning money into programmes. Why not allow the BBC to set the level itself?

It is plain that the revolution in ITV caused by Thatcherite notions of competition has, actually, destabilized one of the nation's most successful, profitable and creative industries. It has casualized a skilled work-force. The effects of the franchise bids will adversely affect programme budgets, and hence what is seen on the small screen, for years. Radio is smaller, cheaper, more flexible. At the same time it has proved itself a source of talent rich and diverse enough to fuel both the BBC and ITV. A prosperous and stable duopoly is what the medium needs to thrive: a BBC securely funded by licence fee; an independent-radio system free to maximize profits in the big market but encouraged to invest back into the development of a new community service.

Listeners would then, and only then, have the choice, the breadth, the diversity and the richness of a radio system which reflects and debates the society it serves. The way to keep more, not less, on the radio is give both sides the freedom to grow and the incentive to remember the person who is listening.

The system as it stands cannot deliver this. BBC local stations are being forced, for reasons of cost, into more and more agglomerations of service, smaller ratios of staff to airtime, taking fewer chances. As ILR stations lose their newsrooms (too expensive and no longer mandated by the Radio Authority) and stream their output of recorded music to compete with BBC and Independent national networks, what is lost is the sound of local voices, the sense your ILR can be a powerful friend. Alan Bleasdale broadcast his first story on BBC Radio Merseyside. A series he later wrote and performed for Radio City, the commercial rival station in Liverpool, gave him his first regular income as a professional writer. The contacts and experience he gained from both led to his first stage play at the Liverpool Playhouse and then, step by step, to national fame as a writer for screen and stage. I asked him could it happen now, could a new young writer get a first start on local radio? He sighed explosively and shook his head. 'They'd laugh in your face,' he said. The pity of it is, he's right. The shame would be if radio were to lose its local voice for ever.

STUART COSGROVE

Shaking up the City:
Pop Music in a Moment of Change

———

Britain's major cities are redolent with myths, and none is more powerful and lasting as that which grows up around a music venue. Hammersmith in London can lay claim to a century of celebrity appearances, reaching a war-time pinnacle during the Big Band era of the Palais de Danse. In the 1960s, Liverpool's Cavern Club had a virtual monopoly on the historic origins of the Mersey Beat; Manchester's Twisted Wheel Club pioneered the secret and soulful atmosphere of the urban all-nighter. In Glasgow, the notorious Barrowlands Ballroom – now a venue for mid-division rock bands – was once the focus of Scotland's biggest murder hunt when the serial killer Bible John stalked the dancefloor in search of female victims.

The modern era has perhaps offered less opportunity for nostalgic atmosphere but has been no less significant. When the Oi! band The Four Skins played in Southall, it marked a turning point in Britain's racial character. The Hamborough Tavern was burnt to the ground by young Asian activists defending their community from skinhead invasion. Live music had a riotous volume. A decade later, in 1991, Manchester's Hacienda Club – a design classic, and home to the city's independent dance generation – closed its doors as the club and parts of the city were blighted by violence, gun law and the human debris of drug abuse. Music had moved inexorably towards the American habits Britain had always imagined it could avoid.

Since its emergence in the 1950s, modern rock criticism has

held on to a simple and sometimes overwhelming metaphor: rock is the sound of the city. But beyond the metaphor lie a thousand untold stories: of towns that defined a sound, of places that tried and failed, of cities that ran out of time and of urban cowboys who learned their trade in the market called music.

Although British pop is inspired by the sound of cities, the music has always been formed by a tense evolution in which the commercial demands of the music business are never completely aligned with the cultural aspirations of the city. At its most oppositional this has often manifested itself as a dispute between London – the capital city and the city of capital – and those muscular cities in Scotland and the North of England whose history and self-image is marked not by the imprint of wealth but by the less tangible currency of 'authenticity' and social culture. It is through the jigsaw of this dispute that some very familiar shapes begin to emerge.

Live rock music and the venues that sustain it traditionally evoke images of labour. Rock bands work, sweat, kick ass and cut up rough. They hump gear from hall to hall and drink hard on the road. It is an exclusively masculine world, steeped in male ritual and prone to the dated work-wear of the past: torn denim, leather jackets, lumberjack shirts and Doc Martens. It is not a million miles removed from the 'mood' of industrial trade union-ism and the spirit of authentic labour that sustained socialism through its industrial phase. In traditional rock music and on the shop floors of industrial labour, 'work' absorbs and reproduces everyday conservatism, but what does work mean when new technology has radically redefined the working day? And what future greets the industry of music when post-industrialism is playing the tune?

Ironically, at the very time that musicians were recognizing the benefits of new technological developments, like the drum machine, the sequencer and the sampler, Britain's powerful Musicians' Union resorted to the historically controversial slogan 'Keep Music Live'. A wedge was driven through the movement. Arguments raged between live music and studio music, 'real' music and synthesized music, traditional instruments and computer-driven technology. It is a dispute that has decades to run, but has already fossilized the image of authentic labour. The live musician is a labouring hero, doing it for real.

By an odd historical coincidence the crisis of identity which beset the Labour Party and British trade unionism during the Thatcher years broadly coincided with a crisis of conventional rock music. As the new technological developments and new styles like rap, hip-hop, house and techno-pop forced conventional rock on to the defensive, so Labour struggled to assert a progressive identity in the shadow of monetarism's apparently inexorable power. At its very bleakest moments, Labour became a political Eric Clapton, a dinosaur out of touch with the present and apparently obsessed with the past. It is a mantle that has not yet been shaken off and it is to the cities that Labour must look for a glimpse of its own future.

The city of Sheffield has developed an exemplary music infrastructure, which not only accommodates the shifting patterns of post-industrialism and the changing sound of music in the late twentieth century but breaks with the legacies that rock music has handed down since the 1950s. Responding to the needs of its young black population and recognizing the impact that soul music exerts in South Yorkshire, Sheffield has built a music base attuned to dance music as much as rock. The experiment involves three separate and profoundly different venues: the Crucible Theatre, the Leadmill and Redtape Studios.

The first of these is widely known as the original home of televised snooker, a multi-purpose performance venue, capable of housing regional repertory theatre, alternative drama and unashamedly populist events from the calendar of sport and light entertainment. It is impossible to say whether Hurricane Higgins-inspired antics in the snooker hall have unknowingly tempted the citizens of Sheffield to try out the more abstract and minimalist pleasures of a Samuel Beckett play. But it is certainly the case that the Crucible enjoys a broad-based, democratic and buoyantly populist reputation, and that televised snooker has played a crucial role in chipping away at the public's long-standing suspicion of theatre's heightened sensibilities.

The Leadmill, which describes itself as 'the most innovative, successful and unusual arts centre in the country', provides Shef-

field with a vibrant repertoire of performing arts and a programme of education and a workshop aimed primarily – though
not exclusively – at a young disadvantaged audience. Unlike
major private-sector theatres, concert halls and rock venues,
nearly every performance at the Leadmill is sold out. It generates
85 per cent of its own income, functioning as a registered charity
with public-funding support and private-sector donation. Its success contradicts the received wisdom of monetarist economic
theory. The Leadmill's enterprising sense of small-scale efficiency
and its founding principles of arts, education and people's involvement looks refreshingly modern and forward-looking when set
against some of the city's chain-store pubs, down-town discos and
decaying dance halls, many of which are beset by the patent
inefficiencies of late capitalism: underfunded, under-staffed, be-
holden to the breweries and burdened by interior decoration that
seemed a good idea at the time.

The Leadmill complex includes the Scotia Works, a City
Council building once earmarked for demolition that has been
renovated with minimal capital and now acts as a venue extension
with a glass covered courtyard and café-bar, and Globe Works, a
post-industrial trade centre, which has utilized a previously derelict Grade II listed building and turned it into a manu-factory.
Globe Works is the theory of post-industrialism in miniature.
Built in the 1800s, it is a remnant of Sheffield's old steel industry
and houses craftspeople and modern office accommodation. It is
currently expanding to house a trade centre, a restaurant and a
public house, which, if the theory of post-industrialism is stretched
to its logical conclusion, will probably be called The Welder's
Arms.

Redtape Studios, a rehearsal and recording facility for music
and the media, is Europe's first local-authority music studio.
Established in 1986 by Sheffield City Council, with financial
assistance from the EEC and the Government's Urban Programme Scheme, Redtape provides recording facilities, training
and information for the city's thriving popular music scene and is
one of the major influences behind the phenomenal rise of Sheffield's dance-music industry. Although its name might program
tremors of digital fear into the traditional business community,

Redtape has been a crucial part of Sheffield's techno-business community and has provided a recording facility for dance-orientated recording artists such as Forgemasters, Nightamers On Wax, Funk Worm, D. J. Mink and The Orb.

The city of Glasgow has also tried to find its own way out of the decaying habits of industrialism and has created its own thriving music industry based around a wealth of local bands, including Deacon Blue, Wet Wet Wet, Hue and Cry, and Del Amitri. Although much of the success of Glasgow's cultural industries has been laid at the door of its year as European City of Culture, there are many other explanations, not least the political sentiment of devolution. If Sheffield's music scene has benefited by defeating the weight of the past, then Glasgow has learnt the politics of decentralization.

Although every major Glasgow group is signed to a London-based multi-national record company – and in that respect they remain tied to the centre – most of them have made it their public policy to devolve creativity and cultural work away from London. Glasgow's small but efficient recording bases – St Clair, CaVa and The Precious Organization – provide studios for the main groups. Increasing amounts of session work, videos, photography and design are farmed out to local organizations.

It might simply seem like the clan system at work, but scratch below the surface and it becomes evident that Glasgow's music scene is driven by deeply held commitment to the principles of self-determination and a social responsibility to Scotland. This was supremely evident in the music scene's response to two very different kinds of live music initiatives, Tennents Live! and 'The Big Day'. Tennents Live! is the biggest and possibly the most ambitious rock music initiative that the private sector has ever attempted to organize in Britain. It is a simple and in many ways admirable attempt to develop a live-rock circuit in Scotland, offering emergent and first-stage groups an opportunity to perform in a 'subsidized' environment. But from the outset the project has been beset with controversy and disenchantment.

The launch of the Tennents Live! project was boycotted by several major groups, some refusing to lend their support to the increasing climate of private sponsorship of pop, others more distinctly concerned with the question of alcohol abuse. Tennent-Caledonian, one of Scotland's biggest and most powerful breweries, clearly saw the live project as an opportunity to promote their product in a predominantly youthful environment. The brewers argued that the circuit of live gigs was targeted at an age-group above eighteen and that significant emphasis would be placed on low-alcohol beer. The dissenting bands, which inevitably included the more politicized Scottish bonds, like Hue and Cry and Deacon Blue, argued that Glasgow's social problems were exacerbated by alcohol abuse and refused to lend their weight to a project that at best was naively optimistic and at worst a cynical marketing campaign designed to sell alcohol to rock's hard-core audience: young teenagers.

In direct comparison, the groups who boycotted Tennents Live! rallied to 'The Big Day', an all-day rock and pop concert funded by the Labour-dominated Glasgow District Council as a populist show-piece within the City of Culture festivities. 'The Big Day' was a free event on four stages situated in open-access public places throughout the city. It attracted over 300,000 people and, as a gesture of civic support, Strathclyde Regional Council provided free transport from the city's peripheral housing schemes: Castlemilk, Drumchapel and Easterhouse. Throughout the day volunteers collected money for the Glasgow Council for the Single Homeless, an umbrella organization run by the council to generate new housing initiatives. It was an event designated to celebrate a city and the spirit of social provision and self-respect that has sustained it despite the worst impositions of industrialism.

If rock music is the sound of the city then it is a sound that is being pulled in new directions by technology and cultural trespassers from outside the predominantly male and white voices that have dominated rock's official history. Voices from the regions, ethnic and migrant communities, and other national cultures have had an audible impact on the sound and shape of British rock and pop in the 1990s. New digital and computer-based technology has changed the way music is made, the way it is consumed and the way it is received in music venues. Whatever changes are to come, the CD player and the Casio drum-machine have insisted that the notion of 'compactness' will join sex and drugs in the encyclopedia of pop.

The Labour Party's response to change has been conspicuously cumbersome over the last twenty years, but they are not alone in that respect. We yearn for easy answers where none exist; we yearn for spiritual guidance and look to Mecca, only to discover that most of them are Bingo Halls and the band stopped playing when the gas ran out. One of the great conceits of modern day Conservatism is that socialism is a thing of the past, a thing of the North, an industrial thing, yesterday's news, an old tune that will never be revived. But one of the most reassuring and truly inspirational facets of the new music from the cities is the way sampled dance music reinvents bits from the past in presenting a regenerated future.

In the political wilderness of the last fifteen years, Thatcherite Conservatism was a new group that believed it had a monopoly on the future. Like every self-deluding rock dinosaur, it believed it had a monopoly on what the people wanted to hear. Fortunately, for those affected by the sound of the declining cities, Thatcherism is a conceit that has run its course: there's nothing more bloated than yesterday's rock. I'd rather be a rap star in Sheffield than bankrupt in Bournemouth.

NOTES ON CONTRIBUTORS

Jeanette Winterson was born in Lancashire in 1959. She now lives and writes in London. Her work includes the novels *Oranges Are Not The Only Fruit* (1985), *The Passion* (1987), *Sexing The Cherry* (1989). She scripted *Oranges Are Not The Only Fruit* for BBC television in 1990 and her original screenplay *Great Moments in Aviation* is currently in production. She is finishing a play for the National Theatre and thinking about her next novel which will be published in 1992. Her work is published in fifteen languages but is much better read in English.

David Edgar became a full-time playwright in 1972 after a short career in journalism. His early work was performed in fringe venues, repertory theatre studios and on tour. His best known plays include *Destiny*, *Nicholas Nickleby* and *Maydays* (Royal Shakespeare Company), *Mary Barnes* (Birmingham Rep and Royal Court), *Entertaining Strangers* (Dorchester Community Play then National Theatre) and *The Shape of the Table* (National Theatre). He has also written for television, radio and film, and chairs Britain's first post-graduate course in play-writing studies.

Margaret Drabble is a novelist and critic, born in Sheffield and educated in Yorkshire and Cambridge. Her father was a barrister who twice stood (unsuccessfully) as a Labour candidate for Hallam, then for Huddersfield. She is the author of several novels, including her survey of the Thatcher years, *The Radiant Way* (1987), and its sequel *A Natural Curiosity* (1989), and in 1990 published a Chatto Counterblast on housing policy and mortgage-interest tax-relief. Her next novel, last of the trilogy, is *The Gates of Ivory*, to be published by Viking in 1991. She is a long-term supporter of the Labour Party.

Ruth Wishart is a Scottish journalist and broadcaster. She writes a weekly column for the *Scotsman*, and presents the BBC Radio Scotland programme *Headlines*, a weekly phone-in programme on current affairs. She is a director of several arts organizations, a member of the Scottish Advisory Committee to the British Council, and of the Scottish committee of the Association for Business Sponsorship.

David Lister is the arts correspondent of the *Independent*. He has worked on the *Independent* since its launch. Previously he worked for the *Sunday Times*, *The Times Educational Supplement*, the journal *Education*, and the *Bristol Evening Post*. Before that he attended the Centre for Journalism Studies in Cardiff run by the late Sir Tom Hopkinson.

Richard Burns was born in Sheffield in 1958. The author of six novels including *A Dance for the Moon* (winner of *The Times/Jonathan Cape Young Writers' Competition*), *The Panda Hunt* and *Fond and Foolish Lovers* (shortlisted for the 1990 John Llewellyn Rhys Memorial Prize), he also contributes regularly to the *Independent* and teaches courses in creative writing at Huddersfield Polytechnic. In 1991 he was awarded an Arts Council Bursary. He is married with three children.

Alison Fell is a Scottish poet, novelist and tutor in creative writing who lives and works in Inner London. Her poetry collections are *Kisses for Mayakovsky* and *The Crystal Owl*, and her novels include *Every Move You Make* and *The Bad Box*. She edited and contributed to the women's collections *The Seven Deadly Sins* and *The Seven Cardinal Virtues*. Her latest novel *Mer de Grace* was published by Methuen in the spring of 1991.

Ruth Rendell has been writing suspense fiction and detective stories for the past twenty-seven years, under her own name or the pen-name Barbara Vine. Three of her novels have won the Crime Writers' Gold Dagger Award, and she has also won three 'Edgars' (awarded by the Mystery Writers of America). Her most recent work, *King Solomon's Carpet*, was published by Viking in

August 1991. With fellow-author Colin Ward, she has written one of the Chatto Counterblasts: *Undermining the Central Line*. She regularly reviews fiction for the *Daily Telegraph*, and is a Fellow of the Royal Society of Literature. She is married, has one grown-up son, and lives with her husband in a 16th-century farmhouse in Suffolk.

David Dabydeen was born in Guyana. He read English at Cambridge, did post-doctoral research at Oxford and Yale and is presently Senior Lecturer in Caribbean Studies at the University of Warwick. He has published two collections of poetry, *Slave Song* (1984) and *Coolie Odyssey* (1988), and a novel, *The Intended* (1991), published by Secker & Warburg. He was awarded the Commonwealth Poetry Prize in 1984.

Paul Bailey was born in 1937 and, after school in London, studied at the Central School of Speech and Drama. He has taught at the Universities of Newcastle and Durham, in Macerata, in the American mid-West and has travelled widely for the British Council. *At the Jerusalem* won the 1968 Somerset Maugham Award and both *Peter Smart's Confessions* (1977) and *Gabriel's Lament* (1986) were shortlisted for the Booker Prize. His autobiography *An Immaculate Mistake* (1990) is forthcoming in Penguin. He is a frequent contributor to the BBC. He is currently completing his seventh novel.

Mike Phillips was born in Guyana and came to Britain in 1956. He went to school at Highbury in Islington, then studied for a degree and postgraduate degrees in English, politics and teacher-training. He started and lived in a hostel for homeless black youths in Notting Hill, leaving that to become a 'community activist' in Manchester and Birmingham. He entered journalism and now teaches at the Polytechnic of Central London. He has published two novels, *Blood Rights* and *The Late Candidate*. He also wrote the script of the TV series of *Blood Rights*. *The Late Candidate* was awarded the Crime Writers' Association's Silver Dagger in 1990. His next novel *Point of Darkness* is to be published early in 1992 by Michael Joseph.

Tim Hilton is art critic of the *Guardian*, 'a paper I'm glad to serve on because of its progressive politics and commitment to regional life'. The organizer of numerous exhibitions and formerly a member of the Arts Council's advisory panel, he is the author of books on Ruskin and Picasso and has taught in a number of art schools.

Richard Cork, the art critic, historian and broadcaster, read Art History at Cambridge. His first book, a two-volume study of Vorticism, won the 1976 John Llewellyn Rhys Memorial Prize. In 1979 a selection of his art criticism for the *Evening Standard* was published as *The Social Role of Art*. His next book, *Art Beyond the Gallery*, was the winner of the RIBA's Sir Banister Fletcher Award. In 1987, when he co-selected the Royal Academy's major survey of *British Art in the Twentieth Century*, his book on the life and work of David Bomberg appeared. In 1989–90 he was the Slade Professor of Fine Art at Cambridge, and his new book on Art and the Great War will be published next year.

Ken Worpole was involved in setting up Centerprise – a bookshop-based community centre in Hackney – which published a number of books based on local oral history as well as the work of many young East End writers who went on to secure national and even international recognition. He was an arts policy adviser to the GLC and later head of the Cultural Industries Unit at the Greater London Enterprise Board. He has written a number of books on cultural policy, and a forthcoming book on the joint Comedia/Gulbenkian Foundation study of city centre cultures in Britain, *Out of Hours*, will be published by the Open University Press in February 1992. He has worked with Mark Fisher on a number of policy studies.

Naseem Khan wrote the first pioneering report on the arts of ethnic minorities for the Arts Council and Gulbenkian Foundation, 'The Arts Britain Ignores', published in 1976. She was founding Coordinator of the Associated Festival of India and is currently chair of the national South Asian dance network, ADiTi. As a freelance journalist, she wrote a weekly column for the *New*

Statesman for three years that covered broad issues of cultural policy and events from kite days to carnivals. She is much involved with arts research and consultancy work, with particular emphasis on South Asian arts and leisure.

Steven Barnett is an independent researcher and writer, who is currently director of the Henley Centre's media group and visiting lecturer at the Communications department of Goldsmiths College. After taking Social Science degrees at Pembroke College, Cambridge and London School of Economics he spent five years in the research department of the Consumers' Association followed by five years at the Broadcasting Research Unit. He was Chairman of the Social Research Association from 1987–9. He is the author of *Games and Sets: The Changing Face of Sport on Television* and has published a number of papers and contributions to books on media and communications issues. He is a regular contributor to the *Guardian* and *Broadcast* magazine, and is on the editorial board of the *British Journalism Review*.

Gillian Reynolds has been radio critic of the *Daily Telegraph* since 1975. From 1967–74 she was radio critic of the *Guardian*. In the twenty months between she was founding programme-controller of Radio City in Liverpool. Born in Liverpool in 1935, she read English at St Anne's College, Oxford. Chairman of the Sony Awards from 1987–91 and of the Charles Parker Archive since 1988, she was made the first Fellow of the Radio Academy in 1990. She has three sons and one grand-daughter, and lives in London with ten radios.

Stuart Cosgrove is from Perth, Scotland. After a career as a lecturer in theatre and television, and a successful career as a freelance writer he became the Media Editor of *NME*. A regular contributor to *The Face*, *City Limits*, the *Observer* and *Scotland On Sunday*, he has written several books on theatre and popular culture. He regularly appears on radio and television, and is currently a host presenter of BBC2's *The Late Show*.

FOR THE BEST IN PAPERBACKS, LOOK FOR THE 🐧

In every corner of the world, on every subject under the sun, Penguin represents quality and variety – the very best in publishing today.

For complete information about books available from Penguin – including Puffins, Penguin Classics and Arkana – and how to order them, write to us at the appropriate address below. Please note that for copyright reasons the selection of books varies from country to country.

In the United Kingdom: Please write to *Dept E.P., Penguin Books Ltd, Harmondsworth, Middlesex, UB7 0DA.*

If you have any difficulty in obtaining a title, please send your order with the correct money, plus ten per cent for postage and packaging, to *PO Box No 11, West Drayton, Middlesex*

In the United States: Please write to *Dept BA, Penguin, 299 Murray Hill Parkway, East Rutherford, New Jersey 07073*

In Canada: Please write to *Penguin Books Canada Ltd, 2801 John Street, Markham, Ontario L3R 1B4*

In Australia: Please write to the *Marketing Department, Penguin Books Australia Ltd, P.O. Box 257, Ringwood, Victoria 3134*

In New Zealand: Please write to the *Marketing Department, Penguin Books (NZ) Ltd, Private Bag, Takapuna, Auckland 9*

In India: Please write to *Penguin Overseas Ltd, 706 Eros Apartments, 56 Nehru Place, New Delhi, 110019*

In the Netherlands: Please write to *Penguin Books Netherlands B.V., Postbus 195, NL–1380AD Weesp*

In West Germany: Please write to *Penguin Books Ltd, Friedrichstrasse 10–12, D–6000 Frankfurt/Main 1*

In Spain: Please write to *Alhambra Longman S.A., Fernandez de la Hoz 9, E–28010 Madrid*

In Italy: Please write to *Penguin Italia s.r.l., Via Como 4, I-20096 Pioltello (Milano)*

In France: Please write to *Penguin Books Ltd, 39 Rue de Montmorency, F-75003 Paris*

In Japan: Please write to *Longman Penguin Japan Co Ltd, Yamaguchi Building, 2–12–9 Kanda Jimbocho, Chiyoda-Ku, Tokyo 101*

FOR THE BEST IN PAPERBACKS, LOOK FOR THE 🐧

PENGUIN POLITICS AND SOCIAL SCIENCES

Comparative Government   S. E. Finer

'A considerable *tour de force* ... few teachers of politics in Britain would fail to learn a great deal from it ... Above all, it is the work of a great teacher who breathes into every page his own enthusiasm for the discipline' – Anthony King in *New Society*

Karl Marx: Selected Writings in Sociology and Social Philosophy
T. B. Bottomore and Maximilien Rubel (eds.)

'It makes available, in coherent form and lucid English, some of Marx's most important ideas. As an introduction to Marx's thought, it has very few rivals indeed' – *British Journal of Sociology*

Post-War Britain   A Political History   Alan Sked and Chris Cook

Major political figures from Attlee to Thatcher, the aims and achievements of governments and the changing fortunes of Britain in the period since 1945 are thoroughly scrutinized in this readable history.

Inside the Third World   Paul Harrison

From climate and colonialism to land hunger, exploding cities and illiteracy, this comprehensive book brings home a wealth of facts and analysis on the often tragic realities of life for the poor people and communities of Asia, Africa and Latin America.

Housewife   Ann Oakley

'A fresh and challenging account' – *Economist*. 'Informative and rational enough to deserve a serious place in any discussion on the position of women in modern society' – *The Times Educational Supplement*

The Raw and the Cooked   Claude Lévi-Strauss

Deliberately, brilliantly and inimitably challenging, Lévi-Strauss's seminal work of structural anthropology cuts wide and deep into the mind of mankind, as he finds in the myths of the South American Indians a comprehensible psychological pattern.

PENGUIN POLITICS AND SOCIAL SCIENCES

Political Ideas David Thomson (ed.)

From Machiavelli to Marx – a stimulating and informative introduction to the last 500 years of European political thinkers and political thought.

On Revolution Hannah Arendt

Arendt's classic analysis of a relatively recent political phenomenon examines the underlying principles common to all revolutions, and the evolution of revolutionary theory and practice. 'Never dull, enormously erudite, always imaginative' – *Sunday Times*

Ill Fares the Land Susan George

These twelve essays expand on one of the major themes of Susan George's work: the role of power in perpetuating world hunger. With characteristic commitment and conviction, the author of *A Fate Worse than Debt* and *How the Other Half Dies* demonstrates that just as poverty lies behind hunger, so injustice and inequality lie behind poverty.

The Social Construction of Reality Peter Berger and Thomas Luckmann

Concerned with the sociology of 'everything that passes for knowledge in society' and particularly with that which passes for common sense, this is 'a serious, open-minded book, upon a serious subject' – *Listener*

The Care of the Self Michel Foucault
The History of Sexuality Vol 3

Foucault examines the transformation of sexual discourse from the Hellenistic to the Roman world in an inquiry which 'bristles with provocative insights into the tangled liaison of sex and self' – *The Times Higher Education Supplement*

Silent Spring Rachel Carson

'What we have to face is not an occasional dose of poison which has accidentally got into some article of food, but a persistent and continuous poisoning of the whole human environment.' First published in 1962, *Silent Spring* remains the classic environmental statement which founded an entire movement.

PENGUIN HISTORY

The Penguin History of the United States Hugh Brogan

'An extraordinarily engaging book' – *The Times Literary Supplement*. 'Compelling reading … Hugh Brogan's book will delight the general reader as much as the student' – *The Times Educational Supplement*. 'He will be welcomed by American readers no less than those in his own country' – J. K. Galbraith

The Making of the English Working Class E. P. Thompson

Probably the most imaginative – and the most famous – post-war work of English social history.

Galileo: Heretic Pietro Redondi

'A powerful and brilliantly evocative book, possibly the most important, certainly the most controversial, contribution to Galileo studies for many years' – *The Times Literary Supplement*

The City in History Lewis Mumford

Often prophetic in tone and containing a wealth of photographs, *The City in History* is among the most deeply learned and warmly human studies of man as a social creature.

The Habsburg Monarchy 1809–1918 A J P Taylor

Dissolved in 1918, the Habsburg Empire 'had a unique character, out of time and out of place'. Scholarly and vividly accessible, this 'very good book indeed' (*Spectator*) elucidates the problems always inherent in the attempt to give peace, stability and a common loyalty to a heterogeneous population.

Inside Nazi Germany Conformity, Opposition and Racism in Everyday Life Detlev J. K. Peukert

An authoritative study – and a challenging and original analysis – of the realities of daily existence under the Third Reich. 'A fascinating study … captures the whole range of popular attitudes and the complexity of their relationship with the Nazi state' – Richard Geary

PENGUIN HISTORY

Modern Ireland 1600–1972 R. F. Foster

'Takes its place with the finest historical writing of the twentieth century, whether about Ireland or anywhere else' – Conor Cruise O'Brien in the *Sunday Times*

Death in Hamburg Society and Politics in the Cholera Years 1830–1910 Richard J. Evans

Why did the cholera epidemic of 1892 kill nearly 10,000 people in six weeks in Hamburg, while most of Europe was left almost unscathed? The answers put forward in this 'tremendous book' (Roy Porter in the *London Review of Books*) offer a wealth of insights into the inner life of a great – and uniquely anomalous – European city at the height of an industrial age.

British Society 1914–1945 John Stevenson

A major contribution to the *Penguin Social History of Britain*, which 'will undoubtedly be the standard work for students of modern Britain for many years to come' – *The Times Educational Supplement*

A History of Christianity Paul Johnson

'Masterly ... a cosmic soap opera involving kings and beggars, philosophers and crackpots, scholars and illiterate *exaltés*, popes and pilgrims and wild anchorites in the wilderness' – Malcolm Muggeridge

The Penguin History of Greece A. R. Burn

Readable, erudite, enthusiastic and balanced, this one-volume history of Hellas sweeps the reader along from the days of Mycenae and the splendours of Athens to the conquests of Alexander and the final dark decades.

Battle Cry of Freedom The American Civil War James M. McPherson

'Compellingly readable ... It is the best one-volume treatment of its subject I have come across. It may be the best ever published ... This is magic' – Hugh Brogan in *The New York Times Book Review*